CAP~~TIVES~~

D0462768

Norman Manea

CAPTIVES

Translated from the Romanian
by Jean Harris

A NEW DIRECTIONS PAPERBOOK ORIGINAL

Originally published in Romania as *Captivi* in 1970.

Manufactured in the United States of America
New Directions Books are printed on acid-free paper.
First published as a New Directions Paperbook in 2014
Design by Erik Rieselbach

Library of Congress Cataloging-in-Publication Data
Manea, Norman.
[Captivi. English]
Captives / Norman Manea ; Translated by Jean Harris.
pages cm
Originally published by [Bucuresti] : "Cartea româneasca," entitled Captivi, 1970.
ISBN 978-0-8112-2047-7 (alk. paper)
I. Harris, Jean A., translator. II. Title.
PC840.23.A47C313 2014
859'.334—dc23   2014036092

1 3 5 7 9 8 6 4 2

New Directions Books are published for James Laughlin
by New Directions Publishing Corporation
80 Eighth Avenue, New York 10011

Contents

Instead of an introduction

CAPTIVES IS OF ANOTHER PLACE and time. It was published in the Socialist Republic of Romania in 1970, when the provisional so-called "liberalization period" was still confusing and misleading, and yet often encouraging to many artists and intellectuals. At about that time, unfortunately, Ceaușescu visited China and North Korea, where he became fascinated by the enthusiastic obedience of the "masses," and upon his return he tried to impose a harsher totalitarian atmosphere back at home. Yet the hedonistic and self-centered nature of the people, as well as external evolution, slowly subverted his nationalistic socialism until its eventual collapse in 1989.

Captives, my first novel, expresses a radical separation from official ideology, drastically departing from all that was heavily promoted and praised by the Party. And although many pages were cut by the censors, it still, by some miracle, appeared in print.

The book's three main characters are vulnerable, weak, and defeated individuals: the complete opposites of the heroes and heroines of the system's exemplary novels. Thomas Mann's statement in *Death in Venice* about weakness—"one might well wonder whether the only possible heroism was the heroism of the weak"—resonated powerfully with me at that time, in our suffocating impasse. These protagonists, connected through a spiral that weaves through three parts, represent complementary faces of captivity: the quasi-burlesque energy of a frustrated schoolteacher, never tiring of her hunt for new illusions despite their humiliating ends; the sensitive and lonely daughter of a suspected war criminal who has committed suicide; and her young colleague, an engineer who—seeing in her the ghost of his lost sister who perished during the Holocaust—brutally ends their brief affair. This young engineer, who slowly comes to understand the perversity of this socialist paradise, becomes one of its wounded outsiders, just as the young woman has.

To create this enterprise, I had to find an adequately unconventional and experimental literary form, and so I propelled these characters through spiraling, self-sufficient, minimalist narratives, each one as larval as our own lives spent pushing our ways through a police state of suspicion, reticence, and submission. I was deeply aware of the political and aesthetic risks such a book might pose: the novel offered a multidimensional contrast to the Party's leadership's cosmetic image of the dynamic social "progress." The book was a challenge to authority, to myself, and to the reader, but didn't Faulkner say that a writer should be judged by the risks he takes, even if risks are conducive to failure?

Sometimes adopting the heavily descriptive methods of the so-called nouveau roman, *Captives* also serves as a document of the epoch, depicting the manner in which a self perceives itself in language and is organized by language. How else can anyone escape from the wooden discourse of an ideological system?

The passive voice, so important to understanding the book, is not routine in English, and the novel's "hermeticism" was an imposing constraint, whereby the object of an action is influenced or even changed, without the voice necessarily pointing to a certain subject that has caused the action. The broken characters are subdued, suspected, and distorted by obscure forces.

I strove to push the reader into a kind of implicit solidarity with my characters, through a labyrinth of twisted narratives, still organic to life in an oppressive environment. As usually happens in a suppressed society, the hidden sides of reality are decoded slowly, displaying their meaning only toward the end of the book, where—I hope—the connections and enigmas open up. Lack of freedom of choice in a country where the State is the only employer, and where citizens are owned by it, endangers *any* individual refuge. My world here is a kind of Kafkaesque "penal colony" with additional local ambiguities, corruption, double-talk, and double-dealing.

By now it must be obvious why I have been somewhat reluctant to publish this book here. Already more than twenty years have passed since my friends Barbara Epler and Griselda Ohannessian decided to bring out *Captives* at the earliest possible convenience of the author, and in the meantime New Directions has remained admirably convinced about the project (or perhaps about the essential and heroic role of a good publisher, ready for "difficult" books, even in a time when writing and publishing seem quite endangered everywhere in the world). In my newly published twenty-five-volume *Collected Works* in Romania, I found the opportunity to revisit this novel, making some minor changes and cuts in order to—at least partially—decode the sometimes overwhelmingly puzzling text, with its allusions and tricks, and its specific blind alleys. I have tried to help today's readers, in the West and even in Romania, to thread the maze of a narrative placed in a closed, totalitarian setting. This English translation follows the second edition of *Captives*.

Aware of the new risks this book faces, now, in my new country and in this troubled time of ours, I can only be grateful to my consistently supportive publisher, and also to Tynan Kogane, my editor, to my excellent translator, Jean Harris, and to my collaborator Carla Baricz.

Let's also trust the patient reader, our peerless peer, who might discover in these pages a reason to think about the strange topics as well as the curious shapes of such a literary adventure.

NORMAN MANEA
BARD COLLEGE, AUGUST 23, 2014

CAPTIVES

❖ ❖ ❖

"She"

Long, intermittent threads of rain, broken and scattered—the delayed perception of rain. His jacket is a soggy bandage for arms and shoulders. The streets meeting at the corner of the building, a likely setting for spectacular revolts to come: the young Christ committed to ironic beggary, deprived of violence, spectacular through the lack of inherent violence in his abandoned gestures—his beard grown wild, disheveled hair covering his neck and ears, the long, gathered curls lightened by gracious, sky-blue flowers—defiant in the confusion of a new day.

He stands on the street corner motionless under the rain and the scrutiny of so many eyes struck by his bizarre appearance, and his arms are as inert as his gaze, which begs for the solidarity of a smile, a flower, some signal of affirmation, or—simply, yet more incredibly—for physical violence, curses, or reprimands for his uncut hair, dirty beard, and limp body exhausted under the rain. The vagrant blankly stares at a place in the wall where a void in the bricks forms a crocodile-shaped hole. Some passerby would like to convince him that he's mistaken: it's just a trace of lime left by some whitewasher's brush, a patch of lime—not a hole, by any means.

This wandering son of the earth yearns to be one with the rain, to see once more the lime spot lapped by raindrops; only later, when he had already started to forget, a little old lady beside him would recall: several years ago there really had been a hole in that exact spot on the wall, which they filled at some point. His hands shook. The horror passed through him again. Then the abandoned gaze came back: hands forgotten, mind blank, glad to know nothing, to be certain of nothing, with nothing to retain or possess, nothing but alienation and sleep, far away and alone—that's all.

Motionless under the rain. Carved onto the street corner like a filthy inscription, with a beard and long hair, indifferent to the ironic looks and insults of all the brave and decent citizens around, spending long hours under the rain, withdrawn, somnolent, in everyone's way: this signified more than the single, unwieldy, stammered, unsuitable phrase cast into the void of the office that he'd just left: "I can't stand typewriters anymore."

Of course, the beholders' terror would have amplified his phrase: *I can't stand myself anymore, and I can't stand any of you anymore, either. I want something else ... like you, frightened of your own awareness ... impossible as it may seem, I want something desperate: poems, grenades, fires ... and on top of that, songs and flowers—naïve songs and innocent flowers, peaceful, old-fashioned flowers, wild flowers, flowers in bad taste, flowers in the hands of parents, beggars, neighbors, colleagues, teachers, directors of one thing or another—flowers growing out of typewriters, shutting them up and striking them dumb.* Only then would the passersby panic—somehow the obese professor herself may have appeared, that burlesque emblem of the stifled, with her suffocating comforts and teary-eyed songs crooned from the cradle to the cathouse.

The street corner could have been the site of a more spectacular revolt than those words left behind in that upholstered office, but the young man was already leaving, deaf and diffident, as though he'd already forgotten what he'd said.

The high iron gate strikes its latch; the narrow, serpentine, spiral staircase devours itself. Hand on the cold metal balustrade, the climber coils within himself. One flight up. Again, the steps rotate uniformly again in the shape of a fan: a point flowing at an even rate along the radius of a circle. Rotating evenly, slowly around the circumference, dizzied by the curved trajectories, the climber's body turns in on itself toward a painfully closed center.

At the door: the oval, raffia doormat. Under the mat will be a small wad of crumpled paper, hiding the key. On the door, the little cardboard rectangle: *Prof. M. Smântănescu.* The metal key clings to his palm. "You'll find the key under the mat!" The door really exists, and so does the mat and the key. *Prof. M. Smântănescu. French and Piano. Quiet. There are other tenants.*

There will be time, time to go back to the corner at least, and from there, with idle steps, triflingly and hesitantly, onto the street now light, dry, and deserted, under the long limbs of tall trees, a tunnel through the leaves, and past houses half-hidden in greenery.

… The building's staircase: step, riser, step, riser—chunks of ice. The final threshold, the wooden door covered in arabesques, angels sculpted from edge to edge on its wide margins. The door opens toward books heaped on heavy iron shelves, vases with slender flowers, a narrow table, a tall chair, a piano raising its oblique tail, the ceiling painted with pastel squares, the slippery parquet: everything accumulated with the serenity of a fairy tale, until chaos imposes itself, until the path from the street corner must be taken again, killing reveries, reestablishing the brutality of things, dispelling mystifications, until the street reasserts its filth, with small, uneven houses doused in fine rain, and narrow, crooked windows; the grillwork of the gates will be damp and cold, and the length of the iron balustrade will cool the hands; the spiral of the narrow steps soiled with mud, the landing with two doors: the one in front with a glass window, the one to the right made entirely of wood.

The door will have to be opened slowly so that no one hears, so that no one comes leaping out, halting or impeding the fugitive's steps, and, as in the past, the door must be cautiously pulled into the doorframe, smoothly and without a sound.

Door closed: obsequiously—a barrier in the face of his pursuers. Escape—even from here—is senseless.

Impossible to keep postponing the inevitable. Here, inside, the fugitive turns back into himself: a vibrating body—that well-known tremor—poised between familiar objects and the need to reinvent and rearrange them again. A hand moves along the length of his throat—that reflexive gesture—the perennial horror of reenacting the spasm that wrenched Captain Bogdan Zubcu's body as it hung from its deadly pendulum, the same gesture that the Captain made before flinging himself into the great redeeming pyre.... Then his daughter's wandering and the exile of this fugitive now, enchained by those two phantoms.

A chair: the body flowing into itself, into inevitable inertia. The green terracotta stove, the thin gas conduit. The valve key over the conduit's screw-tap. To the left, it closes; to the right, it opens, released, it might, possibly ... The dusty piano. The chair in front of it, scores piled in a heap. Symbols and lines, commas, staves and braces: Mozart and Czerny under the thickly settled dust. A crammed bookshelf: vertical, horizontal, oblique, aligned, overturned, tall, thin, small, fat, broken—books crowding each other, suffocating each other: ignored and lost books, dusty from edge to edge, dust on every surface. The cabinet with its glass case: more books, family photographs—false images of a false family—nostalgic funerary relics, papers: a fictitious history, a farce.

A strange, cramped, contorted execution site: the round table covered in soft fabric with its fringe dangling down to the rug patterned with rhombuses and rectangles; circling the table, little round chairs piled with clothes, notebooks, scores, papers, rags, clips, pencils.

The hand has remained forgotten on his neck, the phantom of a routine gesture. Frightened, the hand withdraws. The fugitive refuses to recognize himself.

⋮ ⋮ ⋮

Morning had lurked under the haze. The alarm clock screamed, the shirt rustled. Cold air slapped the dazed pedestrians—neighbors flung into the somber streets. The doorman's brief bow; windblown rows quietly submitting; reluctant fingers on the banister; the queue in front of the sign-in book, the signature, the chair.

Stiffness between ankle and knee, eyelids weighed by sleep, the seemingly careless glances, the hand sliding toward the briefcase—the key to the drawer. The ruler in its brown leather case, the drawing unrolled over the desk. The pink sheen of the paper: two-dimensional metallurgical furnaces in transverse section A–A, B–B; the longitudinal section C–C; the detail, epsilon; the column with funnels, columns, bunkers, dust cyclones, exhausts, blowers.

The dizziness of mornings: the damp that crawls up the bones and the tiredness that crawls down, and swollen legs like leaden bowling pins stiffly striking the stinking, clean parquet. The venomous coffee, black as night, and the sugar cube antidote. His eyelids will begin to flutter. The office worker will recognize his coworker under a smiling mask that asks, insists, slinks between words and smiles, pries, keeps watch, reports. Across the room, a faint buzz; the spy's monotonous voice falters, then comes back flickering faintly with bits of cunning.

—Thank you. Yes, yes. Now I understand. I haven't worked on this kind of furnace before.

Smoke, fog, steam, voices, a telephone ringing somewhere.

—Do you remember? Are the supports for this kind of terrain made on a scale of 1:25 or 1:50?

—1:25.

—And the gradient of the slope?

—2:1 up to four meters and 4:3 over four meters.

Slackness, apathy, pain rising slowly and damply up thin tubes. The dull submissive gestures played in slow motion—at eight-thirty: the lazy day extends itself.

In front of him, the same neighbor becomes the watcher: sallow with thinning, grayish hair, and neutral, serene, submissive eyes. His practiced facade of banalities—the scaffold of a double life: eight hours of detachedly playing the fool at the office allows him the freedom to explore more inaccessible realms than the rest of the chumps.

—I've been thinking, everything they're saying about Kennedy is a bunch of shit. Robert, the brother, is hiding the photographs of the autopsy, and saying they'll only be revealed in '71 because they're *horrible*?

Unobtrusive voice, fixed gaze, astonished.

—What exactly can be so horrible? If it was Oswald who shot him or the other guy, who cares? What's so horrible?

He asks and answers, poses and resolves dilemmas meant to provoke his interlocutor.

—It's clear that Johnson shot him. Otherwise, there'd be nothing horrible at all.

Broad-shouldered, ham-handed, squeezed into a shabby navy-blue suit, the tall man is a caricature and he makes no pretense of hiding it: he emits limpid, self-confident opinions, he notices without noticing, he naps in public. Modest, even humble, proud only of his studies abroad at Tashkent.

—Tell me, how is the overflow threshold calculated?

This formula can be found in any manual, but the request doesn't surprise him, and he notes it conscientiously.

—If I would make it ten centimeters?

—Depends on the debit. You have the formula. Calculate it.

—Well, I have a debit of ten liters per second.

—Good, see how much results.

—I think twenty centimeters will do it.

—If you don't want to calculate, put down however much you like. If you want to guess, there's no more point in asking.

He's silent for a few seconds. His colleague's irritation only reaches him in the faintest way.

—The fact is, theory's one thing, practice is another. I'll make it thirty centimeters.

Mihai Burlacu had learned the textbooks by heart in the Soviet East. He put up with the vicissitudes of fate and accepted burdens as punishments that would somehow pan out in the end. His only virtue was laziness; it kept him from becoming director general, or more. Riding around in the Volga limousine he'd picked up cheap while working as technical attaché in a foreign embassy, he'd gradually sunk to a position where he was simply tolerated in the obscurity of this run-of-the mill department. Serene, reconciled, and modest, he had a way of accepting whatever task and leaving it on the table, untouched among papers, manuals, and drawings. Ten days before the project fell due, he'd announce he didn't have enough time. The project would have to be saved, so the boss would offer whoever took the job a special compensation originally due to the engineer Burlacu. Earning in ten days what he would usually make in a month or two wasn't half-bad for the substitute, and Burlacu was always happy enough with his regular pay. He refused suggestions to transfer elsewhere and seemed wiser than everyone who tried to take care of him.

—You know tomorrow's the Brazil–Ghana match?

Why bother to reply?

—I think Brazil will win.

Offering banal opinions and information, Misha (as he's known), announces things everyone already knows and states them in vaguely astonished, well-informed tones: "I think we'll come to the office tomorrow at seven." Conflating commonplaces with the sensational news, he delivers everything in the same filmy voice.

A rectangular sheet of paper with headings and signs appears on the table. Misha's neighbor has a copy as well. The *Master Statistics Chart*. All work should be accompanied by this sheet: starting yesterday.

Sample Signature Sheet. Time Sheet. Re-used Materials Sheet. Standard Projects Sheet. Worker's Protection Sheet. Deficit Materials Sheet. Awards Sheet. Finance Sheet. Approvals Sheet. Applications Sheet. Completions Sheet. Calculation Sheet. Fire Protection Sheet. New Technologies Sheet. Statistics Sheet.

Now—the Statistics Sheet. (Model) Statistics Sheet. Project Code: 39. Beneficiary: C.S.G.D. Thermo-technical Center (10). Item: 0700 (Metallurgic Lime Factory. Furnaces 3 and 4). Work Category: 470 (Water). Executing Workshop: 21 (T4). Delivery Date. Contracted. Realized. Hours Clocked. Re-use Savings Hours. Value of Investment. Average Hours. Clocked Hours: Workshop P. Average Hours. Clocked Hours: Workshop E. Average Hours. Hours Clocked: Workshop D. Average Hours. Total Equipment. Special Pieces. Tons. Asbestos Cement Plates. Tons. Surface of Pump Rooms. Square Meters. Number of Circuits. Aggregate Units. Flow Rate. Cubic Meters per Hour. Pumping Height. Columnar Meters: Water. Installed Power.

The telephone rings: once, a second time, again and again. Someone stands up, speaks hurriedly, sounds irritated, then continues in hushed tones, whispering facetiously. Two fingers tap a shoulder. Lying on the table, the receiver waits.

—Someone's on the phone—looking for you.

The chair rotates and bumps into the corner of the table.

—Hello! My dear, don't get upset that I'm calling. I have a big favor to ask.

—With whom would you like to speak?

—What? I wanted to ask you if this evening you could …

—Madame, with whom would you like to speak?

Momentarily suffocated, the playful murmur subsides, forbidden, then reappears: serpentine, softly idle, spoiled.

—What, isn't this I.S.P.S.H.C.? Isn't this Department T4AII? And …isn't this comrade …What, no? I'm sorry, you know (and the voice shifts to the formal mode of address), you sound exactly like him on the phone and he usually picks up. Could you, though? You are very nice. Yes, I do have a very youthful voice. No, not exactly, after all. Between. No, it's not possible, please. Yes, since you have the telephone there on the table. Sometimes. Yes. Good. I'll call. Yes. Particularly.

The voice dies away, dumbstruck:

—What, Covalschi? What did you say?

—What? Ger…? Ger-ştan-schi, Gerştanşchi. Yes. Yes. Gerştanschi. Yes. Yes. Gerştanschi. No, No, something frightened me. OK, I didn't understand. Yes.

—Yes, of course. I promise. Please. I'll hold on. Yes, thank you.

Maybe they exchanged first names, addresses, home-phone numbers. Perhaps they joked, swore, kidded each other. Whoever *he* was, he wouldn't have been able to resist such a voice coming down from the clouds of a fairy tale. Nor would the lady have resisted such a chance opportunity to use her voice without giving it a try, encircling it, swallowing it.

Then the receiver was passed to the intended recipient.

—Yes, it's me. Yes, it was a colleague. Yes. They moved offices. I should record?—*The Good Night, Kids* broadcast? The text, why should I check it again? Maybe. I can't promise. I understand. But I can't. I'm not promising. Possibly. Under the doormat? In front of the door, under the mat? In a wad of paper?

The chair rotated back, banging into the drawer. Ahead: navy-blue sleeves, the table scattered with drawings, forms, pencils. The idiotic smile, the sweaty cheeks, the watery, listless eyes. Misha. Misha the spy.

Flow rate. Cubic meters per hour. Installed power. Kilowatt. Circuit Five. Aggregate. Functional Flow. Cubic Meters Per Hour. Pumping Height. Water Column Meters. Installed Power. Kilowatt. Circuit Six. Aggregate. Reference Flow.

Laxity. That's what put an end to the Captain, too. All of a sudden: abandonment. Captain Bogdan Zubcu wanted to end his days hanging from a rope but they didn't let him so he threw himself into a metallurgic furnace, where he finally burned—escaped—that trauma repeated in his daughter's eyes, burning them out. Laxity. Abandonment.

Height. Pumping Height. Water Column Meters. Cubic Meters Per Hour. Air Pressure. Wandering in his daughter's memory, Captain Zubcu had no more air. Meters. Volume. Cubic Meters. Decanting Total. Decanting Time. Hours. Radial Decanting Surface. Square Meters. Flow. Liters Per Second. Cubic Meters. Length of Network. The length of the road to the Captain, to the pyre. There needs to be a permission slip from the chief—Chief Saint Sebastian. Depth of Burial. Meters. Pre-Stressed Concrete Tube. Kilometers. Equivalent Diameter. Chief of Planning Service. Chief, Accounting Division. Chief of the Collective. Chief Adjunct. Chief President. Chief at, Chief of, Chief for.

To the Chief. Finally, to the Chief! Get there quickly, to Sebastian. The chair knocks the corner of the table. Misha naps. The door slams. The Chief. The stairs. Ascending. Ascending the stairs to the Chief.

⁝ ⁝ ⁝

His smile like a slit, Sebastian Caba had personally opened the leather-padded door. Amiable, decorous, well-meaning, he knew right away that remaining in the doorway and refusing to advance would result in the visitor abandoning himself to hastily tell, beg, liquidate; then he would have to offer protection, calm, understanding. Decorously planting himself in the doorway, Caba ushered in his guest.

Advancing behind the desk, he gestured to the armchair on his right. The old games of cordiality would have to be maintained at any price, along with the well-known lines of attack, defense, and encirclement. He knew how to engage the old laws of cordiality. They were Caba's most notable prize.

—What has happened?

"To shatter your will," Caba might have said, as he might have continued woodenly: "This formerly eminent colleague should have been the light of his generation. Through what evil, unsupervised game have all those hopes and promising signs come to naught?"

The formerly eminent colleague, now a humble civil servant, has evidently forgotten Caba's weaknesses or how to take advantage of them, and instead he ineffectually measures out the silence in pencil rotations, as they circle between the two fingers of his current chief—Sebastian Caba's long, fine fingers, made for leafing through parchments, wrappings, banknotes.

—I can't stand typewriters anymore.

The words travel from the door to the desk as if a hired actor had fired off an impromptu line. It falls flat, though the awkwardness assures verisimilitude.

Sebastian Caba can't tolerate his guest's prolonged confusion, arguments, or poorly timed jokes, and salvages as much of the conversation as possible by trying to find convenient solutions to the traps of confrontation. The elegant fingers abandon the pencil. Caba's palms turn upward. He shrugs his shoulders to indicate powerlessness, for Saint Sebastian will have tried fitting words, soothing syllogisms... up to the point of entrapping the subordinate by the side of the door, escorting him through the little foyer, and remaining on the threshold of his office, grieved, thoughtful, and disturbed (as much as necessary) by the other's disquiet and his own ... only to stand silhouetted in the frame of his upholstered door, gazing toward the receding steps that now seem to collapse beneath the guest, who had exhausted his truth or "*truquage*" — perhaps a deceptive trick disguised as certainty — too quickly, in a hurried moment ... and the office worker races down the steps with his hand forgotten around his throat.

The stairs, the street: belated spots of rain. Hands in pockets, the rain streaming down his forehead, his nose, his lips, the hole shaped like a crocodile in the damp wall. Shoulders stooped, the cold, the fear, the hand lifted again to his throat — his sidelong gaze, ready to beg or to bolt upward to the indifferent, dappled skies.

Suddenly: the street appears as useless freedom, fatigue. The wet hand circling the throat ... the narrow, labyrinthine streets under the rain, under the laziness, under the silence. The wandering son of the earth has thrown himself onto the streets like a foreign hooligan, a visionary, an outcast, hunted, happy to belong to this moment of rain, earth, and the lights in the sky.

Just then Monica Smântănescu stepped down from a tram and was about to climb up the little hill; to her left, the racket of the school was breaking out, that assault of little cannibals.

⋄ ⋄ ⋄

The electric switch is to the right of the door. Beside the switch is a meter: a small shiny, black-plastic block with a dial and red numbers. Above the meter, framed in white marble, are four porcelain knobs with serrated edges: the electric fuses. The window, the curtain. The massive desk under heaps of paper. A flowerless vase, black with oily fingerprints. A pair of large tailoring scissors. A small hollow bottle. Two lemons, one halved. Old newspapers coated with dust. A large red handbag with handle. Inside the handbag, notebooks wrapped in blue paper. Books. *Tous le Monument de Paris, Prix 2f50. Dr. G. Coman. Romanian-German Dictionary* (small format, the cover unglued). *Marcel Saras: Lectures en français facile.* Books.

The room drives the vagrant into a state of blind, murderous rage. However, it might only be a trap, in which the assassin no longer gets to kill. The professor will crush her prisoner with her large body. Covering his face with enormous, loosened breasts, she'll whisper smutty little nothings with her fairy's voice—she'll bury him under mountains of hot, soft, sweaty flesh.

A red cap with a large button at the crown hangs from a peg. Every evening, the giantess adjusts the wisps of hair on her upper lip and pulls on the red cap. Roguish, satisfied with her ambiguity, pink complexion, infantile smile, and syrupy voice, she hunts forbidden distractions by night: the small black purse stashed under her pudgy arm hides the powder compact, the condom, the freshly sharpened kitchen knife. Oily arms like tentacles will encircle the prisoner. Damp lips will glue themselves to his mouth. The large naked body will descend upon his tiredness, suffocating his flesh and sating his hunger. The prisoner will muddle through rolls of flesh, swallowed by her bland, maternal groans: "forget it, banish it, erase it all, the Captain turned to smoke, and so did his lonely daughter, we are smoke, caress me, forget it, goodnight, baby, forget, you're smoke, baby, forget." And the cowardly prisoner will forget his desire to kill her, will die *une petite mort*, defeated by her whimpering and will forget everything.

In the middle of the room, the round table covered by thick embroidery, like a blue bedspread on a sandy beach. The typewriter, a sheet of white paper with a carbon behind it—the text interrupted by a hasty departure: *La bonne aventure. / Je suis un pe-tit gar-çon / De bel-le fi-gur-re / Qui ai-me bien les bon-bons / Et les con-fi-tures / Si vous voulez m'en donner / Je saurais bien les manger / La bonn'aventur' / Oh gai! / La bonn'aventure !*

Near the typewriter, a little glass vase filled with a bouquet of slender red and pink flowers: blades of grass sprout between the blooms. A yellow cup with coffee stains on the rim and a teaspoon inside. A full ashtray. Breadcrumbs. A jam jar, one fourth consumed, a teaspoon sticking out of the jar. Between reading two paragraphs of the instructions for an assassination: a slurp from the jam spoon. A transparent mauve scarf. The giantess lightens her nocturnal sojourns with this mauve scarf tied around her neck, the fabric twisted jauntily to one side. A silk stocking gathered into a ball. Somewhere else, its mate. Let the assassin discover that everything in here gets mixed together, covered over, wiped out; one cannot apply pressure to anything, fabric and dust, pastas and sticky sauces, fruit compotes and confectionary. The green terracotta stove, the gas pipe with a screw-tap. Rotate to the left, rotate to the right, the right, always the right—to salvation—all the way to the end! A chair, a white towel resting on the edge of the piano. Lid open, the keys dirty from sweaty fingers. A book: *La bonne aventure.* A little blond boy smiling on the cover. In his right hand he holds a jar flowing with *confiture*, in his left, a ginger cat, dagger between its teeth. Three staves with notes and text. *Je-suis-un-pe-tit-gar-con. De-bel-le-figure. Qui-ai-me-bien-le-bon-bons. Et-le-fi-con-fi-tures.*

Heaps of scores, *Bülow-Haendel: Zwolf leichte Klavierstücke.* A little plastic monkey under a small, plastic tree. A white porcelain vase with painted flowers, violets. Another black vase, empty. Attached to the piano, the bookcase. Shelves full of books and magazines and scores. *K Čapek. Perruchot. Perruchot. Perruchot. Märchen der Brüder Grimm. The Eskimos. Light, Gravity and Relativity, Resin-Scented Canada. Doctor Writers, Writer Doctors. Haydn. Divertissements for the Piano. Brahms, Walzer. Czerny. Erster Lehrmeister.*

The temporary lover will be lulled by her bawdy song about birdcages and birdies, and the bare giantess will lift her short, sausage fingers, and pass her hand through a wig, a shaggy mess of curly red wool. Eyes purified for love or murder. The wig will fall over the piano keys.

She will be big and bare and bald, like someone doomed to the pyre, and then there'll be nothing but sleep; there'll be peace over the earth, peace over the forests, from which the nightingales and starlings and tales set out.

The room doesn't allow for movement. Here, the wardrobe with the mirrored door partly open. Here too, a quarter step away, the bed. The rumpled blue sheet, a pair of green socks, a roll of toilet paper, a bra, a blue skirt. The radio program. A thin book, *Humour en français.* Notebooks in blue-paper covers. The radio atop a bookshelf attached to the wall. Newspapers. Two small reading lamps. A thin, blue sock. Pale blue underpants, a white sock. The lamp's wires hanging over the bed. The stove. A green thermos. A large, red Dutch oven. A white, long-handled pot for coffee. A box of matches. An open jar of salt. Over the stove, mounted on the wall, a wooden rack where the television stands. Near the bed, a nightstand. The phonebook. A thin blue sock hanging off its edge, mate of the one by the radio. The sink. A long-handled comb. A brush. A violet bottle. *Common Lavender.* Another bottle. *Fine Lavender.* Two white plastic bottles: *Nutritional Milk.* A tube. Foaming toothpaste with chamomile extract. A toothbrush with a green handle in a pink plastic case. It will be necessary to wait and kill her here in this ramshackle pigsty—once briefly, once at length, to lay waste this box of piddling junk.

At the other end of the bed, behind the blue pillow, a flowered drapery. It masks a former door on which narrow shelves have been mounted. Boxes. Jars. Bottles. A flashlight. A bottle of cognac, empty. Colored boxes. *Fruit Cocktail.* A green plastic bag. A salt jar. Canned goods. Liver pate. Creeping thistle. Pork. Pork kidneys. Bottles with fruit nectar. Jars of jam. Fruit compote. Confiture.

The absent giantess doesn't have a clue that she will have to pay for the filth and ugliness that her small world represents or that her salvation is being prepared—the bullets, the noose, the poison—which will be announced in the obituaries, so that the children who've escaped from her piano lessons and lullabies can sleep peacefully at night. She'll find peace, finally, in this tomb where so many things are crowded together: the bed, the bookshelf, the piano, the stove, the television, the radio, the armoire, the sink, the books, the scores, the stockings, the confitures, the fats—here, where the spirit of the absent inhabitant unifies everything: dumping ground for delinquents, or conspirators' cell, or multicolored box where children tortuously try the cadences he-he, hoo-hoo on the funereal keys.

⁝ ⁝ ⁝

The professor of French and the piano will have an hour break for lunch. First, however, the stammering hours will come, the hours of gasping *je suis, tu es, il/elle est*. Recreation. Before instruction and recreation, morning: waking in haste, facing the disorder of a new day, not-combing, not-washing, racing down the stairs, enduring the suffocation of the tram, then climbing off and finally approaching the school.

The long limousines appear, braking elegantly in the building's courtyard: reaching maximum speed in front of the square, then suddenly, perfectly braking into the last, lazy, negligent curve—the barely audible stop like a ripple. The driver getting out on the left, slamming his door, running around the front of the car, and opening the door on the right, the vacant and sleepy little girl getting out, stiff and mute, slamming the door, climbing the school's front steps. The driver crossing in front of the car again, opening the door on the left, putting the car into gear, and then hitting the gas and bringing the car forward ... this, the drop-off pantomime mechanically repeated in a continuous procession of limousines, drivers, and children.

It was a matter of vainly having arranged her class schedule in order to avoid this insufferable courtyard motorcade, of preferring to arrive at school after the first hour and leave before the last—to avoid seeing the monsters coming and going. Nevertheless, the unseen automobiles will still be there, in their place, on their way, in her way, in her nightmares full of bewilderment and frustration. They race into the courtyard; they brake suddenly, the drivers dash left and right, opening and slamming doors. A blond boy steps out of the maroon car amidst stifled laughter. From a white car, a thin little girl has descended shyly, stepping fearfully. Keeping pace with each other, the boy and girl climb the school's steps slowly. The drivers open their doors, seat themselves, start their motors, rotate their wheels, disappear. Nightmarish apparitions: the stops, the departures, the phantoms, limousines always coming and going, arriving only to disappear, to empty their delicate, savage load and disappear as if none of this had ever been.

The gathering of the notebooks, the signature in the register, the hasty combing, dressing, arranging, smiling, greeting. Movement will be hindered to the barricaded right of the square. The specters gather: a long limousine, the little savages howl, roar with laughter, rush the school gate shouting at the top of their lungs. Screaming, dozens of invaders hurl their knapsacks in the air and toss kisses left and right. The door slams, the posh maroon car rumbles, starts moving, meteorically reaches the curve of the square, disappears. Now the white car departs—the one for the little girl in blue, who's having a difficult time separating from her girlfriends, chattering, and kissing them all. The little princess salutes her last girlfriend, rips a sheet from a notebook, writes something on it, holds out the paper. They both toss their golden hair, giggle, kiss each other once more. The white car leaps forward. Next a green one appears. There are a lot of students gathered, wild, sweaty, throwing their caps, knapsacks, scarves—a deafening romp.

Now! Freedom appears for an elusive moment among the rows of apparitions. Gaze lowered, among the phantoms torturing her night and day: an instant to consider her movements, humility, lack of grace, and how to pass unobserved to a point beyond the cars with their drivers who would love to insult her—an instant to run horrified all the way to the tram stop, to hear nothing, to withdraw and become unreachable, to pass a hand through her hair, over her eyebrows, over her frightened eyes, to gather the notebooks spilling out of her briefcase, to arrange the collar of her blouse, to remain unknown and unavailable for a couple of seconds, taking a single deep breath, one moment allowed by the gods.

Maybe, then, an hour for lunch. Only then. Barely then. But Monica is always ready to dream of a new spring day: the lilac, suave and sweet, the noble partner suave and sweet, and the owl singing with the cuckoo and the nightingale, suave and sweet, soothing and sinister.

⋮ ⋮ ⋮

"The transcription is in a file on the table. After you record the broadcast, please check that the text matches the recording," she had said. To record. On tape. On an outdated tape-recorder with a black and yellow checkered slipcover.

The big crimes of the day are broadcast live, on the spot, captured by television cameras and hurled simultaneously to millions of famished, hypnotized eyes. Imagination is on the wane, humiliated by hallucinatory reality. The little black microphone replaces and registers the horror ... the tapes will roll on monotonously, memorizing, transcribing, depositing, proving, authenticating.

The opening of the door, the rotation left, right, the click of the lock, the first steps, objects bumped in passing: chairs, piano keys, glasses—eventually silence. Suddenly, the shot—one, two, three—

three tenderly doleful hisses, the fall of a heavy body, the overturned chair. The dull, uncertain recording followed by the rotation of the door—opening, closing—the race down the stairs, the clank of the metal gate. Left behind: the audio imprint, a souvenir attesting to the skill of a professional, the precise, clean, elegant job—executed with gloved hands and rubberized gestures. The supple flight, evenly paced, without a hitch, without haste, without fear. Or: the opening of the door; the rotation—first left, then right—the lock turning, the first steps through the space, dropping the little satchel on the chair, the rolling of a jar, the sliding of a raincoat. Objects bumped: chairs, piano keys, glasses, the rustle of newspapers, the voice of the radio, the creak of a chair, the clink of the spoon in the jam jar. Suddenly: the fall. The brief twitch, rigor mortis. The assassin will have foreseen everything in detail, without shots, without running up and down the steps, without opening and closing doors, just the opportune drop of poison slipped into a glass, in a jar, on bread—anything at all in the victim's path. Or: the opening of the door, the rotation left, right: the click. Closed. Stepping through the space, clothes tossed, chair bumped, the curtain pulled. Suddenly: the leap. The last gasp, suffocation, the body tumbled on the rug. The assassin timidly opening and closing the door, cautiously climbing down the stairs. The swinging of the metal gate. Vanished. Calm, precise, efficient.

The tapes document—not only the shooting, the fall of the poisoned resident, the assassin's leap from behind the curtain, but also the ritual of suicide.

The sonorous voice of the black woman coming from the radio: *Summertime. Summertime.* The painful saxophone: beside it, the voice entering its monotonous lament, then the shot—one, two, three—no, just a single shot fired, efficient, tender: the body pacified, the desperate serenade of the saxophone, the tapes rotating obediently, the requiem. Or: the saxophone's hot, metallic notes lifting the singer's low-down murmur through her torrid gullet; the laceration of a summer afternoon—pure agony, the end of the Captain's daughter on a summer afternoon inside the singer's thick whisper, inside the mouth of the saxophone—suddenly, the overturned chair, the dangling lamp cord briefly strained, once, twice; in the mouth of the saxophone is the dying breath of the man at one with the woman's groan, recasting the Captain's departure with a dripping voice: evenly, monotonously, thickly; the song, sad as the waning of a summer afternoon, sad as the agony, the dusk, and the slow laceration of summer, its rotations in the huge celluloid tapes. Or: the leap over the balcony into empty space, or the knife, or the poison, or the pyre. Requiem for the suicide caught on celluloid tapes that rotate moans, songs, whimpers, shots, whispers, rustles, blows, embraces, steps, slammed gates. Or: the click of the gun … rehearsed from the middle, the beginning, the end of a doleful radio broadcast. "Good Evening, Kids!" "Good Night, Kids." The voice: comforting, soothing, disturbingly sexy. "Good Night, Kids," "Sleep Tight, Kids."

The tape deck—docile witness, efficient, promptly distributing memories, recording live: the last sigh, the shot, the celebrated woman's moan, pink and orange ribbons, the howl of the wolf, the hissing of the cats, anything, anywhere, anytime. Even when the resident is not at home because of the good will of a *histrion*, some theatrical actor, ready to transcribe songs, explosions, slender bedtime stories. Authenticity guaranteed, allowing memories, unaltered sentiments. Authenticity guaranteed: fresh memories, genuine feelings, all live, all the time—life, death, joy: you name it.

The chairs are covered with old clothes. Draped over the back of a chair, a white towel touches the edge of the piano. A plastic trashcan nearby: full of crumpled and stained papers. The bookshelf. The terracotta stove. Nightgowns, dirty rags, a green thermos. Boxes, jars, bottles, a flashlight, a jar of *Nescafé*, an empty cognac bottle, boxes marked *Fruit Cocktail*, a jar of salt, cans of liver paté, cans of pork kidneys, cans of green beans, jars of fruit compote. The objects perched, ready to topple onto the intruder.

The armoire. The wooden door creaks. The interior mirror: covered with fly spots. Dirty sheets, laundry wrinkled and mixed in with the clothes. Under the sheets, shirts, pullovers. The slipcover with black and yellow checks that opens with a zipper running along three edges. A tug at the heavy metallic handle. Things fall into a heap at the bottom of the wardrobe. The mirror disappears. The canvas-covered metal box with a green border, too heavy to lift. The black, twine-wrapped microphone is taken out, and then put back. Tested—it works. Two spools of tape. Buttons. It must be handled with care, with attention; it can't be bumped or damaged: the preparations must be precisely coordinated, the operation must begin several minutes before H Hour and finish several seconds before the end of the hour. The recording must capture everything, must envelop the entire auditory dimension. Discretion, attention, surveillance, skill.

But for now, the lid has to be closed. On the chair, the black microphone. Discretion, control, order, skill, attention.

⁑ ⁑ ⁑

School: panic fills the last minutes of recess. Sound effects added to the eighth or ninth minute of the recording will add to the terror weighing on the poor teacher's thick shoulders and overwhelm her prattle among acerbic smiles and obliquely suspicious looks. Terror pulses under the warm layers of bloated flesh. Her hands mechanically leafing through the pages of a book or hurrying into her purse, scalp rising, shoulders trembling, salivating, her hands moving toward the window—air!—or toward her throat, fearfully trying to free herself from the collar of her blouse or sweater: minute eight or nine signals the sound of a coming bell, the annulment of the truce. After the bell, two more minutes remain, an empty space, in which time continues to carve away at the frozen gaze, now devoid of humanity, blind until the alarm rings. Suddenly: small, savage rings—this is not the worst of it. Pavlovian salivations at the sound of the bell. Purse closed, hand at throat, moving to the buttons of the blouse. The roll book glued to blunt fingers, becoming an extension of the hand. Noiseless steps, as if crushing cotton. The gleam of the teachers' lounge door. The door closing behind … and then consciousness begins to surge: electricity passing through her body like voltaic current. The corridor ahead: long and cold. This will be the hardest moment. The teachers' lounge door will be closed. The corridor will be as cold as sleeplessness: ashen walls, almost black, the chill of footsteps on the white cement. The faint body no longer supporting the pressures of the white flesh; numb and paralyzed by fear, moving one foot in front of the other like a somnambulist all the way to the first door on the left: the exhausted entry into the classroom, mind adrift from fear—but not before one final hesitation in front of the door. The big roll book with blue-cardboard covers glues itself to her sweaty hip.

Blitzkrieg of bread pellets, or a long mouse-like squeak from the corner, or subdued chanting and a cruel choir of whispers erupting in a frenetically murmured chorus … big Moni-pig, little Moni-big, moldy Moni-fig, Moni-wig, here comes Moni-big, here comes Moni-pig, here comes Moni-frigg, little Moni-pig. Another round of bread pellets, mouse squeaks, and a chorus of hooting owls.

Even more dangerous: the cunning silence, a well-calculated diversion. The classroom mute, absentmindedly looking out the window. She'd try to re-establish normality and control, but they'd already know her powerless charade of mock severity, her bloated kindness, her panic, her flurried confusion. The young masters are powerful, free, ruthless: their high-pitched screams or icy silences quickly annihilate her.

The terror of opening the classroom door. Every single time. After the tyrannical hour of class, the horror begins all over again: after recess, another slaughter by chubby-cheeked sadists. They will encircle her, dancing around, following her down the corridor screaming nicknames, questions, and demands—paralyzing her with revolt. The corridor will fill with their chorus: "Missus, missy Sour cream, sour milk makes Sour cream; what's good with cream? What does the dog dream?" They will leave her at the door of the teachers' lounge. Disheveled. Undone. Flabbergasted.

Big roll call book glued damply to hip—her useless shield against the class, disciplined or rebellious by turns: she would wait a moment, caught in the vortex of her ravished mind, certain—as always—of losing allies. They would be rapidly converted to the cheerful, venomous conspiracy—an echo of former days—converted, to the extent of their infantile cruelty, and they would exact their revenge against the authorities who want to domesticate them, subjugate them, tire them out, make them grow old.

The horror before the door, every single time, the repetitive motions: remaining by the window for several seconds, disappearing in the teachers' lounge, and snapping back to reality in the cold corridor with gray walls in front of the classroom door where yesterday's phantoms have been waiting.

⋮ ⋮ ⋮

"The transcription is in a file on the table." That's what she had said, "on the table, is the transcription." Not on the table. On the desk, near the red bag. Under the small, red hardcover book. The transcription among other typed texts: *There lived a little bird in a wood quite removed from the rest of the world. Although she suffered from hunger and cold in that forest, the bird felt that she belonged there. The forest, too, liked to know that the dear little bird could always be found there. Every* tree rejoiced when the little bird ... One fine day, quite unexpectedly, a bird fancier passed through the forest ... the little bird, familiar with the hunger and cold of the forest, but also its joys, refused the bird fancier's proposal. To prove that he was a man of his word, the bird fancier returned to the forest after a while with a new golden cage.

February 28. My Dear Dănuț, Voila! The time has finally come for the letter I've been meaning to write for so long. You have created a footbridge with these telephone conversations: the swallow and the letter symbolize ... sooner than I managed to write you.

Thursday, March 2nd. My Dear Tiberiu. Just got home after an afternoon that you wouldn't wish on your worst enemies.

Sunday, March 5th. My Dear Tiberiu, almost no time has passed— and yet it feels like forever—since I believed you would phone me every morning. I was afraid to believe. Then I felt that I must believe ... one's eyes do nothing but cloud over, yearning cries out, from all points of view ... it dilutes your strength ... a fable that I will use in the school's show at the end of the year ... you'll be quick enough to recognize the characters ... and it would have been very suitable for the evening radio broadcast.

Miss Smântănescu, I alone try to console my thoughts, and hope what you write is true: the lines you've written have awakened ... to request a transfer, or if I do not get it, then through the termination of a budget ... it depends on me, and as the saying goes ... through the strength of will and the ambition I possess, I live in the hope ... for I am on the road of life, like that wayfarer ... stepping as assuredly as the wayfarer. With Deepest Esteem, Grig.

The past, present, and future, tingling with name days, endearments, colored marionettes, imbroglios, and events poured into the telephone receiver, agitation tempered by icy gestures.

Then, cringing-scared-stricken, searching-for-sweet-words, appeals-shelters-asylums.

Then, epistolary ribbons, endearing-cradling-sugary-words.

Then, sticky-fairy-tales-beginning-with-once-upon-a-time, the-

26

suave-voice-of-the-female-announcer, the-bedtime-broadcast-for-children, school-celebrations, carefully-combed-blows-on-the-perfidious-piano.

Then, swooning-tears-for-lost-ephemeral-partners-garlands-trinkets-in-vain.

⦂ ⦂ ⦂

Over there, one swims, splashing too much.

The water: thin and clear, transparent and light. The swimmer's rhythm, barely efficient, with only the slightest appearance of gain, proceeds by tortuous advances only to be annulled right away. In the water his suffering—his alien, minimally harmonious movement—would be illuminated as if on a screen. Only, the aged oil of days doesn't permit spectacular waves and reabsorbs their amplitude. Under the thick layer of fluid, the tiny caresses continue, sloppy and lascivious. The boat rocks. A metal rail supports them, one beside the other. They look at the horizon, and the hill rising above it, where the detainees await them. On one side: an old man with a long, coffee-colored beard and a transistor: a portable piano.

—Handel's Chaconne in G Major.

The man turns in astonishment toward the lovely-voiced woman sitting beside him.

—Music is my business, you know. After this visit, I'm leaving for the Apuseni Mountains. I change trains twice. I'm going to see an old friend.

He is amazed by his neighbor's talkativeness, her logorrhea. He has no appetite for conversation. Instead, he thinks of his father in a prison uniform, and of his relationship with his father, and of the relationship between Captain Zubcu and his daughter. The tension of waiting creates a predisposition to random conversations, he doesn't feel like talking to this stranger about meeting his father again, let alone the father and daughter he can't stop thinking about. Monica Smântănescu misses this opportunity to learn about the Captain's suicide or the man she has just approached. She will, however, note her address and her phone number for him on a bit of packing paper. And to top it off, the sullen bastard will eventually call her. He'll meet her too—intrigued by her puerile appearance, by the demon of her banality. It deserves exploration, obviously: grotesqueness ornamented with idylls; the masks of reality meriting assumption; her miserable ferment—of course it deserves exploration, before being blown up it deserves to be explored, pawed, fingered, maimed, yes, before blowing it up, furiously and ecstatically. Monica is already talking, confessing, naturally; she's going to meet her former colleague and boss, Tiberiu Covalschi, the poor thing, who has finally wound up in prison, which is to say in a labor camp: the pitiable maniac deserves compassion. The music-loving woman knows what compassion is, and tenderness, and what it means to have a sexual urge.

Once maybe, long ago, in the crystalline water of the very beginning, could they really have been so—these great, terrible, unprecedented attempts—or were they, really? Or might they become again, if the past could be played over again?

The talkative woman leaves in plain sight: several sweat-dampened strands of hair protrude from her face, short thick fingers like a bunch of plump sausages, a masculine briefcase stuffed with notebooks and breadcrusts. Just now she crosses the threshold into the school's narrow, shadowy corridor. One pace ahead of her is Tiberiu Covalschi, the Covalschi of those days: the Crocodile.

How would comrade Monica have dressed?—as a teenager might? In winter: a masculine cap, one of those Russian ones with earflaps, or one of the more usual ones with a peaked crown. In summer: simple dresses, with little white collars, lace trim at the ends of her puffed sleeves, clean colors, pale blue or pink or white, vaporous over her bloated body. In winter: masculine ski pants bursting over her swollen thighs, and solid, black ski boots. In summer: laced flats, large enough for her enormous feet, and the simple, light-blue dress with lace collar, slightly wrinkled—with a little grease or ink-stain hidden somewhere. In any case, not very clean, assembled in haste from the wardrobe overflowing with clothes, from the rumpled bed, from beneath newspapers, notebooks, and books, from the table full of dirty utensils, unsharpened pencils, and leftover hankies. From any hook or hanger or corner of the room—the attire of the past, present, and future stand aligned in a pigsty.

She would enter: going through the school's hall in her January boots, with her ski pants and sweater, wearing her red, tasseled beret. Tiberiu Covalschi—as before—would lead. It was his way of making the situation slightly less ridiculous: leading her boorishly ... She would've had enough common sense, even back then, to wonder if her presence provoked vulgarity, if she aroused an appetite in others for cruelty and humiliation. She would enter the hall looking at the rug, the three black leather chairs, the little round table covered with glass, and the two magazines.

Too few, two magazines! Only, objecting was no longer possible after having been scolded for the collection of women's magazines— obtained at the expense of exhausting bargaining. Several days ago, she had shown the comrade boss the colored heaps arranged on the table, but on comrade Covalschi's order, the magazines had to be returned. Her initiative to acquire them had seemed scandalous. We cannot offend the female comrades who come here, Covalschi decreed, looking at the hall where mothers would meet their children. The comrade mothers must not be insulted by heaps of frivolous magazines. On the table there were now only two examples, as Tibi had decided.

The first female inspector. Monica: trembling with amiability. Covalschi: distant and mute, his ascendance as a cunning dwarf, shielded behind his hideousness, seemed perfect for those chaotic times.

—You have arranged things well. There should be more magazines. It looks poverty-stricken. If three people come, there won't be enough to read.

Covalschi levels his gaze at the walls. Monica begins stammering.

—You know, we thought to display only the latest issue. The others should already be familiar, of course.

The inspector looked like she had been struck by a thunderbolt: red-cheeked, suffocating in her fur overcoat.

—Familiar? What foolishness! As if I have the time, as if *I* have the time to read magazines! As if I were the wife of who knows what minister of the old guard with nothing to occupy my time. Who on earth could come up with such a stupid excuse?

The final word gushed out of her with a splash, with an excess of saliva. The Crocodile's silence allowed him to think.

—I haven't had time to stop by here. I was just coming myself to check. It was an initiative of comrade Smântănescu's, a lack of ... We'll make things right—Covalschi stuttered, looking pale. The visitor listened to him tensely.

—Yes! You do that, please—without fail, immediately, urgently: right now! This is unbelievable, unacceptable!

Timid, fearful, there was nothing to do but remain silent alongside Covalschi's hypocrisy. Covalschi could have managed by himself, anyhow. If he had looked differently, or if he hadn't known how to use ugliness to his advantage, he would have been as vulnerable as his submissive, frightened, disoriented peers: the visiting inspector— that menacing authority—would have crushed him like any other subordinate, just as she had crushed Monica Smântănescu. Comrade Tibi, however, continued to act normally, using a mask to cover his secret weaknesses and inevitable betrayals. He went on favoring hard, taciturn, deformed people. His hideous appearance was an insult to conventional frivolity. He was right: conventional forms created the possibility of equivocation, indulgence, and diversion. The dwarf's unblinking eyes knew how to scrutinize the ongoing spectacle with the vigilance of an archangel confronting a secular emergency.

Monica lived in her sickeningly sweet sensuality, in nightmares and lazy illusions. Always hoping for something that would help dismiss memories of school, partners (of one kind or another), and her crazy mother in the mountains, raving in a madhouse—it wasn't possible to slam the door on vulgarity, which leads to running like a mangy goat into some neighbor's sweaty hands, her temples throbbing like pressure columns, the big, heavy body ready to burst through her fat hide.

Covalschi was confident in his intuitions: all he had to do now was sock it to the fat dreamer, which meant waiting for the day when the little cannibals finally went beyond their routine limits and Little Moni-pig Smâtăni-wig was laid out on the teachers' lounge sofa, choking on tears, no longer capable of teaching her next class. Covalschi walked her home, and once inside, he leaned against the terracotta stove and looked at her intently for a long time, smiling slightly and showing the gap between his crocodile teeth. It was warm in the room, excessively warm, as if the little cannibals had built their fire inside her room. Mostly, the plan had been to listen docilely to his colleague's laments and respond calmly at calculated intervals. She had withered powerlessly between his coarse jokes—the imaginary pursuers still chasing her—and only had wanted to collapse from exhaustion, like a hunted beast tormented by thirst and sleeplessness, eager for a moment of peace and refreshment: she would have melted into the earth through the soles of her feet except that the jokes seemed to revive her ever so slightly, like a gentle caress: she was almost his prey.

Today, she was vulnerable to her own weaknesses, ready to be blown off course by a slight change in the wind—and it would happen rapidly, unexpectedly—now, she would believe any of Covalschi's stories, even if they were about hypnosis, sadism, kleptomania, or "preventive, monstrous, necessary evil" as the only alternative to normality. For it was no longer a matter of regarding the stories as simplified, exaggerated rants or the usual posturing of men eager to complicate the monotony of their conquests; no, believing them to be true would be less frightening. In the over-heated, disorderly room, the gleam in Comrade Tibi's eyes would manipulate any trace of vulnerability.

—You know what they call me? *The Devil*. Do I steal, lie, stage sadistic games, intimidate, blackmail, rape? Yes, especially rape. Even sentimental fatties like you. You can't escape. I could strangle you.

Then steady steps approach the victim, who's ready to scream if she still can, ready to abandon herself, to submit, to escape—ready to finish the whole thing once and for all. Once, twice—again and again, until complicity becomes indestructible, to the point of dementia, and even beyond that, to clemency. Consent and closeness mix indecently, melting all opposition into sudden grunting, and ending in the restful release of an embrace that smells of clogged drains.

It would be like a ball sliding rapidly down an inclined plane. The bumps that would slow the fall—remorse, suffering, revolt—would be worth less and less under the curse that persists irreversibly despite the intermittent remains of faded joys and better days. The master will continue to invent new horrors, because this experience permitted no right to any quiet, not even to degradation: the degradation flirts with the promise of stagnation and equilibrium. The fear of tearing herself away, the risk of anything else, and her self-loathing reveries intensify the nights and days of torture temporarily halted by rare gestures of goodwill—the smile, the caress, the kiss. Accepted infirmity ... a stranger's inoffensive smile becomes absolute tenderness, an invitation to repeat the Covalschi experience.

The beads of detail and mechanical analysis string themselves around the third person: *she, the third person—invented, abstract, illusory, bearing any burden, any loan, any pirouette—is nothing but a chubby infant with a faint mustache and blue eyes—innocent and illogical—who transports, conductively and hospitably, the director's needs, ambitions, and the pride of his glory, his garrulity, his pedantry, his perversity.* The slave of the unforeseen, of the other's—or of an imagined—plan, ready to trade everything for a tiny, tender, indulgent, attentive promise of protection, in the hopes of somehow seizing, possessing, binding, and imprisoning him, in order to make herself whole, to define herself.

For this sense of self-definition (or another equivalent), in which we might recognize our own larval panting—agitated by rapid contraries absorbed by their own exhaustion as in sleep—the accomplice backstage would believe himself justified in denying her, in shattering her, in sacrificing her, while assuming not only the responsibility for the execution but even the obligation to redeem or justify his own invisible, useless role in the equation, and in haste might attempt to ignore the fictional alternative, the restaging of a failure from long ago.

... She must return to the beginning of the downward roll, from the peak of the inclined plane—not from absurd, hypothetical alternatives—before she begins to run dizzily after whatever deceptive call, before she pointlessly drifted toward some unknown man: in a boat full of other unknowns advancing toward the unknown, in a train compartment with nameless and faceless passengers. Sly messages in the personal columns of illustrated magazines, fairy tales for little gingerbread pianists. Unless the telephone didn't somehow get her out of one trouble in the nick of time, only to hurl her back into another.

She would find the energy to survive on any conveyor belt — carried from one place to another, from one illusion to another. By taxi or tram or train, ark or airplane or automobile. In any train then, as long as she goes on having the power to utter cries, which is to say, to go on breathing: being reborn after each new failure — she would be the same.

The experience would involve fretting along the corridor, looking for someone to talk to and then rummaging through their good intentions, their gentle, long-abandoned dreams, passing hastily through the compartments of their past — as well as their present — desperately wanting to lean in beside them with vague desires and murky cravings.

She would look for *semblables*, dreamy creatures used to lining up like obedient soldiers, one behind the other, for hours, years, lifespans. The journey seemed to be an act of liberation: her neighbor might be the very person she was waiting for, with whom she might flee, might escape. In the narrow corridor, in the little plush-lined compartments, the strangers look at each other, inquiring reciprocally into each other's hidden identities with fugitives' eyes, eager to roll the dice.

Beside her, the gentleman seems like a mirror of his own silence. The young woman across the way — the very image of a smile gone astray — her slightly maladaptive personality constantly searching for the right place for her suitcase, plump hands, illusions, and small baggage as disorderly as her hair: the long, black, frisky (overly frisky, too curly) ringlets. This overly agitated, overly ample, overly impatient person could be the perfect likeness of the little angel parodied by the poor professor.

It would be in vain to oppose or resist: the voice of this plump traveler might signify the truth of her being. Her restless hunger for the bustle of new things, neighborhoods, and unexpected events, which could be—who knows?—only the explosion of fatigue. She cannot convert her energy—expended in the zigzags of her quests: false hope, false despair like lightning without thunder—into another reserved, potential energy. If she could find the resources within herself for another sadness or dignity, if these deserve to be found, if worthy and true sorrows actually exist, she might have become a bride, a mother, an industrious housewife.

Speculations whirl around her. She grows from the suppositions. Those around her try to remain unaffected by her frayed appearance, by her navy blue ski pants scrunched over her thighs, by her worn military boots. But it would be in vain to resist gasping at the enchanting voice of a disguised goddess in borrowed clothes.

There she is: watching from her corner near the door, wanting to extract a book, a magazine, a newspaper from the crammed briefcase. She will go out in the corridor, pass in front of the other compartments, look at the travelers, and offer herself to their glances. Exhausted, abandoned, there'll be nothing left to do but to lean against the window to the right of the neighboring compartment. The journey will end somewhere, sometime; the heavy iron bird will open its rusty beak and discharge the little group of the deceived. Torn by febrile, spectral gestures, the convoy will scatter. The luckiest will rapidly recognize the end of the adventure. Only a few belated dreamers will try to prolong their truancy, delay their return, prolong their liberty for at least another second. They too will be brought back, more obedient than before; she will see herself multiplied in hundreds of twins lined up in their same old rows, frightened by future temptations to escape, protected by their zealous submission. Standing close to each other now, the traveler and the disguised goddess lean against the metal window bar. Raising the little transistor with his right hand, he has just come out of the neighboring compartment. Remaining silent, they look at the scenery.

—Handel's Chaconne in G major.

She would give him a sly look in quarter profile first before letting her voice ripple forth.

—That's Handel's Chaconne in G Major.

And he would quiver in amazement.

—Yes, music is my business, you know. Where am I going? Me? Far away. All the way to the Apuseni Mountains. I change trains two more times. To see my mother. She's in a madhouse. The war, the camp. Her husband killed before her eyes, in front of the grave he was forced to dig for himself.

Between them, the wheels turn expectation into impatience. Her little whimpers will make themselves heard. The other travelers in the corridor will hear her voice, and they will laugh. Anyone willing to exchange a few words with this unhappy woman will know what haunts her: she'll tell you her story, and she'll convince you that the dead are dead, and will manage to forget everything—it's foolish to travel great distances for something like this: forgetting can be done anywhere and especially where there are crowds of people, possibilities of all kinds; the wilderness doesn't honor mourning—the dead do not exist, even if they were our brothers and sisters and parents: life is and is and is.

The road has barely stretched itself out, time is distant, in the future, tolerant. She will try complicity, she will playfully endure time, and she will find pleasure in her fleshy transgressions. Definitely, the destination has no importance; with an ally by her side, she will always feel free to wander, to run—to the mountains at the end of the world, to submit, to slave, to devote herself, to be able to drain him of sentiment, nostalgia, secrets, and sorrows, to strangle him lovingly. Far away, in the distance, as far away as possible, like the deceptive illusions of childhood. The iron bird, its belly populated by captives, runs on crazily, crazily.

⁞ ⁞ ⁞

Legs sink into the parquet under the weight of morning. Misha: idle, on guard. The statistical sheet, verification, timekeeping, re-use, contract, code, coordination, installed power, pumped power, columns, furnaces, siren, doorbell, kids' bedtime broadcasts, tape recorder.

The key, the radio broadcast, the text, the tape recorder. The stair, the spiral, the doormat. Typed manuscripts and carbon copies and typewriters, deafening and annihilating, ubiquitous. Sebastian Caba, diplomatically asking the clerk to finish everything quickly. The hand around the throat and "can't stand anymore"—period. Full stop. Stairs, streets, another room, cell, or birdcage.

The stranger under the rain, standing on the street corner, with arms crossed—the prisoner of the moment, a challenging deaf-mute, a suspicious person, an outcast dreaded by everyone: the hurried passersby, parents, teachers, wives, lovers, stern mothers, aunts, sisters, neighbors, porters, police informants, office workers, and sadistic detectives. He abandons himself to the streets, hidden on the narrow metal staircase that curls in slow, serpentine spirals; the body follows the spiral of a point that trickles along the arc of a ray, rotated from a torrid center. The room: like the remains of a failed aeronautic expedition. The prisoner confused by the absent inhabitant's stories. The birds, bird fanciers, forests, and the quail's blurted chirping. Every gesture demolishes objects, heaps—avalanches; every step provokes crashes, touches sticky streaks, and upsets dust trails. Notebooks, books, scores, curtains, chairs, shoes, jam, cans, notebooks, buttons, books, teaspoons, hats, *je suis un petit garcon de belle figure.*

Long limousines snake through the sickly fog, through the wanderer's mind, and into a square in front of the school, while Miss Monica is invaded by rows of little lunatic barbarians slamming the limousine doors like cruel slaps. Long, official limousines, phantoms of comrades, intellectuals, and solemn, subservient drivers: officials who dizzy her mind like wandering ghosts.

The guilty party—vagabond, improvised assassin, dime-a-dozen suicide—would have his movements recorded among bedtime stories for kids (tormented by Monica Smânănescu's piano): three tender bullets, the sob stifled by poison, the death rattle of the strangled, suicide's requiem, sung in the low voice of the black woman howling at the end of an afternoon.

She, Monica Smânănescu, traveling the suicide's mind, embodied, materialized under any mask... the guilty one banishes her now, trying to escape, forget. She, the third person, apt for the burdens of her inventor, is overloaded, used, and defiled every which way; enslaved to her role, subjected to terror, siphoning the burden from any character, the nicknames, the passions, the power—or precariousness, preposterousness, plunge, or promise—she: tenaciously dragging her special effects, her tormented acts of tenderness, encircling unknowns, heedless or caught unaware.

The third person, inventing her language in columns of typed text, between missives, souvenirs, cries, sufferings aligned in the typewriter, in two or three of Covalschi's copies. Satisfying her voracity for smells, stenches, colors, and falsettos, little red horns leap out of a word here and there. Her words: pleasantly warm, pleasantly plump, melding, mountains, Tibi, Dănuţ, Tudorica, damaged porcelain, consuming fire—the candy-pink flesh of words goes on multiplying predicates, modifiers, and adjectives in a broken ingestion of the grotesque, half-invented, perverse games, drained juices, the terror of autumn with its torturous classes, and the mute telephone; the trains keep running, letters stray toward one another, and the walls that enclose this space leaven and grow fat. *Lady piano-teacher wishes to meet a kindred gentleman: I await a protector, a partner, a passing affair.*

Suddenly, a moment of numbness permits a brief revolt against her role, but the denial of ridiculousness dissimulates into its own acceptance—a double game, counter-rhythms resumed with the old cunning. The red crayon's tip pecks at the sentences, dilating them, nudging them: the pain should be more pathetic, pedantic, zany, as these chance interlocutors and executioners expect. Her small revenge gives the illusion of momentary freedom as she exaggerates her grimace, sentiments, and stridencies to appear as a poor little girl: an idiot of thirteen or fourteen who has been asleep for twenty years, during which time her hair has grown, and her nails and breasts—all the while preserving the same immaculate heart, the same pure, idiotic, infantile mind.

She will execute the imaginary somersaults prescribed by the fugitive—the fearful man who controls her through calculated detours of weird clowning—the slave of his tricks, a credible abstraction with the appearance of authenticity, the phantom haunting the space in which he struggles. The words of her temporary executioners will be used: *I try to console my thoughts alone. Brown haired, just like the photo taken in 1964 in the park in Sinaia, alone on the road of life, like that wayfarer in the personals, with laser-like eyes.* Everything that can be discovered or invented will be used, and at the end of this ordeal he will climb the serpentine stairs of evening, in a dream where he can prepare the three redeeming bullets, the poison in the jar of jam, the strangling hands—atoning, healing her. Will the executioner arrive as docile as a newborn on the slow, serpentine staircase? Does she exist, does she?

She: suspiciously easy to decipher in objects, thoughts, words, colored letters, and bits of mending, always visible in the chaos of this space, in the nearby fingerprints, the memories on view, the immediate things.

Are her improbably real traces not the deceptions of a trap, of a perfidious track, a delay through which the intruder hopes to escape?

Thursday, March 2, 1961

My Dear Tiberiu,

Got home not long ago after an afternoon you wouldn't wish on your worst enemy. (But more of that later.) Went into the room, where every single thing was still in the exact place you left it (after your departure, there wasn't even time to eat, let alone tidy up).

The two glasses—the little one and the big one—were side by side on the table, so close together that they seemed to be a proof of our unity. The cigarette butts were still in the ashtray on the table, while the other ashtray was still on the bed, exactly where you left it, and it was as if the objects tried to establish your continued presence here among the books, drinking orange juice, smoking and ... the other things (but more later about the other things)—exactly as in the moments when we were conjoined, from all points of view. You ordered me to forget your telephone number (and the other things). Personally, I don't even hope that we should talk. You can't forbid writing, though. Not to anyone! It feels like spring already— the lilac will flower, the nightingales will sing, and from my heart (as among flowers and stars), not one thing will be removed. I'm like a poor, drunken boat under waves of flowering lilac—nothing that's noble and beautiful has budged in me.

The multitudes of thoughts and feelings have united in a whirlwind: I must wage a fierce battle, not to be completely lost. You should know that this afternoon the whirlwind was more powerful than I, and I was 90% knocked out.

The phrase "it feels like spring already" is underlined in red and on the edge of the typed page with a hurried, handwritten note: "Tibi will not understand ... he thinks I am a sentimental goose to walk all over, so it won't give him food for thought, on the contrary, it will make him furious, as it should."

After all our telephone conversations today (four in number, which breaks the record of all other days), I realized that it might indeed be beautiful that you want to be mine, to the extent of your capabilities. The fact that I have felt more and more bound to you has left me clutching the telephone. It's true that all kinds of other voices also find their way there (don't be jealous!). At least there's warmth coming through the phone (remember, yesterday morning I didn't quit until you were happy again). Eating's impossible and so is sleep — in spite of being a conscientious person. Your presence makes itself felt everywhere, and what's more prosaic but true is that you continue to meld me to you, exactly as in those moments of ecstasy when you — according to your own affirmations — sacrificed yourself solely for my ecstasy. I continue to let myself be convinced of the aforementioned sentiments and maintain that the same blaze consumes me, despite having been categorically forbidden them. A fire is easily lighted, but it quenches itself with difficulty (more about that later). You will ask me how I stand with the fire that I lit once in a train and carried far into the mountains? How was it suddenly extinguished when it was still burning several days ago — as proven in the letter about the trinket from the first of March that I had prepared for you and that you opened violently and without my permission?

My Dear Tibi,

There are fires and fires and fires. Some smolder, others consume everything that stands in their way, all at once. The fire in the mountains — when I missed you so, although you'd hurt me badly and I forgave you — was never consuming. It burned intermittently, without storms, and it illuminated my life in a way that was magical, like a fairy tale, if you please, but ephemerally. I was without it once for four months, once for six, sometimes being on the way to believing that it had gone out for good. It never gave the sensation of consuming me more and more powerfully. So you see, the memories that link me to Dănu are stretched over five trimesters, but sporadic ones.

The words "prosaic but true" and "like a fairy tale" are circled in red pencil.

My Dear Dănuţ,

Voila!—the time has finally come for the long-projected letter! The high snowdrifts through which winter howled like a wolf begin to melt: proof that nothing of what is noble and sweet can die. Is it really necessary to spell everything out for you, from all points of view? I wouldn't think so. You're smart enough, and you lived beside me, too, through all the things that happened by chance, and I even went so far away with you, as I had not expected (more of that later). You're too sharp not to understand that the locomotive represents the train in which we met, and the transistor radio—the departure point of our discussions, the heart in a boat—the heart on the little waves that kept getting bigger and bigger after the intervening events and in which you, through our telephone conversations (yes, you see, the telephone), managed to repair to some extent, from a certain point of view. Through these telephone conversations you also created the footbridge toward my visits, from whence my heart sang, every time, and especially the second visit (see the waves of notes and the piano keys). You will realize that the swallow with this letter symbolizes your awaited epistle—rather than my having succeeded in writing to you. The piano is my signature. With much dearness, your

Mica

The phrase "white snowdrifts" is circled in ink, and written above: "Don't worry about that. This one's an engineer!" Also circled are the words "smart," "point of view," and "particularly."

My Dear Tiberiu,

It's such a short time—yet it feels like forever—since I was able to believe that you would call me every morning by phone and that we would converse for a quarter of an hour, at least. It seems like only yesterday that noble spring had come, and that we were slipping like a drunken boat into the flames. The consuming fire had started and the waves carried me with it. Everything in the house is as you left it, trying to maintain, to a certain extent, the illusion that you are still here, that you never left, ever. But most of all, while trying to disengage myself from suffering, I flung myself into my didactic obligations, which were reclaiming me in the most urgent way (more later). If you could only know what I was dealing with, to a certain ridiculous extent, at school, and all because of this scatter-brained head. But it seems that only the head refuses. All my organs have revolted: my liver or stomach, I hardly know which, doesn't do its duty; sometimes my heart aches, sometimes it stabs me; my eyes don't do anything but cloud up all the time, especially when I need them most; my nerves play tricks on me at night when I need sleep so very much. You said it's necessary to forget even your telephone number. So I, your close comrade in joys and sorrows and dreams and happinesses, to a certain extent, am not allowed to know anything—the one who's supposed to believe and understand. But how can you believe and understand if you don't want to know? And how can you know if you've erected a wall between us?—if now as I write this letter at five in the morning you would be by my side, at least to the extent of your abilities. Writing cannot be forbidden, so I write, although there are a million urgent problems to be solved (tests and notebooks to correct, and without fail cleaning the house and putting things in order, because things really can't stay this way anymore; I have two lessons to write, and at eleven o'clock I have to be at school to type some tables for the headmistress (but more later). I don't know if I understood what you were saying about the Gordian knot. It came to me, traveling by tram and *on foot from one lesson to another, as a fable I can use at the end-of-year celebration I organize every summer with the children I teach privately. You're acute enough to recognize this as one of the facts that I've added here and there ... Now, since you're working in your specialty again, in the domain of educational radio, you might slip it into the broadcast where you think would be most suitable—into "Good Night, Kids," I think.*

Yours, always, Monica S.

⋮ ⋮ ⋮

The teaspoon spotted with bits of compote, dirty notebooks, dusty books, moldy handkerchiefs. The television mounted above the kitchen range, unmatched socks on top of colored magazines, the wardrobe crammed with blankets, shoes, rags. The piano. The spirit of the absent mistress breathes from every corner of the narrow cell, from every wrinkle in the sheet, from the unwashed jars, the piles of tin cans ready to collapse onto the imprudent observer, suffocating under the glassy sounds of the piano, under the rotten lace doily, under the cats dizzy from ether. The summer night air stirs the world of the inhabitant's appetites, famished for sauces, preserves, fats, slurping nervously, greedily, under heaps of duplicate books—the second copies acquired in advance for her partner.

If it weren't for our simplistic need to classify—that trap of logic ... the disorder, the libidinous filth, the disgusting need for stroking, salivation, verbal embroidery, and saccharine disclosures, the whole caboodle might be turned inside out. The loneliness under the gray walls, the humiliated tears, the voice yielding to the first phone call and bouncing back under the influence of matrimonial ads: the whole list could just as well characterize someone on the alert to degradation and the ridiculous. Then it would be a matter of conscious provocation, disorientation of intruders—a hidden, revengeful game. Accepting herself in a zealously played role, she would become free to increase her flounderings. Truth and falsehood would expand into perverted farces, malignant complicities, survived sadnesses. She would be presented with a double victory: one having to do with the effect of her scenario on the prisoner and another arising from a vicious dissimulation. Her rebellious spirit would direct the whole series of stories, phone calls, and emotional stunts, which would make her nothing more than a vain and petty harlequin.

Could this be a way of exposing overly direct signals and their vulgar, immediate significance? Or just apparent proof that she plays her role in a state of panic, well-calculated panic ripe with hypocrisy? Or the tactic of confusing the victim by strewing his path with secrets posted in plain sight, which ends in circling around a tangled and hermetic center, the self, her ultimate and authentic value, her burlesque aloneness? The trajectories of her apparent defeats would find redemption in her voice blowing over her usurped body—which is to say, her authentic sufferings, apparent and deceptively mediocre. If only there weren't more—how many more—arborescent hypotheses: words growing like mushrooms, covering and concealing, perhaps just another trick to catch his illusory refuge between even thicker walls. If only it wasn't her—in fact—or just the cockroach that her furious fantasy contains. If only there weren't words.

⋮ ⋮ ⋮

The bitch with red fur might signal the attack on the banks. The *Wangard tire* warns that dissidents are now being tracked. *Spanish* is the watchword for silence at any price. *Exchange of letters*: a signal that the money will reach its recipient. *Middle-aged woman*: the action will begin in the building with two floors. *Only Aurel*: the hiding place. *Two engineers seeking a furnished room*: an order to find a hiding place for the two subversive valises. *The divorce process*: the initiation of public protest.

Starting with a mere whimper in the personal columns of a daily paper or a popular magazine with some blonde celebrity on the cover, inoffensive words can trigger strange initiatives, like a coded curse.

I am buying paintings by the painter Aurel Vintilescu, *only Aurel.* Tel. 13.41.65 (638662).

I tutor shorthand, Stahl method, for foreign languages, including *Spanish.* Tel. 67.51.51 (64280).

Selling three martin skins: beautiful and absolutely new. Tel. 14. 59.02 (65.37.06 61506).

February 28, 7 P.M., lost near the Church of Saint Nicolae, Strada 11 Iunie, Pekinese dog, white breast and paws. Answers to the name Piky. Large reward. Tel. 65.37.06 (61506).

Carensebeş County court summons Liviu Manea, last domiciled in Baia Mare, Strada Cluj, Nr. 25, present residence unknown, for *the divorce process* with Marta Manea at 7 A.M. on March 28, 1968. (918460 ME).

I am urgently seeking an eternal resting place in a burial vault, Bellu Cemetery, for *a middle-aged woman.* Tel. 58.53.47 or 75.70.78 (215).

Lost: *rubber tire, Wangard 590x15* and blue folder containing essays in Arabic. Reward. Call me at 47.55.06 (69294).

Two young engineers seeking a room with central heating, possible tutoring. Serious offers. Tel. 62.38.83, after 4 P.M. (64225).

Professor of piano and French, middle-aged, seeks correspondence and eventual meeting with a serious gentleman with similar inclinations. Tel. 13.31.37, late evening.

Cotroceni district: furnished room to let, comfortable, retirees only, intellectual, cultivated. P.O. Box 62990 (62990).

Young engineer with prospects seeks correspondent, young lady (or nearly so) any field for eventual meeting, serious character, Bucharest only. P.O. Box 62936.

Assistant Engineer and physicist, I tutor mathematics and physics: young lady candidates for the university and fulltime or part-time university students. *Exchange of letters.* Tel. 17.17.77 (64437).

The production personnel for the film *Michael the Brave* is initiating a preparatory course for stuntmen. Candidates selected at Calea Călăraşi, Nr. 11 (218) write to *Aurel only.*

⋮ ⋮ ⋮

She will have an hour for lunch, and will know the insipid taste of mayonnaise, sauces, and creams, the smell or color or taste of any dish capable of arousing torpid digestive juices: spicy grilled meatballs that cause heartburn; white fish sprinkled with lemon, the spine and little bones aligned to one side of the dish as in a tomb.

—Three meatballs and a roll. Or no, two rolls.

In one hand, the briefcase; in the other, a plate with three meatballs, a green plastic basket, two rolls, a knife, and a fork. The buffet line is long. Her big body rubs itself between other famished people.

—May I?

It seems he smiled at her. He's too young—he didn't even see her.

—Give me fish balls, too, a bit of roast, and a beer. Two extra rolls and a pastry with whipped cream.

The briefcase is at her place. The young man has left—replaced by a short man who frequently wipes his sweaty brow. The reddish sauce is acidic; the bread softens ... the little fish balls, cut in half, with the flesh rolled in sauce. The beer comes on time: cold and foamy. Then the tender bit of roast larded with fatty white strips that absorb pepper.

—Can you shift over a bit in that direction, please.

The man has a low, warm voice and the air of a child: dumpy, bald, and blighted with sweat.

Stomach bloated: there's no more room for the pastry. But at least the frothy whipped cream should be tasted, a corner of the juicy,

47

aromatic crust, and another, and another, and just one more. The briefcase, mustn't forget the briefcase. Another furtive glance at the sweaty man bent over his plate.

The rain has stopped. It's warm outside, as it is inside the freighted body that could stretch out in a large bed to sleep, to forget this afternoon of slavery, the spoiled little cannibals, their murderous smiles, the rotten little brats hysterical in the frenzy of the afternoon.

—What the hell are you looking at lady?

Thrown into the bus, crushed, bent over the briefcase crammed with papers, the words reach her from behind: "look at that fatso." The bus breaks sharply at every corner and springs sharply forward: constantly starting and stopping until it suddenly hurls her onto the sidewalk in agitated exhaustion. The briefcase drops, her hands shove air and strike the damp pebbles. Cries. Whistles. A false step, provoked and awry. Down the street. The toes squeezed into mannish shoes have clenched. The right hand extended forward maintains an equilibrium with the briefcase in the left. Having looked worriedly at the cars, pedestrians, and the crosswalk, having made it across the street, the professor of French and piano, slowing her movements, catches her breath, and looks into the little dairy buffet: eggs, yogurt, cheese, sour cream, milk.

—Would you happen to have a Pepsi?

The waiter should have been shocked by the voice's tenderness and rushed over with two frosty bottles yanked directly from the ice, yet boredom leads to looking without hearing, so he missed her angelic voice, and absently signaled her to sit.

—Yes, I'll bring it.

The thin sheets rustle in her briefcase, still imperceptibly impregnated with the odor and breath of their sender. The waiter takes his time, and by now the customer must have opened her briefcase, and would be feeling the thin sheets between her fat fingers, and, as on every day, the delayed gratification was running through her mind—between the words of the letter and the letters of each word, the adjectives and diminutives reviewed in equivocal jubilation: idiotic, willfully idiotic.

The waiter appears through a side door carrying a glass and a narrow bottle with a metal cap. He sets the glass on the table, opens it, and places the bottle near the glass. Now, finally, comes the moment for her to be alone: pulling the briefcase near, passing her hand along the notebooks, using two fingers to draw out the sheets prepared for correspondence, opening the top buttons of her blouse, straightening the edges of the paper, delaying the pleasure for a few more seconds while rubbing her puffy fingers over the little sheet that awaits the rustle of words. The caress of a child, the doltish innocence.

The fire in the Apuseni Mountains and then at the Hotel Dracula—when you hurt me so badly and I forgave you—was never consuming. It burned intermittently somehow, and it used to light my life like a fairy tale, but ephemerally. When I was without it once for four months, once for six, I was on the way to believing that it had gone out. I didn't feel it was consuming me more and more powerfully. The memories that link me to Dănuţ are spread over five sporadic trimesters. A person can't live on sporadic memories alone, let alone sporadic ones with question marks.

The beginning of a smile. The fat lady reads the words, seems discontent with their absurdity, so modest and monotonous, and digs a thick red pencil out of her briefcase: thinks and writes a word, and then another, and goes on repeating the well-known game—writing a word, correcting, erasing. Let's say it was all about burning somehow intermittently *at a low, never tempestuous level.* There follows a moment of hesitation, finding the right gimmick, and quickly adding: *to a certain extent.*

Looking at the sheet, the effect seems weak.

It burned intermittently somehow, at a low, never tempestuous level,

and to a certain extent, it used to illuminate my life, in a magical way,
like a fairy tale, but ephemerally. When it was lacking ... it gnawed a little
from the shore, but assiduously, and then it came to sweep everything in its
path. I saw the danger all too late—nor had I ever counted it as such—
conquering me ever more powerfully, lighting that consuming fire, and
then there was nothing but a final blow. I became a drunken boat through
the spell of the waves, under the eyes of the wharfs, ablaze, crushed.

With her right hand, she pushes the briefcase away and continues looking at the sheet. The infantile jubilation captivates her.

... conquering me ever more powerfully from all points of view, lighting
the consuming fire and then there was nothing but a final blow. I became a
drunken boat through the spell of the waves under the eyes of the wharfs,
ablaze, crushed—the waves hurling aside the last barriers that blocked
our reunion. When you talked to me over the phone we still belonged to
one another.

There's someone behind her. The bottle should have been drunk already. A quick pour. Moistening her lips. That feeling of being watched from behind. Turning to look: confused, frightened. The waiter smiles.

—Would you like anything else?

—No, not yet. For the time being, no. I don't want anything. No, nothing.

Breast lifted, contemplating the words, mouth pursed, her body temperature rises, lips throb, eyes revive—hate, pleasure, play—and the pencil stabs between the words till arriving at the master correction: "When you talked to me over the phone we still belonged to one another, *bodily.*" Miraculous! The word had made a place for itself, mastering the line with the smell and taste and distaste of provocation. The sheet trembles between her fingers. These are lucky moments, repeatable anytime and anyhow, especially when there's no longer any point—when it's too late: only then is it paid back, revenged.

Again, the strange gaze from behind her: better rush. That's how it always happens, the pleasure stops just as it begins, hurried, driven away by hostile conventions without being able to linger in the words, in their revitalizing cleverness—how can there be time for anything but words, to be among and between them, to knead, to inflame, to shape them: tomorrow, the day after tomorrow, Wednesday, Thursday, Friday—again, from the beginning?

The waiter has gone—the fingers move by themselves on the corner of the dog-eared page, nervous, uncontrolled fingers trembling with the impulse to counterfeit.

And you will never be able to throw me in another's arms again. Isn't this so? Yes, that would be perfect, but there is no more time. *As they say about porcelain, once broken, never fixed (more about that later).* Tensed, the pencil moves like lightning across the page. *A broken piece of porcelain can never be glued back in place—it will be very ugly and will have lost its value (more about that later).* This calls for a slurp. The pleasure inflames her. *Today, your rhetorical talent overwhelmed me and I accepted that I still have memories of him—after you left I understood that it was only a matter of the past. I resist neither the destructive waves nor the consuming fire. Unexpected and condemnable, you will say, this fickleness of mine. Perhaps unexpected but not condemnable, too, say I* (say I!). *An earthquake can destroy everything in a matter of minutes.* (Yes!) *On certain occasions a night was sufficient to destroy an empire. Sometimes it only takes a few minutes to destroy a relationship.*

The waiter is idling behind her chair again. She rises, closes her blouse and her overcoat, hesitating with the middle buttons. *I may come back to this. I may come back? I may come back to this ... I may come back to this with concrete examples!* Sure, that's the ticket! With concrete examples! A finger pulls nervously at the second button, hurries to the third that closes the top. Shoved into the stuffed briefcase, the sheets of paper crumple between her puffy fingers. Money on the table, a hand signal, and slinking out, eyes aimed at the ground so the waiter won't see two flushed cheeks.

And now the door is flung open, then closed with her elbow. On the threshold, she smirks naughtily, offering the slightest trace of a smile.

⋮ ⋮ ⋮

Body leaning on the door's edge, Comrade Sebastian Caba slouched against the leather-padded doorframe. Then, imperceptibly, his head, neck, and shoulders slumped along with the rest of his body. Forming peculiar stripes, his white fingers had glued themselves to the dark wood. The bent body, a long, pallid streak against the door's black border. His dreamy gaze follows the one now running away, as far as possible, in frantic haste, far from the silent office.

For the fugitive, it was an experience of running down the wide steps to escape that gaze burning into the back of his neck. Only, at every step, Sebastian Caba's face would appear again, on the wall to the right. Sebastian Caba was following him, sprouting from the walls, motionless and omnipresent, with his body bent slightly to the left, his long, attenuated fingers monstrously white on the door's dark wood. Charging downstairs without making headway, gaze fixed on the white wall, the same tableau hanging always before him: a tall, brown-haired young man, pallid, slouching in sad resignation with his left arm stretching down the length of the doorframe. The long, pale fingers kept poking through the frozen surface of the tableau.

Always at his back, that gaze followed every convulsion of his flight. If only it were possible to escape, to run faster, leap down all the steps, if only each step weren't broken by the tableau floating before him: the bent man with his thin-fingered hand on the doorframe. The tableau was multiplying, proliferating with every footstep, and it was moving, too, descending at the same rate as the fugitive—doubling and redoubling: dozens of identical tableaus had remained behind, projected onto the walls at the height of the gaze that followed the descending staircase. Always the same tableau rising again in front of each new step, or perhaps there was only the single tableau, a single image springing down the steps like a horrifying shadow moving across the wall, continually enlarging his dread.

Descending quickly, without making any headway. On the wall's surface, the pale hand protruding from the tableau, from the frame of coffee-colored shadows. Standing in the outline of the door, as in a picture frame, Caba—still, fixed in place, bent to the left—followed his former colleague's flight with a steady gaze, a stare projected like a terrifying optical illusion from the motionless tableau—motionless except for the gaze and the flinching hand stroking the doorframe: as though in a mirror, the other hand, the hand of the fugitive gleams on the cold banister under the dull gaze from the tableau, moving to the same rhythms, repeating the same movements of Caba's hand in the doorframe. The steps kept sliding like a nightmarish escalator; dizzying and static, the seemingly impossible escape from the tableau ends in a sudden, cool rain. Awakening: tired, on a street among chilly, huddled pedestrians, hurried clerks, and a strange, narrow, suffocating room for losing oneself, estranging oneself in sleep or dispersion or nothing, something, anything.

The upholstered room had perished, along with the wide marble stairs, then the street had passed away, the pedestrians were no longer visible; next, the spiral of another crooked, twisted, narrow staircase, mounting toward a small, hunched room—a coop or cell or birdcage that refuses respite to the fugitive, a prisoner to himself and his own mystifications, a self-made trap full of imaginary hurdles, perfidious obstacles, and mute monologues. And then she: brought to a stalemate, to the transfer of powerlessness and negation, obliged to assume the complicity, fear, and fury of the one who invents her, made to carry sighs, far-fetched charades, mockingly jubilant in the cadence of vain, useless words—she will disown her own imposture, she will host the meeting of the wanderer with himself and his rebellious memory.

For here, eventually, the ever-delayed circles will start to rotate, the colors of the exiled couple buried in fog under a gloomy sky, and eventually *you*, the second person, the refused, recalled, awaited rejoinder will come back. The precursory mystification named Monica is weak, transparent, and false, and her slaves—the books, smells, special effects, pantomimes, and scores jumbled all over the place to confuse the stranger—will not wait for the endlessly delayed confrontation, the painful meetings, the delayed gratifications, the memories and expectations scattered in the sinuous spaces of sleep. Here in the loser's cell, among her negligent belongings, in the hideaway for setups and farces, they will pointlessly recommence their lost youth—the amazed monologue of adolescence that speaks of expectations and desires and the quietly morbid monologue of maturity. Connecting them are the red threads of the pyre on which Captain Zubcu burned and the painful dialog with his daughter: it's only one more step to reach you and nothing will ever be able to be stopped again, no power will ever be sufficient. An hour, a century, an instant, this lapse will no longer be capable of setting us orphans endlessly astray, separating us in the bleak corridors of a destiny without Sabbath: forgetfulness wil be broken. Our dear wounds will reopen.

$$\vdots \quad \vdots \quad \vdots$$

A typed text among other typed texts.

Miss Smântănescu,

I try to console myself and hope that the things I've read are true and that this isn't a … into motion through the intermediation of another person. Why? I can't tell you yet, so for the present I don't have a lady friend, and those who have shown themselves, I haven't liked. I should have faith in you, I should try to create the conditions for us to meet face-to-face, and as soon as possible. Without denying that the lines you wrote awakened warmth in my heart and something…special, which I nourish even though we haven't met. To be as clear as possible, I will seek, in broad strokes, to write my short biography and describe my physiognomy, which should be clarified by a little photograph enclosed in this envelope. I was born in 1933, in the third month, sixth day. I'm filling in the blanks now because, of course, you can't put all this in the personals. So you'll have to trust me. In 1948–49 I had a broken leg and I stayed in the hospital. In 1949 I took an admin. exam for the Bucharest School of Mech. Tec. Nr. 1, 127 Calea Dudeşti. I graduated from there in 1953. Later that year I took the mining electromec. exam, but there were few openings, and being poorly prepared in Romanian, Russian, and chemistry, I didn't pass the orals. In physics and mathematics I scored well. So I presented myself at the plant and I worked there until 1958 as a tech. mechanic. In 1953 my sister went into economic studies and today is director of a school in the city of Bârlad.

In 1958 I took an exam for the Fac. of Mech., T.C.M. Section at the Politech. Inst. Braşov. I attended on a scholarship from the plant and graduated in 1963. Afterward, I returned to the plant. In August 1966, I finished my contract, and by this spring I hope to transfer, or if I don't obtain a transfer, then I will still be able to leave this city as a result of my contract ending. Where? I'm not sure, however, I am sure I can find a job anywhere. I'm not married. I have chestnut-colored hair, green eyes. Height five feet six inches, and I am as I appear in the photo even though it was taken in 1964 at the park in Sinaia. I'm very sociable, modest, respectful. Whether or not you think I'm a nice guy remains for you to judge. In 1964 I stayed for four months in Bucharest at the Expo. of National Economy as a guide on behalf of the Factory.

I was recently in Bucharest on December 21, 1966. I got myself a round-trip ticket, and used my regular vacation from the '66 calendar year, and in September '66, I used the days left from 1964. I had 6 days left that I wanted to use in the course of events, however, my boss at the factory told me to use them all up.

So as it stands I must work till March 9, and then I can come to Bucharest, where I'll stay five or six days in lodgings, even though I have relatives, friends, colleagues, but I don't want to bother them, and I'll see how I get along. On January 3, I found your birthday card, for which I thank you very much and wish you health and happiness in return.

With reference to the several questions you posed, I'll answer now, sincerely and with great pleasure.

1. Age: so, I have reached my 33rd year.
2. Yes! And the idea that you explained is true. I also thought that I could know my comrade for life—this isn't out of the question. To tell you the truth, 90% depends on me in this case. So, as the Romanians say, you can choose from among ... to find someone who reciprocates your love and accommodates your needs perfectly from every angle. In conclusion, I can tell you that I have never sought beauty, but rather, the right person to choose to share this brief life with.
3. If I haven't yet found the road that leads to the right kind of life, I will never become discouraged. Through the will and ambition I possess, I live with the thought that I will realize even this ideal successfully. You have to feel your way till then, though ... getting to know a lot of people, and when I'm finally sure that the person really loves me and is a homebody, as much as me, if I like her, I'll take this step too, for sure, in a short time (one or two months, for example).

In case you come through this city, please look for me at home because I live alone and have no relatives here except for the married brother of my brother-in-law who lives on another street. If you'll be so good, take the time to answer me in writing where you're staying or with whom you live, if you are willing to go on maintaining and reciprocating my desire of not being alone on the road of life like a sad wayfarer .... Yes! However, I have my own preferences too, and for this reason I have not married, because *after that I would never be able to leave here and life would be harder. I have often desired the person who's easiest to get along with, however it has always turned out that I discovered something bad later or that something didn't harmonize with my preferences. Sincerely, to tell you the truth, my hope is to reach Bucharest by the month of March or April, 1967, and I plan on accomplishing this. So it was perfect that we both read the personals in the newspaper and that you desired my acquaintance and that I am exactly the serious gentleman you have been looking for and have similar inclinations if I can convince myself that you have as serious a character as you write in your announcement.*

About my family: I have two sisters, one is married, has two children, a boy in the sixth grade and a girl in the second. The other sister graduated from the school of economics and is the director of a school. Age 35, is attractive but has never married. And then I am the youngest.

It is past midnight, and tomorrow I'm going to the factory. So I must leave you. Please excuse my daring. In the course of events and without realizing it, I wrote to YOU, using the familiar mode of address. In case I've upset you, I ask you to forgive me. I finish this wishing you again health, luck, happiness, and success in everything you wish for.

I remark, too, that I hold you in the highest esteem, especially because you have eyes like lasers, reading my heart directly, with the confidence and bravery of a wayfarer. Health to your parents and to persons who are dear to you (in your family). With respect,

Grig

⋮ ⋮ ⋮

The point moves along the length of the ray that rotates constantly around the fixed pole: drawing a line around a fixed center and evenly rotating in one direction. The form of the spiral depends on the logarithm. The mechanics of a watch measure time, time's passage, duration; the serpentines hook through the space, the upward slope, the aspiration, stairs climbing down curves, cataclysms, crucifixions, clocks, ornaments, more serpentines.

She must be *the third person*, twisting through the curves of the corridors, preparing the appropriation, the propinquity, curving with the spirals—red, wounded, black spirals full of nodes. She is convertible: she borrows, transports, and withstands roles, dreams, illnesses, nightmares, traps, and masks. Time flows along the length of a line that rotates constantly around a pole, the pace increases the spiral, spirals repeat the initial trajectory, enlarged, diminished, cyclically colored, according to the conjunction. She lives the precursory spiral—the access—serving appearances. The spiral grows, falters, and rotates itself, the curve of the mobile point advancing in a codified direction, around a fixed center. The spiral of Archimedes, the logarithmic spiral, hyperbolic, the sentinel cordons, the credible abstractions, watch springs betraying time, ornaments set in stone, serpentines measuring, staring at space, stairs climbing down, climbing down.

$\diamond$ $\diamond$ $\diamond$

Laboriously, like the accumulation of dust, the day advances through her large, heavy body. Sweat rolls down from her hairline. The second floor. Hand on balustrade. Eyes closed. Exhaustion, feet burning from so much walking. Eyes closed. An eyelid vibrates, quivers like the little announcement stuck to the gate: ELEVATOR UNDER REPAIR — ELEVATOR UNDER REPAIR — ELEVATOR UNDER REPAIR.

Break between floors. Stopping to rest, to breathe deeply, just once, like the kids in gym. The inhalation: body raised, arms over the head, as if hanging. Exhalation: languid body, arms lowered, at peace—Ah! The third floor. This climb needs to be imagined as the atonement for a paradise of illusions: one, two, five, six, seven, twelve steps till the landing, twenty-four between floors. But there's no excuse for another break. The steps have to be climbed methodically. Shortness of breath sets in at the nineteenth step: small, suffocated sighs. Hand on balustrade: white wings seem to flutter over shoulder blades. Eyes open, now. Two more steps. Only two more. Briefcase pressed to the hip, climbing. Each step won by the sweat of thy brow, like the bread of one's days—in purgatory. Pressing the bell: once, twice. No answer. Headache. Pressing the bell again for a long time, a second time. Not a sound. Suddenly, the door opens just an inch, as though someone had been waiting, glued to the back of it.

—Good evening.

The grandmother scrutinizes her through the crack in the door.

—I've come for the lesson. Is Luminița at home?

—Not today. She has the flu.

Behind the door: laughter, voices, men, women, and possibly a child. The teacher's cheeks burn, her hand grips the briefcase handle tightly.

—You should have let me know, so I wouldn't make a trip for nothing.

—We couldn't reach you by phone.

—You should have rung me early or in the evening when I'm at home. I can't make a trip for nothing.

—Luminița has a cold.

—I can't make a trip for nothing.

—We couldn't reach you by phone. We don't have money to give away.

—I can't make a trip for nothing.

Choked and trembling, almost screaming. Behind the grandmother, something or someone else shuffles. The grandmother is moved to the side.

—What's going on? What is all this commotion? Ah, you! Luminiţa isn't feeling well.

—I can't make a trip for nothing.

—You shouldn't have shouted at an old lady.

—I didn't shout. But I can't make a trip for nothing. You should have let me know by phone. I'm tired. I work a great deal. I am tired.

—You're unreachable, or the phone is busy for hours at a time. We're finished with this business. German is enough for the child, she has to have fun too.

—Then I'll talk with your husband. He said he'd make sure the little girl would practice the piano two hours a week.

—You'll talk to my husband? You intend to start a fight? And why are you shouting at me? Just because I'm not paying you?

—Please pay me for the lesson. I made the trip all the way over here.

—Go on, leave us alone. Do you think I earn money for doing nothing? Forget about it. You didn't get along with the Bratu family either. You're too emotional—you should get your head examined.

—Please pay me for the lesson.

—I'm not paying for any lesson. First of all you should beg forgiveness for having insulted an old lady. After that, if you want to give lessons at our place, we can talk about it.

And the door slams.

Leaning against the balustrade. Propping the briefcase against it. Getting out the notebooks, the sheets of correspondence, the typed stories, the scores. Resting the heap on the mosaic flooring. Putting everything in its place, making everything fit: the six scores, the folded sheets, the books. The briefcase barely fitting under her arm. The lesson is lost, probably for good. Three hundred per month. In one year, the little girl could have been playing the piano acceptably. If she'd gone inside, she could have phoned the next student that she'd be arriving early. Maybe there's a public phone nearby. Climbing down the first step, the second, holding onto the balustrade. Five times twenty-four—getting the crumpled hankie out of the briefcase and mopping her brow. Going down slowly, one step after the other, hand gliding down the balustrade, prudently, like an old lady. The street. A fine drizzle rains down. The backache, sagging in the damp air, bent over the briefcase. And leaving. Evening rises, assuaged. And she will arrive, depart, arrive, depart, crossing streets, finally return in a daze: another accursed evening when ample and abounding tears will sprinkle the streets, and she will become the same little girl, though her nails, hair, hands, and breasts will have grown. Poisoned, villainous tears. The woman suddenly aged overnight will climb the steps of the narrow, winding, spiral staircase, will prop the briefcase near the door and look for the small, shiny, yellow key. The cardboard notice tacked to the wall will flutter slightly under her panting breath. *Professor M. Smântănescu. French and Piano. Quiet. There are other tenants.*

The key will twist to the left with its teeth facing down. The door will rock softly, slightly: to the left, to the right. The switch. The light.

The whistle of the three sharp, tender little bullets, colliding with the body—collapsed and reconciled with itself—or the teaspoon of poison in the jar on the table, the poisoned water in the glass and the brief twitch, or the assassin's two hurried hands encircling the throat, pressing persistently with an obscure tenderness as the victim's death rattle sounds ever more dimly: the joy of the finale. The saxophone whispers, the voice of the black woman wailing *Summertime, Summertime,* the end of a summer day, requiem for the agony of the murderer, of the suicide. The rotations of the tapes on the tape recorder, the fairy tale, the caged little bird, the negligent assassin, frozen, with a hand to her stiff neck, in that final gesture of horror, of weakness, of suicidal suffocation, dumbstruck by its reality, its image—like his sister who was dispersed in the smoke of crematoriums, like the suicidal Captain, like his daughter reduced to fumes, a phantom.

Perhaps the room will preserve no sign of the stranger, will only remain what it is, her room of adjectives, diminutives, epistles, epithets, her cot and cage, maybe the objects will be pacified, purified: nowhere will they feel, hear, forebode, and foresee the rotations—rusty and relived, the rotations and waverings, weaknesses and wonderings, rotations, reelings, ruin.

"You"

ARTILLERY CAPTAIN BOGDAN ZUBCU came back from the war for you. He returned to his wife and daughter a few months after the fighting ceased. He looked exhausted. He'd shared in the hard campaigns to the East and West: he'd followed the slaughter. For him the war ended in Bohemia. Still, he came home safe. Unwounded. Three years in the murderous whirlwind left no visible scars. He'd never been talkative, so the silence of those first weeks came as no surprise. Quiet and discreet like the Captain, the family went about their lives—happily, it seemed. Zubcu was hollow-eyed, though. An accelerated tick in the left part of his cheek spoke of something more than fatigue. He should have recovered. He slept a lot. He rarely left home, but when he did, he'd take long, twilight walks with his little girl. Sometimes he spoke to you—inventing stories and games—but he tired quickly, and would lower his face in shame, interrupt the sentence he'd just begun, and then bring his hand to his throat, a pale hand with trembling fingers. Not speaking, the two of you would return from those afternoon walks, and days would pass before the Captain left his room again.

He met other people with hasty, tortuous friendliness. The Captain was known to have soldiered through the entire war on both fronts. This gave him a certain status in the little community, so it was natural that local activists approached him. These people, who presented themselves as "initiating plans for popular participation," offered the

Captain a role in the local, postwar reorganization. They saw their offers as signs of trust and esteem. They'd talk briefly with the Captain. Then Bogdan Zubcu would ask for more time. He didn't seem to understand how he might assist "The Effort," although he repeated that he understood their ideas, their scale, and the drastic revolutionary methods through which they hoped to accomplish their goals. He was convinced they overestimated his strengths and abilities. Their increasingly concrete proposals flustered him. The left side of his cheek contracted unpleasantly. He'd blink more and more. The insistence of the new "combatants" tired him. His brow would grow pale and damp. Answers came with difficulty. His pale, trembling fingers would circle his thin, blue-veined neck.

He took to wandering in the alleys, straying from home for afternoons or sometimes whole days. He would return calmer, joking and bewildering his wife and you, his daughter, with his drawn-out laughter. He'd dance them through the middle of the room, and turn the courtyard upside down with noisy, childish games. Thanks to his former comrades in arms—now among the most energetic activists—he'd often bring back foods that had grown scarce in those postwar days when provisions were so hard to find. As the Captain told it, some of his former comrades held new, key positions in the city's administration. Ill-at-ease when they met him now and eager to rid themselves of a person they could only perceive as a problem, the Captain's former pals would give him things he hadn't asked for and put off talking about the proposals of the activists who'd courted him.

Frightened and polite at first, the Captain slid into incoherence. The authorities hesitated to renew their requests. Still, they went on waiting for his answer; Zubcu kept delaying, which deepened their confusion.

The Captain walked around the city. He'd look at the "innovations," those vast new building projects, and try to make sense of the changes.

Then he'd come home full of news about small events that shook the old city's settled order in preparation for its new face. He looked astonished—down to his soul—and disquiet showed in his face. The transient liveliness of these homecomings ended in days of total silence. Then the Captain wouldn't leave his room. He'd avoid his wife and daughter's eyes. Maybe he felt guilty for his passive hesitations. Then he would leave again on long, solitary walks—sometimes he took the little girl with him, and her long, lusterless hair trailed behind her.

The Captain's bouts of drunken liveliness didn't always end in apathy; sometimes they finished in pensive moods, drawn out and bizarre. He kept putting off finding steady work. Since she was still teaching, his wife avoided rushing his choice of occupation. She was convinced that after suffering through the war, he needed more time to readjust, though she waited for the moment when he'd initiate a conversation.

Captain Bogdan Zubcu was never wounded during the three years of war that carried him from the East to the West. He was a tall, slim man with big blue eyes. He had deep, dark circles around his eyes, and his gaze was both open and vacant. Nothing in his appearance or manner justified serious concern. His excessive silences, the nervous throbbing of his left cheek, which amounted to a sort of permanent blink, and the trembling of his hands circling his thin throat as he searched for words—these seemed to be part of a natural, passing fatigue. And the two beings by his side resembled him. The peace of their home extinguished immediate panic. The Captain slept a lot, and took walks on the outskirts of the city, holding hands with the silent little girl hidden under her thick, lackluster hair. Yet with his open gaze and his secret hermetically sealed, the man seemed fragile, unable to find the way back to himself or toward the family that waited for him.

Memories burst from their shroud of ashen fog: filaments of flame. Gestures forgotten for a month, a day, an hour, incidents forever lost—mislaid in the blink of an eye—come back, or perhaps only their undead, rebellious shades. His face welled forth, young and restless, shaken, roused by departures, returns, brief hopes, even if rigid now, wild and mute, or convulsed by desperate wakings. Hard drinking had befuddled him, it seemed, a hand forgotten around his throat.

The days went on, one after the next, like an endless, lazy Sunday. Only with difficulty could he let himself be known and loved, but he used his charismatic voice to maintain his frail ally, his girl, his faithful audience of one in her state of sickly admiration. Then the long day came when freezing silence barred the door to his room and the heavy door to the shed where he now gazed at the dusty scooters, sleds, and wooden horses—which his little friend played with while waiting for him to come home.

The hanged-man pendulum would vibrate and reel in the shed filled with old toys. Thirsting for death, the body would swing in its frantic haste toward oblivion. Then the rope broke under his serene face—perhaps the last favor granted to his daughter: her victory over his desire for death. A red streak encircled his neck, a magic sign of salvation. The dead parent rose before his daughter's eyes like a curse and a mockery.

You would have to forget the body shattered by weakness and the fearful exhaustion of the following months. The teapot would escape from your hands, the fork's jabs went astray, and the rows of books overlapped nonsensically. Forget what was and what followed, down to the final traces. Escape to the mountains and stare for hours on end at the empty room and the tall, polished wooden bed in the house that belonged to the schoolteacher, Vasile Obreja; listen to the swish of the small rubber wheels rolling his wheelchair; look at the mountains, the spring, the forest; lose yourself in the silence of the evenings under the pines; gaze vacantly without seeing or hearing, as if nothing could have been, nor could be. Forget the feeble little girl executing instructions from a book of popular medicine, panting over the half-man, giving rhythm to despair. Forget her obstinate will to revive him, the miracle of salvation, and the somnolent weeks when the dead man reeled, teetering in his second birth, under the care of the child who had brought him back. Forget the extravagant laughter of the suicide with the beautiful face whose noose you untied to bring back a pale, waxy countenance, which lacked the ugliness that turns hanged men's cheeks to stone.

You can't lose if you understand. Everything would have been lost if I died: you can't lose if you hold out, he used to say. You, the girl addressed, should understand, and you shouldn't lose and you should lose: you should want to lose what you don't understand, you shouldn't want to understand, you should forget that you lose, that you leave, that you are climbing the mountains of exile, abandoned, lied to, cast out of the game of lying, without defense. You should forget when and who and what some people say. You should look for other words, objects, hours, habits, and you should tremble once again beneath the resonance of a nearly forgotten word—that thunder—a word from the past, from so long ago that it never existed: you should tremble once again so that the whole thing can begin anew, from the present, from the past, from the past passed in the great sleep.

Those brief, rapid, cunning gestures would have to be forgotten too, and those tenderly paternal movements with their unbearable lightness: the pale hands trembling on the throat, the redness that marked the failed suicide attempt, the duty to start again, despairing and dying all over again, the gestures of refused salvation, of forced rehabilitation, the demented stubbornness to revive him, to punish him, to deny his peace, to force his resurrection, to prepare another death, the same death—his drunkenness and fairy tales and walks and promises: they would all have to be resumed, restarted, reset, without rest and without end.

Looking at the mountains, the orphan girl remembered the Sunday-ness of some mornings on the bridge or at the station, walking with her tender father, that traitor; she saw, once more, the mountains, the narrow hall where Mr. Obreja's wheelchair rested, the race of spring, the wind blowing through the pines and words—words that were shared with that coward. Among the drifting aromas of long, straight candles, like frozen pine trees in the mountains: there you should forget your hands that once supported the dead man's heavy body, your burdensome memory of death.

You should forget and memorize everything, ransack the hiding places, undo the knots and rip open the seams, you should understand in order to forget those places where nothing can be recovered, ever; you should forget what you've forgotten and what you've understood, empty yourself of thought, of the past and the present, look at the unseen mountains, the wooden bed, the madness of spring, the schoolteacher Vasile Obreja's silences that were as cold as massive graves.

It was necessary to gather memories, to rummage through them, to understand them so they could be forgotten, and then the amnesia would have to be checked again and again, for it would have to cover everything so there'd be no need to cheat or engage in the farce of little passing deceptions. You'd have to understand yourself through the suicidal father, destined to pain like a favorite of the gods. The only way would be to forget him—and yourself—so that you'd climb down the mountain estranged from that former girl, aging now into the past, undermined, reborn—in transient, transpired, transpiring time.

You'd have to understand the one you'd lost—unforgivable, incapable of being forgotten—and then you'd understand your own attempt, and assume it to yourself. Because there was no other way to scrap and forget the alienated girl inside yourself that you hated so much and chased away. By now she was a kind of phantom twin. She clung like a shadow. She caught up with you wherever you went, and then you had to feel her breath rise through your body to your nauseated mouth. You would have to feel her mocking gaze burn into the back of your neck, making you feel like a stupid orphan as she rubbed her transparent palm against the whitewashed wall, lost in the mountains at the end of the world.

⁛ ⁛ ⁛

Death sends a servant to test the victim, to prepare her, to rotate her slowly toward the nearby faces of the deceased, to stun her with suppressed hopes, to cloud her vision and obscure her desires, to make her fragile and hollow like something that can be triumphantly lifted up.

You were still a solitary little girl, clumsy and hostile. The sap of your femininity rose slowly, with difficulty, always delayed. Seeing the future, you wrapped yourself thinly with a moistened mouth, with large eyes, and that sheen like a shower of lunar snow. Pale as moonlight, you dressed yourself in a nervous body with sinewy legs, transparent hands, and gestures abruptly broken off. Death's servant worked on your profile, on your body's curves with their coiled air, the curves of a sad, wounded feline.

You would have accepted isolation as a redemptive tombstone. Or, conversely, impatiently, furiously, you would have started a war with humility itself, to humiliate yourself as much as possible, embracing humiliation while dreaming of a train corridor: an obese woman professor naively babbling lewd provocations and infantile tales in French into the first stranger's ear. Fear, disgust, depravity. You would have remained withdrawn, faded and dry, otherwise you would have turned into a mad woman or a whore in order to ruin that fat phantom of life.

You had to remain just one moment on the icy threshold of isolation to understand its torture and its weight. Having taken refuge in fragmented gestures and rapid, frightened spasms, you huddled in the cold, waiting, crouched in silence, in sleep … to understand and receive the gift of suitable trials.

Death drew your father back so that you could see him, stand before him, shake him, resurrect him, so that you could lose him again, irreversibly. Death returned him: to hurt you, to overwhelm you with pain so completely that you'd forget any other form of suffering. The generous gift of death—suffering, your partner on the bleak mountain—makes you ugly without realizing it, leaves you famished, tired, frozen, mocked, and forgotten. The pain erodes the nights, changes and surprises, sharpens senses and thoughts, and prepares a concealed femininity. The men, all the men on earth, had perished in a violent hell, smiling like beautiful cadavers, and the only man worth protecting had collapsed like an ordinary deserter at your feet, his image eclipsing the sun.

You come down from the cold mountains, disgusted by how easy it is to leave, by your lack of regrets, the absence of any nostalgia, humiliated to have found nothing in the mountains' indifferent silence other than the silver of water, the darkness of poverty, and the failure of your journey to find tranquility. Somewhere, death waits for your moment of fulfillment.

In the mountains, you passed through the white border under the moon, leaned exhausted against a tree, lifted your gaze toward a branch, and felt a vast, tired astonishment in your new being.

You remained puzzled by what seemed to have happened or was happening to you, without being able to take the next step. You would have to remain a slave of expectations, for years to come, and sometimes still catch glimpses of the nomad's thin silhouette at the end of the long corridor and the streak of his blue shirt, which marked his passage down the corridor. And that was all, for years and years: the silence of a long corridor cut by a young man's haste. A colleague, an engineer, that's all.

… Lazily the sun rotated its rays in the wheels of Vasile Obreja's wheelchair. You went on advancing blindly, not knowing where you were going or where you came from. At the burial, Obreja had accepted your pushing him around in his wheelchair, and it was the only time that the schoolteacher had said more than simply *good day, yes, no, bon appétit.* He asked, "Do you read stories?"—and, before you could respond, he stupidly added—"you should've known that babies can't tame crocodiles, and that some illogical people can be and are despised."

Without glancing your way, the dead man's relatives accepted your presence at the service in that mountain village because they could not forget that the dead man's belated passion for books had been roused by an elementary school teacher, whom they'd driven away so many times, and convinced themselves that the deceased might have lived longer if he hadn't let himself be won over by this last silly stunt.

… A sleeping sun kept rolling in the spirals of the wheels, and you continued to perceive nothing else, as if the old peasant, Abesei, had never existed or remained as alive as he was on those evenings when he'd take a crumpled copy of *My First Book* out from under his woolen vest and start practicing his ABCs.

With maybe twenty meters to go, you raised your eyes. A couple was just coming out of the village store that served as a pub. You quickly recognized the forestry administrator, Dan Vasilescu. The couple halted. The woman moved closer to her partner. They remained glued to the spot. Your pace slowed as you got closer to them.

"Danny, you understand," "Danny, I always," "Danny, you must," "Danny, it wouldn't be right." Your hands clenched the handlebars of the wheelchair. For an instant, the woman shifted her gaze. She was fat and middle aged, or rather ageless, perhaps she was even still young. The white lace of her collar lit her bright cheeks; hair aflame in the red dusk, eyes intensely blue, for a moment she had been radiant. Linking arms, the couple resumed walking. "Danny, I can't believe," "Danny, this beginning," "Danny, this flight," "Danny," "Danny." In the blink of an eye, her lamentations had purified the surrounding air. Impossible to understand exactly what had made you freeze: the voice of a fat and unhappy princess out of a fairy tale, the nickname *Danny* used for *Dan*, the voice *in lamento*, that innocence of an angelic child. Vasile Obreja's hands trembled nervously. You started pushing his wheelchair again. Perhaps the crippled elementary schoolteacher wanted to avoid meeting the forester, who had a bad reputation in the village, where he was trying to absolve himself of some political guilt.

You might have met Monica Smântănescu back then, in one of the moments she believed she was being healed ... then, as she leaned tenderly on the shoulder of the new Danny.

It's impossible to come down from your hiding place in the bluish mountains, remembering only the face of the old peasant with kind eyes and a forgiving smile, a timeless man, anyhow, a man lacking old age, who had crossed the threshold of time—one as quiet as his native mountains, clear waters, forests—an old man healed of hate, fright, or decay ... Marveling at the capital letters of the alphabet, who would go on repeating the letters like a magic spell that could open the magnificent realm of youth. It's impossible to leave the mountains that are silent except for the sound of damp earth covering the grave dug for Iorgu Abesei, who spent eighty years traversing five kilometers of hills to end up flipping through the ABCs. It's impossible to leave with the memory of teacher Vasile Obreja's shoulders and his wheelchair, pushed through the abrupt, narrow alleys, toward the locked doors of villagers bored by talkative do-gooders who disrupted their tranquil poverty.

Not even the hypothetical meeting with Monica and her pleasant voice — after her visit to the clinic where her mother Rebeca Smânânescu vegetated — could change your feelings of disgust with human beings, your disgust with their love and betrayals, so that you might come down from the mountains healed, emptied of the past, indifferent to any present or future.

Alone, frozen in the mountains' lucid silence, among people desolated by poverty ... A meaningless refuge at the end of the world ... The silvery water, the snow's hush on cold evenings, the tremor of an old man charged with wonder: none of that offered anything to your despair. In their silence, the tall, pure mountains stood indifferent: those huge specters, from whom you couldn't expect a thing, so that you went on twisting those sparse strands of thin, weak hair, and your bits of fallen hair reminded you: the struggle goes on; there's no miracle cure for memory. You must accept the disintegrations, even if the simple gesture of passing a hand through your hair turns out to be prohibited as well, just as the gesture of a passerby was once like some spontaneous combustion — long ago, recently, by chance — when he brought his hand to his throat. You were leaving the wilderness of that precarious stopover empty-handed, yet carrying everything you hadn't yet managed to lose, replace, or forget; hands trembling in sparse hair, quickly withdrawn, frightened of the shedding; hands stiffened on the bark of a tree.

The hours there taught forgetfulness, however — gradually, slowly, hesitantly — crumbling, separating, unraveling, and scattering partial gestures, voices, and smiles. The struggle with memories went on sending small signals ... strands of hair kept falling when you least expected. The lesson of forgetting would have to be lived, forever, without end.

You stood with a hand on the bark of the tree. Wide eyes, lips damp with expectation, dread, amazement: your lunar face prepared for the greed of a new era, prey to another present.

You would have to open the door on a spring morning and show the newcomer and stranger the place near the window where the boss, Caba, bent over a desk, smoothing a small heap of banknotes with long, pale fingers. The stranger, the new engineer, brought a hand to the collar of his blue shirt. Your hair rose. Your hand pressed the wall.

After that you leaned in the cool corridor for days like years, your hand pressed to the wall, waiting for the stranger, now your colleague, to momentarily appear. The weight of the suicidal father began to lift. Your arms freed themselves. Curse, burden, and despotic memory fell away. You were becoming free ... for the phantom of another impostor.

⁞ ⁞ ⁞

The father with the luminous gaze hung himself one autumn morning in a shed in the courtyard. He was found by his daughter, who tried to reanimate him with resuscitation techniques for the drowned. For the next two weeks, they tortured him with emergency care: he came back to life gradually, miraculously. It wasn't easy.

Captain Bogdan Zubcu didn't do anything to suggest he'd try again. He lived through a prolonged convalescence. He no longer left his house, except sometimes by chance and only for minutes. He withdrew to his room. He became even more silent. The family avoided asking him questions or making tiring demands. His nervousness seemed to disappear, along with the grimace that contracted the left side of his face. He no longer hastily brought his trembling fingers to his throat. During his short appearances, his startled reactions abated. It was the end of autumn, 1952.

That winter, two officials visited the Zubcu house. The Captain left with them after a long conversation. He didn't come home after that for several months, a year, maybe more. The authorities conducted an investigation in several cities, the capital included. It wasn't possible to find out what the Captain was accused of, and he refused afterward to comment on the facts. There were rumors about the Captain's conduct during the war, about which he hadn't said a thing. Some said the investigation had to do with the military administration of a camp: that survivors had appeared, trying to denounce him. Mrs. Zubcu stubbornly protected her daughter against such insinuations. It was hard to say what the woman had found out, since they asked no questions and she displayed no change of attitude.

The Captain returned after a long time, and told you that he had not been found guilty and that he recovered his civil rights. You no longer believed him. He added that he might be interrogated further, but in the meantime he would try to find a job to help the family's financial situation. He was blinking again, almost non-stop. He couldn't find the right words and paused all the time. Conversations tired him — that was apparent in the precipitous way he rubbed his hands and then brought one or the other to his throat. Indeed, he took steps to find a job. He remembered those who had come, several years ago, to solicit his participation in the construction of a new type of society. Most of them were no longer in the same positions. The few who remained seemed to be involved in investigations similar to those he had been involved in, and they seemed to be trying to avoid him. His old comrades in arms made vague promises, but they never followed through. He decided to try getting a job on his own. In the end, he was hired at the large factory nearby. He quickly accustomed himself to the new job. He worked three different shifts in rotation, obediently and conscientiously. But all of these self-imposed efforts wore him out.

⁝ ⁝ ⁝

The official room: smooth desks, silence. Two women, whispering. The papers on the desk shifted slightly in the breeze as the door opened.

—The comrade can take you to Engineer Caba.

A subdued greeting. Your fingers slid into his. You looked at him, astonished. Unshaven, looking tired, the stranger wore his blue shirt open at the neck, the fabric spotted with lime or cement.

—Yes, I'll take you.

The two of you climbed down the steps. He kept quiet. Maybe he was thinking about Caba, his former classmate's free and easy way of passing among the school benches with his open smile and pleasant, cordial handshake, and the formality with which Caba approached each of his new classmates, and Caba's amazement when he shook hands with the head of the class, and that classmate's surprising reply to the handshake, so different from the others' awkwardness. The stranger's silhouette cut through the quiet classroom like a breath of fresh air. He was alive and cheerful, polite; he thought quickly and understood in a straightforward way: he seemed like a tennis player hopping off his bicycle near a grassy tennis court where girls were laughing. You would learn all that later.

The stranger was climbing down the steps, remembering his classmate's voice from long ago:

—*Is that how you imagine marriage? You work together for several years, you speak rarely or not at all, and then one day you invite her to the movies, and as you exit the theater you propose marriage in an off-hand way? Do you believe in such unnatural simplicity to avoid formalities and solemn engagements?*

He went on descending the steps. You had both arrived on the second floor, yet he was still wandering through the memory of a winter afternoon when he had impatiently waited for a visit from a school-mate who owed him an explanation. There were ice flowers on the windowpanes. The rustle of the impatiently flipped pages filled the room. Caba was not going to come .... The lines of print had a way of projecting themselves on the window frame: *It remains a problem for professional thinkers to know if a hermetically sealed can sitting on a shelf is or is not outside time ... and what must we think of a son of the earth ... entitled to feel one of the deepest worries.*

On the ground floor you turned slightly to the right, and followed the dark corridor to the last door. You were waiting for the newcomer to grab the doorknob and say: "after you." He stopped, caught himself, smiled, looked at you.

—Ah, yes.

Near the window at the end of the room, slouched over a polished wooden desk, Sebastian Caba was piling up bits of paper: counting banknotes. The two exchanged smiles. Taking each other's hands as they had in the past, they anticipated each other's voices, waited for each other's words. They seemed to share a tacit understanding. You stayed by the door. Suddenly the stranger grasped his blue collar with his hand. Your rough, wiry hair rustled. He looked surprised by you as you supported yourself with one hand and leaned against the wall, your fingers whitened by lime.

After so much time, this reunion might have clarified the past, and maybe that's why they looked at each other amazedly: to see each other, to understand each other, all the way back to the tangled knot of their adolescence.

Maybe the stranger was hoping to finally understand the secret of Caba's friendliness, which had won over everyone, even himself, or maybe he was hoping to discern the substance of the answer he had waited for in vain one winter evening long ago. Whatever the case, the stranger had let himself fall into Caba's affable net. Realizing that he wouldn't understand, even now, the stranger returned to himself, with difficulty. He had already become overwhelmed by the disarming friendliness Caba used to ensnare his opponents—again, he had fallen into Caba's trap, helplessly and inescapably becoming his former self, maintaining the rules of their established relationship . . . the stranger, the fragile son of the earth, might confuse or conflate "yesterday" with "ten years ago," when they were still classmates, and "tomorrow" with "three years from now," when they would again separate without his understanding—more than he had previously—the true and hidden logic of Caba's hollow words and politeness.

Or maybe they said nothing to each other because there was you, another person in the room. When the stranger had tried to bring his hand to his throat, a gust of wind had blown near the door: the wind of dry leaves, rustling hair, vaguely metallic, and they were forced to look at the thin girl, slumped against the wall. But they would say nothing to each other in any of their daily meetings over the following years—even when there was no witness to distract or embarrass them. Nor was anything said as they separated again three years later, when Sebastian Caba had become intrigued and curious, and tried to understand the mysterious stammering of his colleague, sickened by the typewriters' patter. At this last meeting—both were hoping it would finally be their last—Sebastian Caba eventually adopted the other's tactic, letting himself be caught in the invader's silence, and acting surprised by his unique phrase, itself too clear to be credible. Having decided to present himself in a pleasant and benevolent light, and being careful not to ridicule the runaway's first, childish argument, Caba hoped that other arguments would follow (however twisted and stammered they might be), from which he might be able to discern the real, present, and past face of his onetime former protector and learn how his old classmate had renounced the chance of success for which he had been destined. Caba would try to understand how and why this former star of the school had lost himself, and why he now saluted him as a resigned subordinate, why he recoiled from any closeness or affection that would remind him of the past.

The stranger never moved beyond the superficialities of their first reunion. For the next three years, Chief Engineer Caba, moreover, did not succeed in clarifying their positions. Now, all his previous protector and schoolmate did was repeat the one ridiculous phrase, stubbornly persisted on leaving it behind, and repeating it correctly and distinctly, like the words of a magic spell. Just as the stranger became terrified by the continuously increased complicity that followed their initial conversation, which led him, then, forced him, to raise his hand to his throat to defend himself, similarly, three years later, Sebastian Caba was hiding, sheltering himself in the soundlessness of the room and in his interlocutor's silence, becoming transfixed by the phrase about the unbearable typewriters which was paralyzing him in the paradox of their past circumstances, except now the roles were reversed. Caba hurried to raise his hands, yielding himself, conducting the stranger to the door, regaining his politeness, his amiability, and standing frozen in the doorframe, resigned to himself, abandoning words that weren't useful, because they couldn't explain what can't be said.

There would need to be a new morning, further delayed, a morning like all other mornings: the fatigue, the noises, Mişa the comrade spy, clocking in to work, pumps, projects, and masks, and little Monipig, the fat teacher, typing stories as though sprayed from a machine gun and pounded into the walls. And finally the damp, illusory street.

You were far away or nowhere or had remained there, in the shadow of another spring, slouching against the walls, waiting.

⁝ ⁝ ⁝

Shoulders, hands, hair: your entire body glued to the cold, damp wall. You were watching the stranger's hasty passage, his particular passage measured against everyone else's passage, all in the friendly blink of an eye. By now, you were used to that hallucination, repeatedly present and in its smile. You were wading in the waters of your old terrors, which were abating. Your arms were becoming weightless, disburdened of your dead father's memory. The forgetfulness you craved was catching you as you were becoming free, fearful, about to scream from visceral terror, suddenly light, yet available to recall the dead man—he who is always with you, in you, against you—like an outstretched shield, a casing, a shell that stifled as it defended, like being enclosed in an evil force-field that separated you from a riptide of hatred and loathing that no living being could resist. You were becoming corruptible. Another death was on the threshold, heavier than any burden on earth. You were frightened for him, the stranger—for tomorrow's dead, brother of an instant. Another liar, loved with no way out.

You felt the conversion's beginning. The obstacles that stood in your way would have to be reinforced to keep you at a distance, far from the center of the earthquake, from everything except the shadow's oblique passage through the long corridor. You should remember the dead man, place that memory in front of you, so his cowardly, tired, parental face can defend you with his death, the final escape. Until the days when the recollection of the lost one—that last powerless despair—becomes a lamentation full of longing, and you will be able to think of them together. The dead man's final revenge on the threshold of becoming unforgettable: he forced you to wait for your treacherous new ally, being swept away by the stranger.

Yesterday, a year ago—which is to say "once upon a time"—the dead man would have to be brought back to life, as a warning to the man still living, to understand his kinship with a hypothetical, unseen parent, at least for now, when you fling the shield of an absent corpse in his face, so that he can recognize himself quicker, defend himself or run away, so that he can see his own resemblance, and while there is still time, run away from the weakness that may be his fate.

Father is still tall—this thin, careless, negligent, weak man with elongated hands who crosses the cool corridor of bygone, youthful days, spending evenings in his room absorbed in his books (whitened by the lampshade), holding them with nervous fingers. His face is handsome, full of lunacy.

Difficult, tiring evenings: he hangs over his little girl like the burden of damnation.

Suffocated by loss, wounded by incurable guilts, no longer able to find his rhythm, he tried everything and nothing in those postwar years. His breath is like the lazy, dusty city's. It stinks of death and hard work. He would like to live in an empty house somewhere in undulating uplands, disentangling trees over crisscrossed streets.

There in an enclosure of nights with gusts and gales where the dead meet the living to exchange places, where you can strike a bargain with the insomnia of the little girl from back then, he returns, leaves, returns, pursues, alienated from himself, wanting to hear his daughter's laugh again. Maybe he would have arrived at the other end of the country and would have met a son—a fervid and reclusive son, if there had been time for such deluxe forms of hopelessness. But there wasn't.

The war left him dazed, as though he had forgotten how to return to the rest of humanity: thoughtless, careless with words, indifferent to songs, flags, slogans, or prosecutors, burdened by noises, and mistrustful and deaf to the promises of spies and interrogators, silenced by their tiresome, monotonous exaltation, as if he had landed among them by mistake, ready to flee at random, to anywhere else, to nowhere. In their company, his face contorted with memories and

81

hesitations, he collapsed into laziness and became odd and defiant … they cast him aside like a tiresome phantom, a suspect that didn't even deserve a trial.

The tall, nearly transparent Captain passed through layers of exile, a jailbird only seeing a small square of sky, an outline of color, changeable with the hours. He had grown used to the reduced landscape. Enclosed in the damp tranquility of narrow spaces, his gaze had fallen into the square of sky, into the realm of sleep. He'd been left to wait for his sentence. Then they threw him back, to transform him into what he could no longer become. After that, he avoided talking about the pitch-dark cells just as he had avoided talking about the war. The rupture of his being was barely the beginning of the expiation of his guilt or non-guilt. He threw himself into heavy drinking again, became exhausted, happy, tired of feeling powerless and ashamed, and spent near-catatonic days in silence. He would say "I'm going," and then later he'd say "I've come," and reprises of apathy would follow, cut by Sunday walks … rarely illuminated by startled reactions, dizzied by the sun, by words: satire, station, bridge, and promises, particles, pigeons.

The young man in the familiar blue shirt quickly crosses the corridor again. You linger there. He hurries or runs carelessly. Sometimes his hands squeeze his throat … and you saw the jump rope. You pulled him down. The cord fell over the waste of childhood, so you turned him over, rolled the jacket under his back, and you went on repeating the movements you'd learned for saving the drowned. It was clear then: Father had died. No daughter had ever been born. He was a lifeless puppet worked by an adolescent female stranger. His livid face sought resurrection from a thread of blood that oozed from the corner of his lips. He would writhe for weeks until his unwanted rebirth.

The agony of endless weeks: liquefied gestures, milky mornings, dispensing with objects, people—annihilating their movements, swallowing their haste, rarifying their muddled signs. Work shift one, shift two, shift three, shift one, shift two, again, shift three: Wednesday's day and night had passed. Thursday evening he kept laughing. That was the final vacillation, the hesitation of the finger on the trigger, the rope that had yet to lengthen into a knot, the poison still licking the bottom of the glass—the last moment of weakness. By then, though, he was waiting for the end: his plunge into the industrial melting pot. No one could bring him back from that sea of flames. A final embrace: ash, smoke—ignition.

The freezing walls burn; your fingers tremble. And the stranger passes hastily toward nowhere, once more through the dark, silent corridor. Still young, unapprised, prisoner of increasingly difficult, deadening mornings: Thursday, Monday again, Tuesday, Wednesday, an engulfing fog. Years of delay, until finally one Wednesday, one Thursday, at around ten o'clock, amidst the tumult of spies, the rustle of papers, the whistle of the telephone, the cadence of the typewriters, everything becomes unbearable: alone, a solitary man in the scorching rain faces his destiny, his reconciliation.

The young man goes by. He doesn't suspect he's being watched. He hasn't seen you, embittered in your mourning clothes, cursing the way people go cheerfully about their games as if skipping a rope made of days. You are an outsider to their appetites and pleasures, discarded among books that enchant and lie, lie and enchant, just like the grownups, the cowards, the runaways, the idiots: those paternal braggarts—those cheaters.

Frightened again by the power of death that brings your hand to your throat (withdrawn quickly, uselessly, too late), you come to yourself. There you remain, resigned to waiting. The stranger doesn't see you. He can't see the smooth wall of this vestibule where a blizzard of waiting scorches your fingers. Hidden by the shadows of the corridor, you repeat the gesture spasmodically and quiver, startled as if the intruder of tomorrow had snuck between the deceased past (as well as the past deceased) and the daughter deserted by the present. In a rush, the stranger goes by, blind as a forgetful ghost in an abandoned corridor. But he's not like you. He hasn't held a suicidal father in his arms, and if he had, it would have meant that he was retrieving his parent from the alienation that separated them.

Whatever we think, whatever we do, we drag them behind us. We deny, curse, forget them. Their ballast oppresses us, bends us, joins us. Time is nothing in this equation. After fifteen years you find yourself repeating the verbal tic of the dear departed, and the same pain in your left leg torments you the way it did him. Maybe your fictive brother repeats the words of his absent shadow, too.

Back when you had to wear schoolgirl pigtails with mournful black bows, which you hated so much you chopped them off, the stranger was a young Party star, the wonder kid of his little town. The offspring of correct, zealous parents, you were on the way down: even then you shrank into yourself. He was rising, though, unknowing, blind, burning with big slogans he believed were his own, ready to denounce his parents for any deviation. He had no hesitations, and he would have been ready to give *you* away if an intransigent code demanded it, *you*, with your politically dubious parent, *you* and all of those like you—or the hypocrite Sebastian Caba, who used his winning cordiality to hide the secret of his dubious parents, relocated as enemies from the banks of the Danube on the basis of who knows what varying suspicions. He'd have sent all of you down the river, with your cunning loser airs, ready to sneak into the crowd, hiding behind sacrifices and towing the party line.

The cold of his own ascension shook him. Dislocated, he turned fragile, lazy. He threw away his chances. Your spine suddenly stiffened, meanwhile. Refusing to sink, you understood you needed to resist, to die again, many times over, until you could return to the others, without ever actually being among them. At the same time, rounds of amnesia spiraled, redoubled. Precursors of birth, recognition, tropisms lazed by warm currents, undermined all chances of revolt. Or maybe his halt wasn't voluntary. Maybe an unexpected accident, a family nuisance, or some unlucky swindle flung him suddenly into the camp of the defeated and the wronged where he adapted just as easily to the reversal of fortune. Sadness, obsession, humility, fear. Perhaps even your return from defeat didn't signify a choice, but only happened because it could be no other way: the unbearable had gone on for too long and something had to be tried—anything, because time kept passing. You cursed the cowardice of a father who abdicated: caught up inside himself, without escape, ignoring his responsibility, his promises. Perhaps the hypothetical brother was cursing the perseverance of a parent who didn't abdicate but who was eager to raise protective walls, spaces of doubtful safety.

How is your isolation different from his indifference? To what extent is indifference an end and isolation a beginning, a way of waiting without hope? To what extent do they stand on the same crumbled rock?

You went down into the damp tunnel, groping. Each step took you further from the patch of sky left in the little window of aloneness. Distance narrowed that rectangular eye. Another slope closed the distances behind: the vastness increased. The light grew scarce. Whoever says there's a moment of terror greater than this is a liar. You look back and see: there isn't enough time to turn back. That would take more than a lifetime. Whoever claims they're tough is a liar: they've made up their loss. They've recovered from abandonment without knowing how the cold pours over you when you can't find a scrap of light from behind. You two have met in the risky game of banalities, though, and have both heard the suspect's nightmarish undertones where masked figures bark at the funeral masquerade.

Damp, high, close walls: the course descends; there's no right or left. Time grows dark, cold. Your skin covered with sores, dregs, you fall prey to stammered, startled gestures. In the distance: the torturers' carnival. We cannot lose what we have understood and gotten close to, you said once. Yet only this do we lose—we have nothing else to lose. We squander, we abandon what we've understood and have grown close to: closeness dies over time. Understanding flutters for a deceptive instant. You can live in the mountains for four years or forty, always ransacking the same false idea ... what miraculous powers could have grown in the lonely little girl in a year, or two, or ten if what happened could have been delayed, if Time allowed itself to test her later, but Time raced through the defeated Captain's damaged laugh. Nothing could support him or keep him upright. He didn't have time, however much he might have been watched over. He needed to speed toward the moment when he'd finally embrace himself in the pyre of forgiveness and atonement.

The walls close in along the corridor. Fingers splayed, your hand slides over the narrow, moldy wall; nearby other fingers grope; a slippery step, another slippery step: your breath trembles. Your hand and the other's should meet and clasp. You listen to the drumming of fingers on the walls, fingers bloodied by another fall. Shortening the distance, you try to reach out.

This new death will no longer be lost! So you believe. It will regain time, it will remain, it will be stopped. There will be delay or resurrection by an ardent sister who is not sixteen years old anymore, nor twenty. She has learned to defend and preserve! Joy and terror expand—the terror of meeting the other's joy and terror. The cold doubled, the mirroring in the other, in a narrow place, condemned, where one can't stay or go, except into an embrace of terror that's worse than death.

The shadow embraces the emptiness as it was at the beginning, as it was long ago, as it will be tomorrow and forever.

The factory heaved great columns of smoke and flame at the sky. It demanded the worker' hands and hardships, not to mention their complete attention. The city would soon hear of the terrible event. At the beginning of the night shift someone had plunged into an enormous pot of molten metal. The burning liquid consumed the man's body in an instant. All that remained was a brief hiss and the smell of burnt flesh.

On closer investigation, inquiry established that it had been suicide, possibly premeditated. The worker was capable and serious, his behavior uniformly correct: he hadn't attracted attention. His coworkers sympathetically recalled the way he obstinately gathered his strength to keep up with them and almost always succeeded. They, acknowledged, however, that he was smothered by tiredness, and then he would hurriedly rub his throat as though trying to catch his breath. He would blink rapidly and purse his lips in a way that contracted half his face.

A previous suicide attempt came to light. This essential detail should have curbed interest in the case. It had horrified many, who suffered nightmares for several weeks. Rumors continued to fly. There were vague whispers about some sense of guilt from the war. Some maintained it had been proved; others that it was nothing but an insinuation the authorities pinned on the Captain, who had refused to collaborate.

It was the beginning of 1954. The Captain's daughter was in her last year of high school. She passed her exams and tried to become a schoolteacher. That would have suited her well. She was calm and coddled by hours of reading. She had a deep respect for her mother's vocation. Though she was admitted to university, she was soon dismissed: her father had taken an unsolved guilt to his grave. The university advisors told her to find a job—there were enough in the country, which was at the peak of reconstruction. The girl withdrew to a quiet village in the mountains. Several peasants seemed ready to rent her a room, but as soon as they heard she had come as a teacher, they fobbed her off on their neighbors. The village had recently been disturbed by peculiar "teams of agitators" from the distant cities of the plain. Wary of showing their faces, talking in an urban, intellectual way the peasants couldn't understand, and delivering sly slogans, a host of these "foreigners" had then settled into local households.

The new teacher eventually found a place at the end of the village in the home of Vasile Obreja, an elementary-school teacher like herself.

... You entered the little vestibule. You heard "Forward!" shouted from somewhere behind the walls. There were two doors on the left, two on the right, and one facing the entrance.

The voice seemed to have come from behind this last door. There, indeed, there sat the master of the house, at a table facing the door. Snowy haired but still robust, he offered you the first room on the left. He wouldn't hear of money—except, "I have one rule of my own," he said, "never try to push my wheelchair." The girl settled comfortably into Obreja's empty house.

The stubborn villagers refused to send their children to school, let alone come themselves. The young teacher didn't lose her poise: she kept coming back to them. Despite her slender body, she confronted snow-covered roads and the biting cold. She didn't make friends. For one of them—a certain old man named Abesei—she showed particular attention and sympathy. He seemed to enjoy their conversations and came to the evening literacy classes regularly. When he was absent for more than a week in a row, she became worried, all the more so because Lică Abesei, his nine-year-old grandson, wasn't coming to school in the morning either. She climbed the hill to their house. She was forbidden from entering their gates by the father of Lică Abesei, who practically shoved her and yelled that he didn't need "communists" coming to visit. The peasant was living morosely as a wronged man. Poor, but still the wealthiest householder in the impoverished village, he had just lately become a *kulak*. Bearish and violent, he hid his son's boots to keep him from attending the communist school. He kept quarreling with his elderly father, too, who was amused by the relative socially damaging wealth of his son, who had finally enriched himself, just when he shouldn't. Overjoyed to infuriate his son and to make fun of him, the old man was jubilant. He was enchanted by learning the ABCs and had made a secret pact with his grandson. One of the violent father–son quarrels ended badly, and in the end, very badly for the old man's heart.

Under Vasile Obreja's protection, the young lady teacher was able to attend the funeral, which had immediately improved the classroom attendance of Lică Abesei, a weak boy who stammered but was still the smartest kid in class.

Only then did the grumpy loner—the teacher Vasile Obreja—accept his tenant's request to talk in the evening. More than that, he uttered some of the most curious phrases: "You should read fairy tales, miss. The people who write them are the only ones who teach us morality. Remember the syllogism of the mathematician: Babies are illogical. Nobody is despised who can manage a crocodile. Illogical persons are despised. Therefore, babies cannot manage crocodiles. That's what the mathematician said, and I will accompany you to those crocodiles."

The young teacher used to run from one edge of the village to the other. Once in a while, when she came into the village, a cheerful and energetic vitiated man would help her: the forestry administrator, Dan Vasilescu, who had come to the mountainous village and its clean, fresh air, to cure himself of a morphine addiction. Her neighbor, Vasile Obreja, helped her more often with the literacy classes.

She stayed in that village for two years. After that she was hired to assist in the construction of a factory in the capital. She worked as a low-level technician, a job that could have been handled by a high-school graduate with some capacity for drawing. Her modest diligence won the sympathy of her superiors. After the factory was built and put into operation, she remained in the "technical department," which was an unusual reward, because the privilege of residence in the capital was almost impossible to obtain. She took classes in the evenings at the technical school and when she graduated she became a knowledgeable technician, because she knew—from her time on the worksite—many more details about the construction of the factory than any of the other employees who were hired later.

To everyone's surprise, however, a few years later, she left the factory and the city: after a month of medical leave, she returned friendly and energetic, but on her first day back on the job, she requested the vacation days that were due to her for that year's work, and after that she never came back. Her former coworker Sebastian Caba, who had become the chief engineer of the factory, probably approved her transfer, because the big city was too noisy for her anyway.

After a while, they no longer talked about her. Someone who had visited the factory where she ended up confirmed that she hadn't changed, and hearing this news, they never thought of her again.

⸭ ⸭ ⸭

The chair, the desk ... the comrade spy in front of it ... the nearby coworkers swallowed in white mist the way that mountains rise from fog at dawn among the trees after a chilly night. The somnolent prisoner among confused, rising voices like stray tones in the woods, barely plucked from night.

The bustle of the early hours: drawers slammed, voices, telephones, rustling paper. Between dry lips, the bitter white pill to chase away sleep, bodily fatigue ... soft steps, treading the white misty waters. Soon there will be earth under his feet. A narrow strip of light will insinuate itself on the peak of the hill, the color of a delayed morning. At the middle or a quarter of the way, words will suddenly come through the receiver raised to his ear.

You see him. He's close, a step away, near your drawing board.

In the pocket of his portfolio, a bundle of white pages covered with signs, understandings that came too late. The envelope from Donca, the sister that he'd told you about. Stepping toward the door, hesitating, and turning back, his hand again on the gleaming white envelope. The door closed, shut—the avenues of retreat: blocked. Nothing could be delayed anymore. The gong had sounded, the due-date arrived. Stairs, the upholstered office. The phrase, rapidly, negligently hurled out:

—I can't stand typewriters anymore.

We can't stand typewriters anymore, those machines. We're lunatics. We fall asleep within the nightmare of machines listening, recording, printing, and classifying. We go numb toward dawn, as though paralyzed. Speeches, fairy tales, and lullabies: traps at every step. We sleep in haste. We rise pale and groggy from the ritual of tiredness that subdues us like hypnosis, from which only murder could revive us.

He climbed the stairs, suddenly, disconnected from the tiny, senseless event resembling any other, like the drop that finally makes the water spill over the edge of the glass. The avoided meeting with an imagined sister banished between the sheets of a belated envelope—and the grotesque, the surrogate, little Moni-pig, Monica.

Anything could have been said, even the truth. They might have recapitulated the months of years, the days of weeks—the years of months of weeks of days—when the lunatic had gradually lost the strength to climb the hill of captive mornings anymore, and he heard, ever weaker and more distant, the words that once gave him strength:

have to, and a bit more, again today, again tomorrow, maybe tomorrow, maybe the day after that ... until the sky would suddenly grow dark, thunderous, and the postponements would finally explode: that would be the end.

The interim and hierarchic chief, Comrade Caba, would have to listen to the warning and pass it on to his own interim and hierarchic bosses, for the warning was not addressed to him alone, or to them. Nor did it belong solely to the subordinate who delivered it. The cryptic lament would have to be uttered. It was, in fact, a threat.

Then, the first steps in the rain, the fugitive's cadence, the liberating refrain of a moment in the professor's moldy cage: I-can't-stand-anymore, once, twice, the cadence ever more aggressive between the cold walls of the event that presumed you as witness and accomplice.

He could have said anything. Caba might have given anything in response—seeking a joke, a diversion, a recollection. He might have concocted any surprise—if anything he said could still surprise ... attempting one last chance, hoping that it's never too late to mislead once again, to sweep away the foolish target, to manipulate and deceive.

—I knew then what you risked for me. We were only high-school students, but back then, any obstacle might have been able to delay me for several years or maybe even cause a definitive failure. Who on earth knows?

The subordinate to whom he was speaking wasn't susceptible to surprises. He knew his interlocutor too well—and all of his worn-out tricks—about which he had explained to you over and over again.

Sebastian Caba might have complained about the way relations between them had been made too official: the subordinate's hasty and obsequious daily greeting, and the distance that the subordinate maintained.

—I don't understand what happened. We were proud of you, envious even. In a way, we may even accuse you of allowing mediocrities to get ahead.

Raising his hands to mime helplessness or bewilderment, Caba rose to his feet behind the glass-topped desk: he knew how to listen and answer, and he continued maintaining perfect, benevolent, well-meaning, well-shining camaraderie, while assuming the appearance of amazement, with the perfect balance of emotion and expression, with studied cheerfulness, and with calculated compassion. He fell silent opportunely, understandingly, wisely. He went on listening.

—I can't stand typewriters anymore.

His manicured, long, white hands rested on the thick glass covering the desk. He went on listening.

—*I can't stand typewriters anymore.*

Concern united his hands, intertwining them, even and pale.

—I can't stand typewriters anymore.

This stubbornly repeated phrase seemed like a sign of madness. Palms unclasped, Caba's hands opened upward, showing him distressed and powerless in front of this strange mumbling.

—I can't stand typewriters anymore.

The superior led his colleague to the door and raised the fine, pale fingers of his left hand to the doorframe, where he leaned his shoulder and head in a sad gesture.

Static finale: the left hand leaning against the doorframe like a thoughtful and frail branch.

⋮ ⋮ ⋮

Just like another time. The massive desk covered with a thick sheet of glass. The sentence settles over the glass rectangle, over the pale, manicured hands with the palms motionlessly waiting on the gleaming glass. Just like that other time.

Back then, he was counting banknotes. He had lifted his eyes and recognized a forgotten colleague. His gaze suddenly brightened the room. The air vibrated with his cordiality. You remained near the door, beside the unknown newcomer you'd accompanied to meet the chief, directing him toward the window at the end of the room, and then remaining forgotten near the door. Filling the room with words, Sebastian Caba had started exercising his amiability right away. The unshaven guest in a dusty blue shirt with traces of whitewash or lime was struggling—shy and awkward. Caba's hands waved through the air, practically aflame, encircling the guest, weakening his opposition, and asking the questions, while his former colleague brought his hand to his throat, a defensive reflex.

Near the door, something rustled, like a cat's hair. The stranger turned, amazed, and only then did he look carefully at the features of the girl who had brought him there, and your wiry hair seemed almost metallic.

Caba had the hands of an adolescent: thin, velvety—as though they'd never perspired—protected from cuts, eczema, or chilblains, untouched by warts or boils. He shook other people's hands thoughtfully, slowly, patiently. It was perhaps the conquerors' first surprise and his first triumph in the class of timid provincials where he'd appeared. The class followed him with their eyes, enamored from the start, and when he took his seat, his gaze lingered on the classmate right in front of him. Perhaps he suddenly wanted an ally, or believed himself to be discovered, endangered.

Now, he had raised his left hand, his pale fingers contrasted against the coffee-colored doorframe. He bowed his head, shoulders, and body while remaining dreamily in the doorway, unmoving, as in a picture, watching his subordinate rush down the stairs.

A chill ran down your spine. Your wiry hair rustled, as it had at the stranger's first appearance, when he brought his hand to his throat, in defense. The gesture shouldn't have ever been repeated.... No one had the right to mimic the well-known gesture of your dead father, and no one had the right to record him. You had imagined—over and over, too many times—the moment of triumph when some stranger would involuntarily bring his hand to his throat and you would be able to watch—uncaring, apathetic, able to live again among the living. When the stranger suddenly brought his hand to his throat, you grew pale. Your delicate palm rubbed against the whitewashed wall, and the fine plaster dust stuck to it.

You went on gazing at the stranger—frozen, with his hand on his throat. You pressed your hand against the wall, hoping this could somehow save you, while listening to the galloping of a hostile future—that moved along the length of the cool corridor—the specter of an awaited, unwanted, unknown, beloved executioner from whom you did not know how to flee in time.

You went on gazing at the stranger. You gazed long and far away, chased back into the mountains that kept refusing refuge.

$$\vdots \quad \vdots \quad \vdots$$

You will run toward the glass building. You'll fling your jacket over the back of a chair. You'll see if he's alive, if he's somehow still there—the man with the bandage around his neck that you spotted from a crowded bus. You were trembling, eyes wide with fright. You looked bewilderedly at the back of a blue shirt, at the wide strips of rustling tracing paper. You wanted to imagine and then absorb an image able to chase away the phantom that had sprouted in the bus window. But the recently hired engineer was there at his drawing board.

He'll be there, and you'll be there on other mornings. You'll talk and listen. And you'll receive a ticket to the movies: the danger will come one step closer. You'll have to comprehend everything that's incomprehensible, everything that can't and shouldn't be understood. And you'll only ask once, hastily and timidly:

—You were a child during the war, weren't you?

You won't expect an answer. And there will be a movie theater, a summer afternoon, and on screen, the border area where the wanderer could no longer escape. Daily war stories flow from the movie screen: smokestacks of crematoria, skeletal bodies, nocturnal hunters, barbed wire, sentinels and executions, howls and hatred, beasts, eyes wide with fright: archives against forgetting, films viewed in respectful silence. The average moviegoer doesn't want to know more about the war. The people who sit in the dark theater all the time want entertainment. There's a sob, a squeal from a girl with a short skirt. Ravished in the dark hall, tonight she'll expend the pain in the frenzy of some dance hall ... When the girl quiets down, an old man dozing in his seat lets out a smothered cry—woken by the thundering of cannons that remind him of the mud of two forgotten wars.

—You were a child during the war, weren't you?

Blond, thin, and from another era, the boy on the screen looks at himself in the mirror of the well. His mother's laughter suddenly bursts into the canon peal of water, and long, lonely horses eat apples by the seashore.

The question went unanswered. Your date only wanted to know as much as those cinephiles of summer afternoons, gladly going to the waters of Lethe to forget. He had seen people buried alive and resurrected, detached from despair and hurled into depravity, impatient to touch each other, to rub against each other, to enter each other.

Obsessed once, as he'd said—long ago, in an ancient and forgotten adolescence—by his own capacity for alienation, he'd dashed through his youth, inventing dilemmas and disquietudes for himself, gathering obsessions that could occupy his need to understand—what should be and what shouldn't, what is and what isn't—and he doesn't want to know anything more about the war, *he doesn't want to know it*. Words travel with difficulty, detouring around him so that nothing can reach him: slave to oblivion—which shames, humiliates, and soothes—its trophy and glory.

How could he be like the other: the obsessed, the prisoner, and the master of memory, swinging in the past's vertiginous pendulum, imprisoned by the ravaged waters of impossible forgetting?

He'll climb the stairs behind you on a summer evening. The door will remain open. Someone should close it behind him. His hand will seek the handle and he will pull, slowly, fearfully, as though anticipating an ambush. He'll twist the handle till it can go no farther. The bolt should enter the slot unheard, the door should remain stuck in the frame. Almost closed ... pulled slowly, the door nearly flush with the edge ... yet powerless to finish the motion, aligned with the doorframe, noiseless, in perfect silence, without disturbing or awaking ... tiptoeing, eyes lowered to the ground, fingers gripping the handle ... don't move too suddenly, don't slam ... everything should flow as silently as a dreamless sleep. Closing the door, the same way each time: frightened, cautious, with humility ... startling at any sound of a slammed door, shaken by the first loud noise, by any powerful gesture. The humiliation of silence, the humiliation and habit of forgetting, the humiliation driven to the point of forgetting. Noiselessly, the door pulled, slowly, in terror, stuck to the wooden doorframe—an interrupted, unfinished, fearful gesture.

You were waiting for a sign from the forever departed, still frozen in your memory so that you might be able to break the curse and detach yourself from the cold that belongs to him. Daughter, orphan—abandoned by whom? Unknown sister of which unknown man? Who squeezes his hands around his throat? Which stranger sends such unremitting alarms that pass hastily down the corridor of your expectations?

You were waiting for a blue shirt. The forgetful passerby, the passenger in permanent haste and change, the wanderer zigzagging across soluble days, without participating and preserving, wandering in a foggy labyrinth and indifferent to where the serpentine pathway leads, docile and foreign to himself, moved by strangers that he's able to instantly forget, as if he were actually the stranger, the other, elsewhere, in another's dream ... without parents, without brothers, incapable of keeping a sister.

Your hands descend from the wall and wrap around your body. You belong to no one, and you're for no one. Orphaned by yourself and by everyone else, you're a solitary female in a tunnel of silence, crossing paths with them for just one instant. You feel the walls swell, enlarging to the left, to the right, wide enough to allow narrow shoulders through. A dead man's daughter, prisoner of this death, you've delayed absolution, and been terrified by such a useless and drawn-out recovery. Discarded and forced to wait, the dead man is your mirror: he is apparently alive, resembling you and you resembling him, as if the resemblance isn't another kind of death. Should you all be *semblables*, the likeness of each other, which is to say made the same, for you (the lone female) to die in the peace of resemblance, in its order, peace, and equality? — the identity frozen, the synchronized howls, a landslide united under the same mask? Let contraries and contradictions perish! Should you remain the daughter of the dead man and the sister of the one not yet alive? Should you draw them closer together under the cover of night? Why should you resemble them when death waits to make us all equal? Unless the dead are somehow trying to call us before the appointed time, unless, in his state of reconciled non-being, the dead coward can't bear our pride, our living protest, the eulogy of our uniqueness born of solitude.

The despotic vengeance of the one who has strayed into the labyrinths of memory, the putrid prince, burned there and dispersed as smoke, far from you, has become the waves that stop you, make you return, prevent you, rope and rock your thoughts, make you submissive, steal you away. They make time pass, age your bones and gestures, quash your revolts, make your hair fall out and rot your teeth, lower your gaze and dry the leaves and trees and waters nearby, wreck landscapes, murder mountains and miracles—down to the sea it-self—and make you resemble him and the stones. Pulverized into the great silence, he no longer knows anything but blank oblivion that covers cadavers and disasters, that doesn't heal and doesn't give birth.

And you gouge your nails into the slippery walls to avert him, to defeat him, to retrieve your freedom and uselessness, terrified of wait-ing in the lightning flash of a single, blue instant in a corridor of silent perdition.

⋄ ⋄ ⋄

The dream began with a streak of light. You caught a glimpse of the bustle, oblique and smoky, through the slit, cracked open like a door. The pedestrians crossed rapidly, noisily, the way they used to. Their eyes were lowered, as though inspecting insects with cyclopean curi-osity that you rarely felt. In the evening they were tired: they panted and grunted inside their cabins and cells and coops. You snuck out of your hiding place. The moonlight fell drop by drop. The pathways kept descending: all paths headed down. You heard voices confront-ing each other. You heard severe summonses and punishing blows, and you went on stammering like a mute who tried to learn how to speak far away from the ravaged fortress. You would return late, feel-ing your way through the braided knot of oblique streets.

A long hall like a silent tunnel or a tall, milky glass. You were a regular at that underground shelter. The waiters and patrons knew you. The smells of roasted goat, of beer and rum, the aromas of plum brandy, vodka, vermouth, kebabs, cognac, spiced meat, pickles—a redolent mix—mastika, ouzo, syrups, and slivovitz: everything mixed together and then dispersed.

A cold, empty hall, fresh and clean, it smelled of nothing. You clutched the chilly glass several times. You raised it slightly. Behind you, someone brayed like a mare, a hostile laugh followed by silence, and then somewhere in the back, the sudden laugh again. You turned to look.

That's when you saw him, young as ever, the collar of his blue shirt turned up. His partner had bleached-blond hair like an unkempt haystack, and a chubby child's ruddy cheeks. Her swollen, sausage-like fingers played rapidly over the table. Far away, at the other end of the hall, maybe farther, they sat—though in the peculiar architecture of the place, they might have been a step away, as if you were sitting right beside them. He hadn't changed. Young as ever, he was embarrassed by his painful perpetuity. She was all suave voice. Ready to kill her, he kept looking at her who was looking at you, stock-still, the frozen glass in your hand.

A babble of stories swirled through the air. Reflected in the half-open eye of the victim whose voice kept whispering like a fat fairy. The young man from long ago hadn't moved an inch. The victim stared at you without blinking, though there was flirting and clinking glasses, too. Dumbfounded by their byplay, you stared unmoving, and your glass grew warm.

Multiplication of intimate sounds: wine swishes, bottles clank, her speaking, her breath striking glass after glass, and in the peculiar time of that place, the encounter goes on a little while that's also long; you watched them again after who knows how long. The waiter wrote something in his notebook. Then the young man in the blue shirt paid. The waiter bowed down to the floor. You could see his white jacket bend forward. They took the first enormous step: the distance between you and them had compressed, or perhaps they had been next to you the whole time. The blonde's mouth opened and closed over her yellow teeth, but you couldn't hear a single word; he was watching her as if there was no one else around, and he couldn't have seen you. They moved forward—but somehow, as though fixed in place, without making progress — and suddenly they were no longer there.

They disappeared. The restaurant: empty, mute. They had passed within a step of your table. They were beginning to climb the steps toward the hole of light that led to the street. When she looked at him, you could see the white of her eye. Smiling, he bent to settle the red jacket slipping off her shoulder. He put an arm around her shoulders in a delayed, gentle, weary gesture — a protective pause before the crime.

They were climbing the first step. The room filled with your dry, old woman's howl.

—You didn't caress *me* like that!

Hurried and powerless, you moved your lips in hatred. Without raising, your voice struggled, suffocated, crying into the void, strangling each syllable.

—You never caressed *me* like that!

A thick voice, an old curse, inaudible, internalized.

—You never caressed *me* like that!

Again and again, with every step they climbed. They weren't turning around, and they weren't hurrying, as though they couldn't hear your thunder from beyond the grave; you could still see their legs, his shoes and her bare feet with filthy nails that had grown bent and crooked like a wild animals' — enormously wide feet with warped, black nails.

Your scream broke off, useless as baying at the moon.

You wrenched your hands from the icy wall, touched your forehead with your fingertips. Your eyes had closed ... You were in the corridor once more, inside the nightmare of a long, vaulted corridor. Your fingers felt for your lips and throat, in case they had somehow grown old and shriveled. Hadn't some friend or brother crossed the corridor too, hearing how you cried in your sleep, ages ago, before you turned into an old woman trapped between narrow walls and buried forever?

There hadn't been anyone. Not one person heard the cries of your pitch-dark terror. But day invaded. The illusion broke: light struck your eyes, amazed by this repeated, recognized dawn. You were the same as yesterday, punished by the long wait, the cold and endless corridor.

⁝ ⁝ ⁝

Out of the stillness or disquietude of waiting, the red orb will follow the rotating ray. The advance opens purple curves onto the burned sky of stars and lights still-becoming: incandescent trajectories.

That waiting was just the hesitation at the starting line, a premise that begins with possible death or liberation for other births and other deaths. The moment for movement had to come: for the blood or fire to become a red projection that gives birth to curves, spirals, serpentines, stairs, and steep trails for the hurried traveler heading toward nowhere. It had to come, for *YOU* are the mate, the partner, the *second person* who names the living or the dead, the *dialog* that separates and gives birth, the mobile point, a step away, a rest stop: you are *THE OTHER*, come to disrupt our sleep, attack our panic, you are isolation or indifference, the confirmation that we exist.

They would have to set out: the rotating spirals on which you must arrive at the moment, *YOU*, the change, the transition and transaction, the offering from somewhere remote, distant, and unknown, or from the unstable—doubling or dividing—self, from duality, or the choreographed special effects with which we contain ourselves, divide ourselves, make ourselves whole, fragment ourselves, multiply ourselves, and destroy ourselves.

⁝ ⁝ ⁝

The one who delayed would need to be punished in the end.

He will go downstairs in the morning—the son of the earth will run toward any shelter where he can be alone and free. An ordinary morning: the mannequins, Mişa the comrade spy, then the exchange of calm, cretinous words, the rumble of typewriters, the rotation of upholstered doors, Sebastian Caba's smile. From the neighboring workstation, you would continue stalking the fugitive, who couldn't be stopped by you.

He will meet the rain, crucified on the decayed wall, Christ-like among the ruins, exposed to pedestrians and patrols.

Smiling, he was running away from your expectations, likeness and light, greedy for a violent and total gesture to shatter reality, the out-of-tune melodies of submission and hypocrisy, the deaf-and-dumb complicity of the suspects—finally ready to kill the grotesque caricature of the fat, needy, puerile dreamer and the places for senile caresses.

The room of topsy-turvy objects, piano keys yellowed by blunt fingers, solemn candlesticks standing like telephone poles, jam jars near the towel stained with shoe polish, teaspoons choked with grease. Strange little creatures with five eyes and thirteen wings, oozing yellow liquids. In such a cell he will try to remember, but the past is without return. Pencils tipped with marmalade, socks wrapped around sugared rolls, needles perforating the pages of books, scores with sticky covers. He'll pull a book off the shelf and find a knife blade between his fingers, he'll move the chair and clay buttons will plop to the ground, he'll look for the electric outlet and an alarm clock will ring, his hand will be swallowed by dust, and his shoulders will hunch as though weighted down with heavy armor. The fugitive will pound the walls to find out if the fruitless day isn't just a mistake or some hallucination, if destiny has prepared the right place for crime and salvation.

You know his story. You see him. You foresee him. You are the shadow that pines for betrothal.

The stranger—the absent one trapped between the four hundred walls of a random cell (as among four or forty mute winds)—will be refused the answer left behind with the second person, the counterpart from whom he has fled.

$$\vdots \quad \vdots \quad \vdots$$

A summer morning, a vast marble staircase, a white screen catching the faintest glimmer of light ... somewhere a dark corridor ... somewhere, fragile windows continued rotating the light. The girl in the dream leaned on a wall somewhere, just as she had once leaned on the thick, rough tree trunk in the east of the plain. The encounter was announcing itself, finally: there, at the end of some infinite stairs, the victim awaited the end of the summer day. In the sunless tunnel, a hand had clutched the walls. Suddenly, a cheek appeared: impatience illuminated moist eyes. Then the blue shirt gleamed. The familiar rustle, smile, the momentary hesitation. It seemed he was remembering something. He stopped, came closer.

—Won't you come with me to the movies this afternoon?

You understood: it was no longer the customary wandering among books and chimeras and questions without answers; it was no longer the circular residue of coffee in which *you* looked without the courage to pronounce the name of the expectation, in which *you* continued your precautionary wandering. You squeezed the ticket stub between your fingers. You were smiling, relaxed, as the chosen of the gods used to await the fulfillment of their foretold deaths. The death sentence should be fingered, fondled, ridiculed, chased away like a phantom, like a false storm, but the victim is smiling, the mistress of fatality. She's the princess from a fairy tale, from a living and lucid dream whose finale will freeze the readers' blood.

You laughed, you joked, you dispatched words—that was the game. The palm of your left hand rubbed against the oily wall. The ticket fluttered between the trembling fingers of the other.

The summer afternoon halted as the lights came down. Suspended hours, whitewashed air: windows open, the rooms seemed to float in the inertia of the day. In the silent corridor, a thin, elongated being with a white face and wide-open eyes floated freely, until swallowed by thin, aromatic winds.

The new movie theater's waiting room was high and long. Because of the burning heat, only a few people attended—many people were at the stadium or dancing in the outdoor cafes. Or perhaps it was because of the obscure Russian title of the film, or because it was about war, and somewhere else they were playing movies with romantic knights and beautiful ladies.

Words had breathed their last that morning, so you took your seat mutely, glad to have nothing asked of you. Images flowed from the screen, so you couldn't look at anything else: the mirror of the well, the bucket drenching the boy's fair cheek, then the powerful, fresh-faced mother, laughing—the two of them momentarily reflected then blown apart by the explosion of water under the smoke of war. Little Ivan passed through the nights to the gentle purling of occupied rivers, his face increasingly fierce and aged. You gave a start without looking at your neighbor, who didn't seem to react in any way.

—You were a child during the war, weren't you?

Your whispered words came out like a tremor. He didn't reply. On the screen, the boy's fair face eclipsed the darkness and silence, along with the long, sad horses eating apples down by the seashore. When the darkness dispersed, the audience rose, reconciled, ready for other stories.

You stood. You kept silent. It was almost evening. Together, you crossed through a long, deserted street, passing under the tall buildings. Cars rushed by. Steps resounded on the sidewalk as if on glass. The shop windows were coming alive. To the right, a side street opened. He followed a step behind, a step below. You opened the apartment door. He came from below, a step behind you.

The opening of the door should have made a noise. You knew the sound exactly. You expected it, heard it, and yet you didn't. You stepped across the threshold with your hand on the switch. The room appeared. The door was hinged to the frame, rotated with caution, almost closed and yet only pulled to the edge.

To the left of the door, the wide bed covered with a red blanket. You sat on the bed; he sat on the chair, both in silence. You looked at the wardrobe, the wall facing the door, the one narrow bookshelf, high on the wall. The small table. The balcony. You turned on the radio to break the silence but couldn't find the right station and gave up. You rose and leaned into his chair. Keeping quiet, he propped himself for an instant on the lap of your skirt. You passed a hand through the buttons of his blue shirt. You turned off the light.

Fragmenting the darkness, horizontal bands of light from the street came through the slatted blinds. Penumbrae traced outlines of objects. Evidently looking at you, he stayed on the chair, motionless and probably absorbed in his own thoughts. Without looking at him, you moved toward the edge of the bed, where you remained standing. You unbuttoned your light, short-sleeved blouse. You took it off. It fell to the ground. Your hands parted the zipper of your skirt, which slid down and fell on top of the blouse. You lowered your arms. A small clump of silk coiled over the white skirt. Starting at the waist, you moved your hands down along your thighs, over your small round haunches.

There was no movement, not a sound. Maybe he looked at you. You remained in front of him, a naked statue. You were beautiful—your small breasts, full warm shapes. Long, toned legs. His eyes dilated in his lunatic face. You knew you were beautiful then. You looked at him, smiled timidly, guiltily. You raised your arm and slid your fingers through your hair, letting it flow down your back. When you brought your hand back down, your hair came with it, clenched in your fist. You let the wig fall over the little heap of clothing gathered at your feet, and shrugged your shoulders slightly as if to say, what can you do? And went on smiling the same level smile you'd worn all along.

You were truly naked now, and so you remained straight and silent. Your short hair—like an army recruit's or a pale, adolescent prisoner's—increased the intensity of your gaze ... The body of a Greek statue, slim and unreal, with sweet breasts and rigid legs ... Naked, whole, ready: you spread out on the bed, crucified under the white-washed ceiling, oppressed by the total silence ... Later: something or someone rustled. The pain of hearing made you close your eyes. Something or someone was moving nearby, and it hurt, unbearably.

Once, he passed his hand over your eyes, which had been closed for a long time. You felt the skin of another body against yours—an instant of kindness, of peace. The body rolled over, time after time, clenching wildly, dissociated, famished, furious. The summer night roared.

Fingers were growing from the foreign body, probing for elbows, shoulders, arms; the body had drawn close, collapsing upon itself ... the arms continued curving into caresses, the legs, shaking. You were breathing at the same time, brother and sister, until the shock hit him: a sudden earthquake, horrified by the nightmare of kindness, unexpectedly abandoned, abandoning.

Again, the weight of silence: the ceiling suspended you. Again, the body twisted, the hand slid on shoulders, cheeks, eyelids, the strange hand climbing toward the damp eyelids and stopping, trembling like the wing of an injured bird. The neighboring body was trembling, withdrawing, returning. It was caressing your thighs, looking for your heat in some hiding place. You, with the hair of an army recruit or a prisoner, had damp shoulders, breasts weighted with weeping.

The tears flowed from the beginning, from before the beginning, from all along: from the moment you stretched out on the bed with your arms spread and soft things rustled over soft things, dangling on the edge of the bed ... you were waiting with closed damp eyes ... the strange hand had grasped your hands—first the left, then the right—and things fell down again ... *you* opened *your* eyes in the white ceiling, the summer night galloped alongside with tears like drops of sleet and hail. Out of the friction and spasms of bodies, the sudden disengagement of shoulders, arms, and chests: fulfillment had culminated. You were crying ... maybe you cried the whole time, from the beginning, unheard crying, inaudible even to you, the same as the closing door that should have been clearly heard, but somehow wasn't. The movement of clothes, arms scrounging through fabric, the sheet, the body by your side, distant steps—no, first he touched one of your fingers, trapping your finger, squeezing it lightly in farewell. The footsteps moved toward the door; the door should have opened, as you knew it must, for the sound of closing to be heard. But the sound had disappeared, perished without a trace. The stranger had remained in the same spot, near the bed. Silence passed: time and silence.

You sat up halfway, you looked at the door, stuck to the edge of the wooden frame. It seemed closed, but it was only brought to the edge of the doorframe, shut too gently, almost closed, just enough to let a strip of light into the room. You remained in the same position, oppressed by the white ceiling, by the darkness and silence. Then the summer night broke open. Through the wooden blinds there were two young faces to be seen, ravished by the crack of the moon. A thousand stars on the blue background in the hole of the well. You closed your eyes, fast.

Easy sleep without tremors or dreams. You woke at dawn, at the same hour as always. You felt your shoulders, your cheeks. Dry: in their proper places. You lifted the wiry mound of hair from the floor. You sat the wig beside you, on the bed. Your feet landed on the chilly wooden floor. You picked up your clothes from the floor, and put them on. Smoothing your cheeks with your hand, your body began to awaken. You took the wig from the bed, and put it back on, straightening it approximately. You looked at the room, opened the door to the balcony.

In the fresh air and the light of a summer dawn, you crossed the room. The door was open, almost imperceptibly. The fugitive had left this as evidence. You walked to the window and went out onto the balcony. Busses were just beginning to leave, bicycles set in motion. The commute was beginning again, the same as always. In the street, the rat race was livening up.

You might have been able to face the astonishment of the heavens by leaping beyond the eventless calendar, beyond the crowds of hardworking, famished, overly submissive rodent workers. The earth without paths or surprises, without beginning or end, a resigned collapse, a silent tomb, the delirium of everyday absence.

You looked at the white walls and then at the street again. You panicked, you ran down the stairs: another morning, the kneeling of the slaves approves of the sun.

⁝ ⁝ ⁝

Smoky shadows, starving office slaves returning to their nests. The patrols and pickets to their posts, the spies running in high gear: the amnesiac mob. You can hear the clank of spoons and glasses, doors bumping against beds, and ringing telephones.

In the mouth of the stove, something revolves. It looks like a ring-shaped loaf of bread: a small curl with leaves of ash. The pile of burning pages rotates: burnt letters, fairy tales that have become black powder in the wastebasket under the piano teacher's instrument. Ash-colored smears: the paws of a carbonized monster.

The fugitive gathers strength for the great, unfulfilled deed. The surrounding apathy prepares for retribution. Hatred promises to fulfill the dreams of explosions. Here, the door closed itself: the lock turned itself, the door fell back into its frame with the short piercing sound of pinched metal like a pistol's click ... but that was long ago, a century ago, at least. Games of forgetting, of giving birth, of remembering, of revolting. He should stick his temple to the cold metal of the tape recorder, the sharp corner of some table, the wardrobe mirror, the telephone receiver, the door handle—any solid object that will confirm his existence. Then he should pick out the buried histories that he didn't have the courage to utter and that he'll carry with him forever: the treasure and the guilt.

He would also tell you the story that he forgot to leave behind in your room.

It happened long ago and far away, when everyone should have been glad, yet too many have managed to forget. Remembering the images is exhausting. The narrator grows tired quickly, too. The chroniclers write that back then arrogance had served the movements of the day and had been unleashed onto humanity. The cry of hoarse voices, suspicious people who hunted their own kind, suspected people and banished them into foreign lands ... into an unknown land where the cemetery would be their final home. Gathered into prison camps, far from the rest of humanity, they saw only barbed wire, trenches, common graves, common dormitories, common crematoria.

The few survivors were cadavers on liberation day. Immense beards, wild hair, ghostly faces. Rags hung off their skeletons.

Their perplexity continued for minutes and hours and days. They looked at the tanks covered with leaves and tree branches and at the incomprehensible smiles on the faces of their liberators. Some of them rushed to the gun turrets of the tanks to scatter the leaves that masked a great red star. The gates were thrown wide. They raised their rickety arms to feel the soldiers' bodies. They saw everything *clearly*, they heard the cries of happy beasts; they danced for joy: unanimous madness. They crowded toward the gates, toward the hands of the saviors. Everything was seen with limpid clarity. There was no room for doubt.

They sensed the smell of burning clothing. They saw how everyone was throwing their striped clothes into the heap, which smoldered at first and then rose to a high flame. They saw, heard, felt, and understood everything that was happening. It couldn't be otherwise, and in the following years—those shameful years of reintegration—they showed no trace of madness. They had endured, first clinging to the hope of such a miracle, then out of habit. Eventually, the rumors that spread during the final months would justify the panic on their executioners' faces.

The light of the survivors' eyes had grown brighter, reflecting the tired smiles of the liberators with their short haircuts and the peculiar commands that were issued in a noisy language—their uniforms dusty, their rifles and voices coated with dust.

They stared at youths that spilled out of the tanks like entrails. They tried moving slowly. For several moments or hours or days they remained well-behaved and tame—staring at the metallic letters strung above the iron curtain of the gate, sounding out the words that they had repeated so many times: "To each what he deserves." They slipped by the others, who weren't paying attention, and made for the gate. The disorder of collective joy protected their flight.

They went quietly for about a hundred paces. They seemed calm: three yellow cadavers with eyes bulging from their heads, their chins invaded by dirty hair gleaming with white strands. Just a bit more, and then suddenly they began to run, all three of them ran automatically, just as they had moved harmoniously before, without words, in terror that this fairy tale would fall apart. The perplexity that had affected each of the fugitives might have been their only sign of madness—hard to explain in the end, except through the perfectly aligned mechanism that was driven by their separate instincts.

They ran for a long time without looking back, without stopping until they came to the edge of a forest. They entered the forest panting, without slowing their frantic pace, harmonizing their slow, heavy steps. Fatigue and the coolness of the woods struck them simultaneously, and the father of the one running away ran on while sleeping, like an automaton.

He woke with the sun beating down on him at the edge of the forest. He had crossed the cool forest like a sleepwalker, as he told it. He had slept under the trees, dreaming in the shadows and shades of green that surrounded him. He had lifted his left leg, lowered it, then his right and lowered it, pummeled the air with his hands—first with the left, then with the right—following the same cadence of his stride, aligning his steps, one after the other, feeling and dreaming the coolness of the forest, and it seemed as if he had crossed the forest in a single leap.

They ran, they rested. They ran again. They sat on the grass or on tree trunks, without speaking, terrified of any omission or word that would reveal their humanness, weaken them, knock them down. They halted to rest and then ran again for almost thirty kilometers, until dusk, when the first houses popped up on the edge of a hill. The beginning of a village, or the remains of a village, or a lonely hamlet. They seemed to simultaneously understand that they would not pass beyond the first house, that they would fall down exhausted by their long race and terror. At this, their movements tripled, spontaneously: the only trace of the passing madness of the three men who were safe and sound. They acted as one, instinctively. They didn't have time to think or speak. When they finally entered the house, it had grown dark.

They saw the women: shadows spread on the floor. They didn't come near the women. They didn't even show any trace of amazement or violence or timidity. There were five or six women. They each approached one particular woman, and took her by the hand. Silent, calm gestures. Even, monotonous breaths. Suddenly, one of the men gave a start. He stopped himself. He passed his hand one more time over the woman's back, and then he cried out. He recognized her and himself. He wanted to howl for a long time, till the walls fell down. He passed his hand again over the woman's back, he howled again—which is to say, he wanted to howl again, but nothing came from his throat except a suffocated growl. The others looked at him indifferently. He shoved them. He hit them like a madman. These were the women who had escaped two days ago. They had heard about them in the men's camp. This woman was his wife. He had not seen her for three years. He had believed she was dead. He had forgotten her, obliged himself to forget her forever. The woman had a little growth on her back, which grew like a round acorn, and was only known to him.

The sluggishness of dusk. The soft walls close in. Soon silence will descend. We will be able to fall asleep, far from stories of the past, alien to our coincidental sisters, as *you* weren't able to do: so alive you remain, real and eternal.

The son wanted to tell the story of the father's escape during *your* incestuous night, but he wasn't able. He already knew about Captain Zubcu, there was no more to add. Guilty legends do not bring ease. The dark will receive him soon. Lethe will bring to rest the absent one, far from the empty days through which no one passed, ever.

"I"

BLACK AIR, LEFTOVER TWILIGHT, and the wan ribbon of
street: blinded by headlights and honking, pedestrians momentarily
crossed paths. As in wartime, the neighbors' radio played an English announcer's voice—tuned low. Suspended over the street, the
narrow room with fuzzy walls: a gentle kick would have gone right
through. The objects cowered. The scaly, reptilian bed. The curtain
of coiled worms. The nightlight: the throat of a creature ready to
screech. Darkness: obscuring forms, flattening volumes. My body
wedged between table and piano. Closed my eyes and felt the piano's
edge. Passed a hand over the ebony bars. A finger's pressure made a
thick sound. Another: thin. Piano keys: black and white.

Had sprawled on top of papers and laundry, to sleep: perchance
to ... wake as another, to wake no more. Got up. Stepped in front of
the bookcase. A shelf lamp cast light on the spines: double titles, as if
the music teacher always bought two copies each. Found a book with
a familiar name, looked at its letters, repeated the title several times.
Had read this book once. Knew whole passages by heart back then.
On the table, a folder with papers. Opened it. A typed letter, a carbon
copy. Another copy of a different letter typed on the same machine.
Another letter: awkward masculine script in a trembling hand. A story
in typescript. Took the folder and the book from the shelf. Put them
together, on the bed. It was peaceful in the apartment. Outside, the
cars kept up hysterical alarms. The neighbors' radio went on playing
forbidden news.

Drew the sheet of paper toward me and lifted it between my fingers. *There lived a little bird in a wood quite removed from the rest of the world. Although she suffered from hunger and cold there, the bird felt akin to the wood. The wood, too, liked to know that her dear little bird could always be found there. Every tree rejoiced when the little bird said "good day" or "good evening." The little bird would grow stronger when she saw that a tree had grown a shoot or that another had put forth buds, and similarly, she felt as if her own body were injured if a tree were hit by a bolt of lightning or some woodcutter's axe.* A bedtime story. Would reread it once or twice and fall asleep, at last ...

In the eternal present of bedtime stories. Close my eyes ... A bird fancier passes through the wood. Charmingly convinces the little bird to come with him. But there's already another pretty fowl at the bird fancier's home! In the end the bird fancier tires of his new little bird as well, abandons her, and goes out into the world with the pretty fowl, all the while forgetting to open our little bird's cage. The little bird waiting for his return had refused him at first, because she had only felt at home in the wood. Only, like an insistent wizard, the bird fancier had come for her with a golden cage. Having left her home and friends, there was no turning back. The hesitation at the beginning, the humiliation of abandonment. Seduced and abandoned, just like the movies.

We don't know if the bird fancier returned on time to bring the bird back to life. Her heart beating with emotion, the little bird waited for him and went on hoping. What do you think? Did she wait in vain? That all depends. If he was really far away and it was raining, he wouldn't come back. But if a yearning for distraction overcame him again, then he would have hightailed it back to the melodrama.

The thin sheets in my left hand ... crumpled into a tight ball. Threw them away. Couldn't sleep though worn ragged. Among the books on the shelf, spotted the one read long ago. Did this prove the necessity of what was happening to me? Had found a book by chance in a chance room, a book known long ago, in a long ago life. So ... how could this experience signify nothing at all? Recalled an anecdote from a text having to do with the calculation of probabilities: George D. Bryson makes a business trip from St. Louis to New York. His train passes through Louisville, and since Bryson isn't in a hurry, he interrupts his travels for a day, heads to the best hotel in the city, and at the front desk, by way of a joke, asks if some correspondence hasn't arrived for him. The smiling receptionist hands him a letter: George D. Bryson, Room 307. Exactly the room that he had just been assigned to. As luck would have it, the preceding occupant of Room 307 was another George D. Bryson, traveling for a Canadian insurance company.

The two Brysons meet and then have to slap their own faces, just to make sure they aren't dreaming—what's going on? A sensational occurrence, a coincidence that doesn't prove or validate a thing? Would it have been any different if these gentlemen were named Tiberiu Covalschi or Bogdan Zubcu? Is there any reason to find an event like this interesting? "Yes, if the event concerns us," the probabilist wisely replied, to which he added, "always taking into account that the notion of interest is enormously subjective."

Should a reunion with a book—or a life—read long ago on a winter evening interest me? Winter evening then, expecting a visit from a classmate ... thought he owed me an explanation ... went on expecting him to make important confessions. Is it worth caring about this old incident that sends me back to a time when there were still memories in my head? Or is it better to look for significance within this absurd room? Only if one wants this room, this day to lend itself meaning ... as in the probability narrative: the George D. Bryson associated with New York discovers years after the meeting in St. Louis that his grandfather had left his hometown on his way to the Civil

War, before *his own son*—the New Yorker's father—was born. And on top of that, it so happens that many years after the war, the grandfather showed his grandson a photograph of a second family of his, who were conceived during his time in North Carolina, where he had remained for several years during the Reconstruction. Then, a second possible coincidence appears: two George D. Brysons could be grandsons of the same man, the father of the Canadian George D. Bryson being the illegitimate son from North Carolina.

Recall the words reserved for my classmate on that winter evening. Recall them exactly: *What should we think of a son of the earth who is also at the age when a day, a whole week, a month, or a semester should still play an important role as they yield so many changes and moments of progress—and who, one fine day, should get in the ungodly habit ... or who at least from time to time should let himself fall prey to the pleasure of saying "Yesterday" instead of "a year ago" and "tomorrow" instead of "in a year."*

Pulled the book toward me. If it were a question of interest—that it would be best to fall asleep as soon as possible. But maybe it'd be better to believe in rare events and that leafing through this book would yield the desired revelation. Would have to open to Chapter seven, after page five hundred. Kept recollecting the words and phrases from another time, from a time when there were memories in my head. Leafed through the book page by page without reading a single line, all the way to page 582. The lines danced before my eyes.

Time has an objective reality, even when objective sensation is weakened or eradicated because time "presses on," because it "flows." It remains a problem for professional logicians to know if a hermetically sealed can sitting on a shelf is outside time or not. But we know too well that time accomplishes its work even on one who sleeps. A certain doctor mentions the case of a little girl, aged twelve, who fell asleep one day and continued to sleep for thirteen years. In this interval, though, she did not remain a little girl but rather woke up a young woman, for she had grown in the meantime.

Back then, footsteps passed before the frosted windowpanes. They startled me but didn't halt. The lines danced before my eyes. Completely still, drowsing over the letters, rereading each line—not once or twice but ten times. Except, the inhabitant of *this* room full of remnants will not come. The murderer will lose his power and desire, his madness and patience. Back then, frost flowers were etched onto the windowpanes. He wasn't showing up. It was his right to use all possible lies to escape. It was time for battle, and he knew it, and I knew that too, yet I went on waiting in vain.

It wouldn't be too hard for us to imagine hypothetical beings who live on planets smaller than our own and who have a compressed measurement of time, and for whose "brief" lives the lively rush of our watch's second hand would have the complete, invisible slowness of the currently advancing hour. We could similarly imagine certain beings whose sense of time is extended in such a way that their conceptions of "Immediate," "Shortly," "Yesterday," and "Tomorrow" would acquire an infinitely enlarged duration within their existence. But what must we think of a son of the earth who on top of that is also of an age when a day, a week....

A day has gone by, a week. Am still a somnolent high-school student. No, only a day, a week, a Saturday has gone by, and talk of confusion would be justified. Everywhere, machines for typing and checking and intercepting and photographing and following and reproducing: their monotonous patter is here, and myself ... fugitive, lost, stalked from every corner, unable to sleep.

"You walk, you walk forever, you have lost time and it has lost you ... a terrain, sprinkled with seaweed and tiny shells; hearing thrilled by that unbridled wind that freely roves ... we watch the tongues of sea foam stretch to lick our feet."

Under the waves, under the stroking foam, the sea roars in the great castle of water.

⁙ ⁙ ⁙

The sea boomed. The thick castle walls kept out the noise of waves, but other sounds collided and crossed paths in the great hall: the release of bolts, metallic clanks, keys turning in locks, latches, heavy springs. Between them, odd, erratic breaks. One, pause. Two-three, pause. Four-five-six, pause. One, pause, two-three, then four-five-six, pause. Over and again, perpetual clanking, a continuous murmur from the right. To the left, short breaks; to the right, the crowded taps of many fingers, hammering.

Raised my eyes. Found myself on a chair placed to the right of a medium-sized table. Gazing across it, a powerful, broad-cheeked man with big hands. The discontinuous noises from left and right never stopped. Turned to see what was happening behind me. Small tables in two rows. Metal blocks vibrated on each table: calculators, type-writers. Backs bent over all the tables, and the anonymous, hunched bodies kept moving their arms, beating the keys of machines for writing, calculating, and checking.

Spun around and bumped against the arm of the man who sat on the other side of the table. He held a large sheet of pink paper. Examined him, twice. Dressed in a worn-out, navy blue suit, his floppy shirt collar with its points twisted over a dusty Bordeaux-colored tie: my cellmate, the spy, Mişa Burlacu, set to report on my "good behavior." Smiled at him. Mişa smiled back. Extracted the sheet of pink paper from his large, sweaty fingers. A form with many horizontal and vertical columns, covered with statistics. Under the printed letters, filled out in ink, between parentheses: (Model). Job Code. Beneficiary. Object. Job Category. Executing Workshop. Project Number. Date to Return for Processing. Figures filled out in ink. Wanted to ask Mişa what it was about, or—smiling as his mission required—Mişa wanted to ask me.

Worn-out, navy blue suit, as his mission required. Mişa held a rectangular sheet of pink paper. Took it. The Statistics Sheet had

120

many horizontal and vertical columns. The machines kept rattling on: calculators and recorders to the left, typewriters and trackers to the right. Scanned the headings and columns. Job Code. Suddenly something rang. Some adding or writing or transmitting machine had started signaling errors. Turned around: the row of backs on the left hadn't moved an inch. Arms twitched rapidly, mechanically, at every table. At the end of the row to the right, at the back of the room, a huge specter held a receiver to its mouth—probably the telephone. There was, indeed, a telephone on each table. Large as it was, the whole room was saturated with thick smoke: on every table—to the left and right—a cigarette burned in a round ashtray.

Rotated back to see broad shouldered, broad faced, sweating Mişa—smiling as he continued to keep watch. Gave him a look. The noises grew louder. There was no telling left from right anymore: calculation and typewriting everywhere. Held out my hand. The Statistics Sheet. Circuit Five. Installed Power. Kilowatt. Felt something soft between my fingers. Stared at my hands: a tuft of silky hair, a wig. Mişa was smiling, wearing gloves—in evening costume now. His wig hadn't passed completely into my hands. Both of us held it. Would have to ask him, whatever it might be—to talk to him ... to talk to him at any cost. Opened my mouth. Too late. The siren was ringing—or maybe it was the phone. Would have to move, but couldn't. The sound came from nearby, at my feet. Mişa smiled, bent slightly toward me, took the wig in his immense white-gloved hands, left it on the table, and leaning slightly under the table, he raised the sharp, black tail of his dinner jacket. He placed the telephone on the table, took the receiver in his right hand, and lifted it. For a moment there was nothing but the sound of our breath and the others' panting behind it.

Through the earpiece, a man's voice commanded:

— Covalschi here. Tell that dopey woman that there's no radio broadcast. I piss on her idiotic stories.

The sordid remarks thundered clearly out of the phone so that the whole office resounded with the echo of the rhythmic voice that kept saying the same lousy things, over and over again.

—Tiberiu Covalschi here. You can tell Auntie that she's never gonna hear her foolish stories on the radio.

Covalschi kept cursing. It was horrifying. Something had to be done: break the earpiece, the office, the voice and—all the voices panting in the background.

—Covalschi here. Tell that plucked chicken that her little stories...

Palms dampened with cold sweat, flung an arm around the telephone receiver. Closed my eyes halfway. The wardrobe, the stove, the radio. Kept holding the receiver in my hand. No one spoke. Background noise. Dial tone. The receiver slipped from my hand ... again, my shoulders relaxed. Stroked by gentle waves, my feet among the seaweed. Never to return, covered by eternal waters, dipped under the silky water. Complete stillness. A long hall, a castle with thick walls, a table. On the table: a heap of pink pages. Picked one up. A form. Statistics Sheet. Code. Beneficiary. Circuit One, Two, Three. Circuit Four. Raised my eyes. In front of me a man smiled. He had a wide face, sleek hair, and he held the pink sheet in his hand. Was supposed to ask him what it was about, but the bell or siren had gone off. In the rear there were little tables with small, vibrating machines. My neighbor's smile was dead.

Was supposed to put out my hand, pick up the receiver, move my arm, and bring it to my ear, but now blows were raining on the glass walls. Sprang to my feet. Came to myself in the bulb's weak light. Someone was knocking on the glass, on the glass door. Was there in a step. Flicked the light switch. The light blinded me. Twisted the spring, the lock, the spring. Pressed the handle, the door, the handle. The door opened in. Pulled it a little more.

Dressed in a navy blue suit, the tall man had a wide, blotchy face.

⋮ ⋮ ⋮

Solid, freshly shaved, smelling of the hairdresser. Dark suit, white shirt. Under the soft collar, the tie pulled tight. Mid-weight coat and a briefcase in his right hand. Hair: sleek, thin.

—Mişa, how are you?

The person standing in the doorway to the right of the stairs opened his mouth in shock, accidentally left it open, and straightened his shoulders to deal with the obvious lunatic.

—Doesn't Comrade Professor Smântănescu live here? The suit-shirt-collar glanced at the small piece of cardboard attached to the door.

—Aren't you Mişa? Mihai Burlacu? Fell silent, came to myself, clung to the wall, made excuses: Pardon me. Excuse me. Yes, yes, the lady lives here. A mix-up. My misunderstanding ... a workmate. Confused you with someone from the office. Forgive me. Yes, do come in. She does live here.

Hurried to invite him in: an act of absurd, hasty compensation. The door had already closed behind the stranger, who entered and was now waiting.

—Ah, the things one forgets. My sister isn't at home right now. But who are you?

Ready to attack or defend, the guest looked at me suspiciously.

—An acquaintance. Engineer Grigore Butnaru. Grig.

Let him rattle for a moment or two. The visitor evidently feared a trap. What fun to watch him deal with Madam Professor's husband! Farces leapt to mind: all equally good. It was hard to choose.

—My sister told me about you, the madman finally remarked. Personally, I don't live here.

—Mhm. She didn't write anything about having a brother.

Should have seen that one coming. The end of the letter had been clear.

—Make yourself comfortable. Perhaps you'd like to wait. Have a seat.

Proceeded to pick a pile off the chair. Miscellaneous trash. Couldn't find a place for it. Threw it on the bed.

—My sister's getting ready to clean house. There's a bit of mess ... wasn't expecting visitors ...

—Ah, no. Just dropped in ... unexpected.

Ill at ease and uncertain of the situation, Mr. suit-shirt-tie took a seat, with a distrustful glance in my direction. Wondered if Mr. Grig wasn't a total idiot, after all.

—She didn't mention anything to me about a brother, the less-than-complete idiot said for the second time.

—She's my step-sister, actually. My mother died a long time ago. My father remarried right away.

—You seem younger.

—My appearance ... Healthy skin.

Grig gave me another long look.

Had a crazy desire to draw him into a sincere conversation, wanted him to expound his principles—to win his confidence: there'd be confessions, promises, and he would slap me on the shoulder like a future brother-in-law. Managed to say:

—Grig's the name, right? My sister told me about you: she holds you in high esteem ... said something about your letter full of elevated thoughts.

The guy loosened his grip on his coat and set his briefcase down.

—Yeah ... kinda like to say everything outright, especially in writing, because it lasts.

—Good point. My sister told me about *your* sister as well, the one who's a professor at Ploieşti. And you're close with your sister, too—that says a lot about a man's character. Also heard you're successful: a guide at the exhibition, several factories calling to hire you.

—Not exactly, but the bit about being able to transfer anywhere is true.

There should have been a glass of slivovitz by now, dirty jokes, tales from the army. However, Grig was starting to look around, and if he got too curious, the jig'd be up.

—Have a seat, please. Have a seat. Monica will come any moment now. Have a seat. Was at Ploieşti myself some years ago. Met your sister, the ISEP graduate, at a youth action meeting—it was a great pleasure for me. Who'd have thought there'd be a family tie one day? To have met your sister, who's even the director ... can't figure out how great the family resemblance is, but it was her, for sure.

Hand on briefcase again, the guest gave me another long look.

—My sister never worked at Ploieşti.

—That's what you wrote, no? Your sister's the director. There can't be a mistake. Monica was saying ... as I know very well.

Was ready to strangle him. There was nothing else to do, and the words grit between my teeth like sand.

—There was no accident with your leg either? No poor grades in Russian and chemistry? Which means that nothing's for certain anymore: not the stupid letters, the ads in the personals, not even the spelling mistakes? So maybe your Excellency's the Swiss ambassador, or some long-lost brother of mine, or maybe the prosecutor who'll be asking for my head?

All that was a useless bother. Everything was already lost. The obliquely, vengefully smirking visitor looked me straight in the eye and said:

—Mhm. That's how the first letter is, till we get to know each other. My sister's actually a manager in Bârlad. Doesn't have anything to do with Ploieşti.

—Whatever, whatever ... my mistake. My memory lets me down sometimes. In any case ... remember very well that the director said her name. Still ... won't insist if you don't want to wait ... Maybe call and drop by tomorrow ...

Resumed a more respectful tone. My words kept dragging themselves out, but the burley, wide-faced engineer was already at the door, ready to leave, briefcase and topcoat in hand. With his hand on the door, he turned to me and smiled. Yes, he'd drop by tomorrow or telephone.

The door clicked behind him. Should have broken down the door, run downstairs after him. He couldn't leave like that, all of a sudden, without explaining himself—it would be necessary to say: "You mean to say that back there, where you are respected, advanced, and distinguished, no one jumped into the flames? You know nothing, as if you were the Swiss ambassador or something. You were on another shift, in another section, at another factory, in another city, the other madman, the other, at some other time, somewhere else? Have you have no memories of anything, you sentimental fool? My dear fellow citizen, you are a crocodile."

Time passed: had it been a special meeting, with this navy-blue visitor named Grig, Grigore Butnaru?

Hence: had left my office anyway. There were machines and mechanisms of all kinds. For me, unbearable . . . because babies can't stand typewriters. Repeated the phrase without being able to explain it: it was a watchword, an excusal from indiscretion or refusal. The Chief Engineer watched me run all the way downstairs. That fateful phrase had force—those words had struck him. The crocodile despises me (even now) because of letting myself be pushed into anonymity, because of my correct greetings every morning, my way of bowing sanctimoniously, *comme il faut.*

My lying and insulting makes me the ideal resident of this coop, but the chief remains cushioned and cordial; he didn't even want to acknowledge that stupid phrase which did, of course, have force. The powerful and twisted phrase didn't even touch him; it didn't strike him at all. The boss remained amiable, absent, self-assured, comfortable, logical, as he went on playing with his fine, fragile hands in a melancholy way. Since long ago, since infancy, he's had long, nervous fingers. We were classmates once, and back then he had perfect, pallid hands. We were like a bunch of newborns then, and we had memories, we believed in logic to the end, to the bitter end and beyond.

$$\vdots \quad \vdots \quad \vdots$$

The new student made his way down the row from the teacher's desk to the door. He wore a perfect, aggressively white shirt, starched like a board. This new classmate was slender. He had brown hair, and bowing ceremoniously in an almost courtly way, he shook everyone's hand, a smiling comrade, brisk and manly. Slowly but surely, the others began to fall under the sway of his smile, straight into his palm: conquered. Shrewd, sullen, timid sons of peasants—with hands used to the hoe, the plow, and the scythe—bent over their books till late at night, they regarded him prudently, then with hostility, then mockingly, and after a few more seconds they instinctively wanted to become his future admirers and bodyguards. He shook my hand, and for an instant he looked startled. Our gestures were identical. We bowed. We smiled. We shook hands. He seemed momentarily moved. But he smiled again, walked on, and, after sitting down in his corner, flung me another brief glance.

The new boy was a mediocre student, I understood after a few days. That put him in good standing with his classmates. I asked him during a break if he had brought the "transfer slip" from the political youth organization. He wasn't part of the organization, he replied. I asked him why. He smiled: in Giurgiu they only let swimmers in, and he didn't know how to swim. The guys laughed, and I laughed with them. I asked him what his father did. He wasn't smiling anymore, and he waited until the last trace of cheerfulness had left our faces, and then he answered: his father was working as a laborer in the salt mine nearby. The bell rang. I shot him a brief, friendly signal.

He respected my position among our classmates from the start. Admired and followed by them, he took part, of course more distantly, in their way of following me.

We were then in the last year of high school: Sebastian Caba had acclimated perfectly to his neighbors at the dorm. He became one of them and lost himself in the mass. He didn't excel at anything. His attentive manner and his cordiality distinguished him. The intensity of my political participation was already descending toward neutrality, but it hadn't gotten there yet. I'd become despondent when I conjectured that the enthusiasms that had projected me to the front would vaporize so quickly.

Looking at Sebastian, I'd see his father among the workers pushing their barrows among colossal vaults of ice. I'd imagine the nightmare of putting in a hard day's work under those Gothic elevations. I kept seeing the laborers' exhaustion, their frozen faces as wasted at the start of the shift as when they all trooped back to the light. I'd hear their blows hacking the great castle of ice, their voices seeking each other among the blocks probed by picks and drills. And so I went on feeling them: abandoned by their kind, aged, occasionally lifting their eyes to some worker nearby, who might die one day, buried among the glaciers of salt.

Our new classmate seemed worthy of the greatest attention. My desire to climb down into those vast, refrigerated burial vaults was greater, though, than my curiosity about the newcomer—greater, too, than any curiosity about the larger social experiment in generosity, compromise, and guilt. I was in a hurry to meet anything that might put the blindness of our poor textbooks to shame, along with our unfledged, youthful ignorance.

The visit to the salt mine could have been arranged right away if

I'd spoken with Father. Only, I wasn't in any shape to attract his suspicions, again.

⋮ ⋮ ⋮

Two years had passed since the end of the war. Only at the end of the first year of peace did we return from the camp on the steppe where we had been banished. My new sister was born several months after that.

My parents' whispering came through the half-open door. I understood they were coming up with names—peculiar names: Katyusha, Sveta, Agnita. Sveta sounded Swedish, masculine. The others were downright incomprehensible. They never had much originality, so I didn't understand what had gotten into them, or why it was necessary to have another child. I went into their room. The plank bed, somewhat larger than mine, had been made by the carpenter neighbor. The familiar old dining table on which we now ate and the three chairs were all in my room, together with the cupboard made of planks. Ileana, our friend and neighbor, had hidden our beautiful old table and chairs from before our deportation and gave them back when we returned.

There was a mirror and a baby carriage in my parents' room. Mama was in bed, convalescent. My parents looked at me. They understood. They gave each other a look, and Father, who was sitting on the edge of the bed, turned toward me.

—What do you think? Is there a name that you like?

—No.

If I were smiling, they might have taken me seriously. But the frown on my face and my solemn answer seemed childish.

—Really, what would you like?

—Dona.

All the blood suddenly fled from my mother's cheeks. Realizing a crisis might break out, Father clasped his hands together tightly and gave me a disdainful look.

—What do you remember about Dona? Do you even know what she looked like?

Indeed, more than a few years had passed, but I hadn't forgotten: she was slender and wore the crown of a great, black chignon. She had large eyes, black and grey, and thin white hands that stroked lightly, like a rustle. Dona was almost a young lady although she was just a kid. She swayed, like a wonder that would have to disperse, and was the first to scatter. She clasped my hand, on parting, in despair. I forgot how the next girls who were sacrificed looked. They were almost young ladies too, and slight as chicks, like her. Their eyes had grown huge and gray, transparent. I don't remember how they all looked. They were light, made of glass and air; they separated from us in despair. Dona would have done anything if she thought it would help save me. Dona wouldn't have believed a word the executioners said: she left us in a state of despair. She had great black and grey eyes, light hands. She wore a crown—heavy and black. We have been separated for so many years, and she still has great, black eyes.

Footsteps in the kitchen. The noises came just in time. Father opened his hands and stood up happily. I was near the door. The guests were beside me in an instant. I shrank against the wall so they could pass: Ileana and Virgil Mehedinți, our friends. Tall, very tall, white hair, black mustache. Like a highwayman. Small, thin, fragile as a doll, with brown hair and white skin, Ileana stopped conversations when she appeared among strangers, and it was as if amazement circled her delicate being . . . people's knees gave way under her beauty and charm. I snuck into my room. Just then the baby carriage began to fill with the baby's cries. They fidgeted around her; then everyone quieted down. Father went into the kitchen to make tea. He looked at me. He stopped for a few moments to think.

—Dolores, would you like that?

—No.

He went on his way. Sveta, Dolores, Agnita, Katyusha: I'd have liked to know where he found such names. If these were names, it meant that the baby could be anything. Why not Dona? Or Eva? If everything still had to be forgotten and started over from scratch, as Father kept saying, then Eva sounded very good. He went on repeating so many times a day: "we have to forget in order to start anew." Fine then, Eva was the very thing. There would be no need to go on inventing complicated foreign names. We had one all lined up. If I'd have told him so, he would've looked down on me from his lofty height, convinced I didn't remember a thing. He'd already headed back with tray and cups. I heard them talking till late in the evening. I think it was then that they first focused their still uncertain, vaguely troubled attention on me.

⋮ ⋮ ⋮

So ... Ileana Zaharia. She had been our neighbor before the war. She used to work with my parents at the bank. She'd invited us kids over to her place many times. She used to take care of us, playing, running around with us, and giving us baths. She had much more patience than Mama. She entertained us with stories in the evenings. She loved us. After our disappearance she tried to save our things, and even tried to find us, to contact us. Someone denounced her for wanting to help. She was lucky: they acquitted her for lack of evidence. Her obstinacy was not only proof of her enormous contempt for danger and her fidelity to us: there was something else, too. Amid the general hatred, she had felt alone, astray—besmirched. She was so incompatible with the morbid chaos that she seemed to come from another world that denied theirs.

Ecstatic, her cries met the cadavers dressed in rags that paraded down the city's barely pacified streets as the deportees returned to the living. She was the first to see us again, the first who wanted to see us again. During those early months she fed us in her own home, gave us everything she had. She tried to get us used to life. She listened to me for evenings on end, and asked me to tell her about my sisters Dona and Eva over and over again—about every day and about their last days. Again and yet again: she wasn't afraid that I would die as a result. Relentlessly, she went on asking for more details.

She used to come with the young carpenter who hadn't hesitated to make us the cupboard and beds even though he was already quite an important person. A tall, powerful man with white hair, he convinced Father that he didn't have the right to remain a modest bank clerk, and that he was destined to do something else. She repeated his words—she was completely taken with him back then, several months before their marriage. The calls for change were bursting out on all sides, catalyzing everyone. After hesitating for a while, my parents quickly found themselves a mode of frenetic devotion. I was ready for another start, too. The eyes of the boy of eleven or twelve were burning with enthusiasm.

⁝ ⁝ ⁝

Squeezed into my tight collar, I would return home late at night. Back then, we used to go out to the villages where we'd assemble the peasants for our recitals, dances, and performances. After that, a truck would drop us off at the formerly Austrian town hall. The nights were cold. Thin and impetuous, I used to slip along the sidewalks, hugging the walls. Then I'd huddle between the coarse sheets, exhausted but sleepless, reading in bed. Those were the ardent, impatient reading sessions when I first experienced naïve and turgid rhymes, and felt the pulsation of words.

The public demonstrations soon struck me as frivolous, though, so I watched Virgil Mehedinți tensely. I studied his movements. He was a great model. I tore up my pathetic poems: their violence and solemnity seemed ridiculous. It was time to take the next step. I realized I was making a fool of myself—singing and dancing like an idiot for the benefit of silent, dignified workers, so I gave up the cultural activism that was driving the nearby villages crazy. I was busy studying Virgil Mehedinți's gestures, words, and way of looking when I came upon my passion for mathematics.

I rarely saw my parents. Father was often gone. It was hard for Mama to divide her time between the house, the bank, and meetings. I was one of the leaders of the political youth organization, but didn't neglect math, and came home late on a regular basis. We'd talk sometimes, and then I felt my parents' concern. One evening, I heard them whispering: "He'd be ready to do anything." Of course, I would have to be ready to do anything. Two honest bank clerks couldn't very well understand what I was up to. We were building a new society, and the frenzy of postwar reconstruction was liberating in its way. I had a part to play, and it cured me of my humility. In those hasty years, I learned to speak loudly, declaim publicly, and slam doors.

My parents used to come home late and exhausted. They slept little, ate fast and plenty. Fat and bloated now, agitated sleepers wrenched from bed at dawn, beaten by the daily rat race, they had no time to regain their physical balance, and when they got home they unloaded all their tiredness and discontent and the suffocations that come with age: alarm signals of endangered health. For them it was a matter of sadness and collapse. They were dumbfounded by their teenage son, who saw them as ruined statues. In their moments of exhaustion, he'd confront them with questions and distrust. We were caught in a barbed circle, with no way out.

During the day, I used to rush around, leaping over every hurdle—from the folkloric show to political meetings to mathematics and then back to the meetings again and those first awkward kisses in the city's dark corners. Vitality kept changing its direction, but I wouldn't forget that the world needed cleaning: we were the angels of purity destined for a new heaven, impeccable and pure, safeguarding consciences as crystal clear as my little sister's eyes and soul. Named for the communist heroine Donca Simo, my sister Donca had just turned seven.

⋮ ⋮ ⋮

Our gray loden coats with little military collars would flap over our long, wide trousers and work boots. We were like bundles of immense sleeves when we took each other by the arm. An embracing couple turned into a topsy-turvy scarecrow of flailing clothes. Fingers intertwined, racing to get past so many layers of fabric, to liberate some corner of skin, to sink into flesh. We'd interrupt our scuffle when we got to the unlit spaces at the edges of buildings, where we'd pause for a hasty, ravenous embrace.

I kept dreaming of naked bodies, soft arms, the classmate who unbraided her pigtails while laughing, dizzy with desire. In dreams, too, we were horrified by the forbidden closeness, paralyzed by prohibitions. We lacked the courage to share the iniquity we craved. We'd wake exhausted between damp, crumpled sheets. The next evening we'd see each other again at yet another meeting or in the stinking lair of the cinema. Frozen, we'd solemnly listen to the crunch of snow. We'd use big words—principles kept rarifying the air. Our bodies would slam into each other again, and then we'd be looking for ravines, dark courtyards, and tall church fences. While mixing breaths, our teeth would clash; we'd scratch, blinded, frenzied by the panting that turned us into wild beasts. At home, frightened parents would inspect their child's tangled hair still damp with snow. The tension would rise, the room would get smaller. I'd hate the thick, damp walls, the food that tasted like washing water, the hostility of the guards. They thought I was abnormal, an enemy. The torment of chastity went on exploding between thin, fiery sheets. Yes, I was abnormal and their enemy forever. Their little domestic habits revolted me, their suspicious looks, all the slurping at table, the snoring, and those little nightly groans through the door.

The way things stood, the wish to visit the nearby salt mine would have provoked another crisis of suspicion.

⋮ ⋮ ⋮

With small steps I was making my way across the uneven stones with my eyes glued to the ground, fiddling with the metal clasp of my satchel. Always suspicious, my parents were expecting me, and I skipped from crooked stone to stone as if this could have helped me defend myself from what lay in wait—all of which became, in its own way, a superb novitiate for the strict devotee who kept refusing his parents access to ideality, principality, and reality.

—Sir! The woman had waited for me to pass in front of her without noticing, and she said, can anyone be that distracted?

This lady was one of the city's three destitute aristocrats who had barely maintained themselves by giving German and piano lessons in the other wing of our building. All three of them were crammed into a single room. It was said that there was nothing but filth in their room crammed with junky, old, mismatched antiques, that they were a laughingstock, not only on account of their eccentric dresses but particularly because of their delicate manners and because they were afraid of any new bit of news in the papers or on the radio. The neighbors said that two of the sisters were old maids, but Colette Triteanu was the widow of a former minister.

—I've heard you're a studious young man. I could lend you interesting books. I still have my husband's library, which is actually quite extensive.

The aristocratic lady was trying to put herself on a good footing with a young militant and maybe his parents. Her white hair fluttered youthfully above her thin shoulders, and singing lessons had "educated" her voice.

—Give me one.

I waited while leaning against the wall of the building. Father had been gone for three days. He was due back, but I wasn't in a hurry: I also wasn't interested in exploring the rumors about how our aristocratic neighbor lived. My dry response had flustered her. She returned quickly with a large, blue hardcover.

—This one's decisive for a young man. I imagine you can read German.

—Of course, ma'am. With your permission, I'll visit you to return the book. I'd be delighted to meet your sisters as well.

I left quickly, without allowing myself the pleasure of seeing her face.

Lunch had already been served. At the end of the table, Father was laughing at the silly face that pudgy little Donca was making—she was miming the adventures of her first months of school. She displayed proof of her skirmishes and games with the boys on hands, nose, and knees, and they enlivened the monotony of our lunch times. Right now, she was covered in ink, down to her shoes.

I asked Father where he'd gone. He told me he'd had to stay three days at the salt mine. I went out to wash my hands. When I came back, I told him we had a new classmate whose father was working at the mine. He asked me where he came from.

—From Giurgiu, I answered.

He nodded his head as if he knew. When Mama went into the

kitchen to bring the second course, he told me that there had been an accident at the mine. The accident had happened because the majority of the workers were new and unprepared for such work. I asked him why. He told me that most of them had been relocated from other parts of the country: they were part of the former exploiting class that needed to be liquidated. The class, not the people, he added, but Mama had just returned with the dishes.

Goes to show: it's good to get home on time for lunch and eat with the family. I no longer had to visit any salt mine. I'd have to visit classmate Caba during every break to decide where he belonged. My duty was to divide people according to strict criteria. That simplified things: love to the left, hate to the right. I had the right to use cunning when necessary so that the guilty would cast off their concealments and repent. The goal was an exhibition of warrior virtue, a spectacle worthy of both the masses and those in power.

Preparing his tirades, the coward in me entered a state of jubilation.

⋮ ⋮ ⋮

Professor Laurențiu Sofronie was a worn-out old crocodile. During his lessons, we often found ourselves forced to listen to his youthful adventures on the streets and in the libraries of Paris. His voice and eyelids would begin to tremble, and we knew he was about to digress, once again, into some speech praising "the true humanism." He would glorify the "exemplary discipline and honor" in the camps of the Romanian monarchy's "young guards," the rightist movement of his youth. His reek of a desecrated corpse, the smile he used to close his "allocutions," and his never failing "dear children, you must learn what life is ..." would have nauseated us if the combination hadn't boiled down to a tremendous waste of time. Paris had of course been hospitable to this landowner's son, accustomed from the time of his school vacations to the delights of "honor" practiced in the camps of the monarchial guards.

The old reactionary's trap would have to be shut. At home, however, I didn't have the courage to talk about what was going on in anatomy class. That would have forced me to admit to my parents' horrified supposition, that I was "capable of anything" right now.

Virgil Mehedinți, the councilor, would have been astonished that I hadn't acted independently, that I hadn't stormed out of the classroom and let the administration know what was going on. As it was, the coward in me feared the consequences of defeat as much as the fullness of victory. When the coward couldn't stand it anymore, he let himself be pushed by his desire to become a paragon of virtue—though not in a particularly steadfast way. He'd fail and then try again—a matter of half attacks and half retreats.

In the middle of a class about the circulatory system, Laurenţiu Sofronie lifted his elbows off his desk, straightened the label of his crumpled jacket and took out his eyeglasses. The classroom waited. The professor's thin, dirty, salt and pepper hair fell in greasy locks. He smoothed them with his hand.

—Dear children, you must learn what life is.

Sofronie rattled on for fifteen minutes about the heroism of Japanese pilots during the last world war who had hurled themselves at enemy warships and depots and blew themselves up in their planes. The souls of those kamikazes (in their jerkins with seven metal buttons, stamped with the three-petaled cherry blossom) deserved our admiration. Symbolic death, divine afflatus, contempt for pointless lives, the sacrifices of those who not only confront death—"which is natural in a war," as the professor was saying, "but seek it out …"—the reactionary argument drove toward a single conclusion: death was the trophy, the flower of courage.

During break, the director listened to my denunciation with horror rather than attention. Professor Sofronie came back the next day with all his buttons closed and his hair neatly combed. He dictated the new lesson slowly, starting sentences over again whenever he stuttered. He didn't look at the rows of desks, and he behaved this way through all the following lessons. "Very well, children." "That's it, children." He had raised grades: "Be more careful, dear child," "Please respect me, dear children." Sofronie didn't cast an eye in our direction, didn't look at me once. Anatomy class had become something else, the professor, someone else. Following him tensely, eyes fixed on the professor's face, my colleagues listened to him with their hearts in their mouths as they watched his tired movements—so ill at ease—his frightened old walk, his dread of words. Something had changed him; someone powerful and perfidious had changed him: someone who should have been feared had become just that.

I made myself small. I was afraid. I was ready to grovel at the feet of the victim and beg for forgiveness, to try joking with him, to find a moment when no one would be able to see us, when I could whisper (in some corner of the hall) that spies had forced me to denounce him but that he was actually safe: I knew him and would defend him.

I was ready to do anything so that my classmates in their rows of benches would recognized me as one of their own, so that I could be one of them, so they'd let me into their fraternity. Terror of remaining alone forever mixed with an unshakable fear of a slow, disgusting collapse, a state of half-heartedness, negligence, abandon. I kept wanting to be left alone, to forget, to escape the pressure of my ambiguities, to meet with myself, to avoid confrontation, to fall asleep. My classmates had no way of knowing my remorse, but they seemed to accept me, sympathetically even. I was, after all, a prize winning pupil who chased girls and was willing to lend my notebook so they could copy the answers to the next day's math problems; as for my political role in the school, by reducing Party meetings and going easy on discipline, I managed to perform it in an approximate way without overdoing it. The torture of great hardliner ambitions only wracked me in secret. My rigid determination only exploded at home, as attacks of fury and contempt. Outbursts like the anatomy class incident would take place rarely enough that their effects would wear off in the meantime.

That wasn't all. The class turned to stone several months after Sofronie had changed. I stood up at the end of a history class and proposed that the professor change his grading system: since we all knew when our turns were coming, all we had to do each semester was learn two lessons each by heart. Popovici, the kind priest who had become our history professor, turned red to the tips of his ears. It was true that he used this system of calling on us in alphabetical order to let us off the hook. Now, he remained silent for a few moments and then stuttered something, vaguely admitting that I was right, because after all "we had to master all our subjects as well as possible." The class was now being forced to give up easy marks, which were evidently in their own interest, yet afterward, in the following days, my classmates spoke to me in the same way they always had. They must have understood it was the head of the class's duty to strike out at the former land-owning, exploiting class, and if he gave away a few of their advantages, that was his right, which was inevitably the basis for his becoming a caricature of "the little proletarian hero."

In the end, Professor Laurențiu Sofronie had rounded up everyone's grades, and he wouldn't have had any reason not to raise the grades of his best and most dangerous student. The priest-turned-history-professor now wanted everyone to correctly recite a long passage from a book, and it was natural to give the highest grade to whoever recited with the best diction and without messing up the grammar. But when the professor of anatomy or history, or even the director, with whom I was going to all kinds of political meetings, listened to me with fawning attention and handed out exaggerated praise, I didn't know where to run, ashamed as I was of the prestige I'd won. And I couldn't find the courage to endure or accelerate my stubborn, solitary rebellion either. I would have run to all my subordinate classmates, ready to share smiles and answers to final exams, to organize excursions, dances in the evenings with the students from the girls' school, or athletic competitions with the neighboring town. I wanted to feel them around me, to witness and approve my betrayals, and understand that I always wanted the best for them and that I only acted out of pure idealism and in complete candor.

They may have perceived my openness toward them despite the inconsistency of my behavior. Otherwise, Sebastian Caba, who lived with them the whole time in the school's dormitory, wouldn't have listened to me as peacefully as he had when I told him I'd visited the salt mine where his father worked. Pale and worried, Caba would have cornered me with all the questions he could have stammered out: how the mine looked, how long I stayed there, what they said to me, if I'd met his father. He should have pestered me with all kinds of sly questions to clarify whether I knew the one thing he was trying to keep secret. He had heard how I talked to the history teacher. He saw how Laurenţiu Sofronie, the former landowner, wisely acquiesced, bowing his old shoulders. He should have been frightened by these warnings. Yet, in the middle of his first winter among us, he had asked if he could join our organization. He had seen right through me. And he ignored the fact that I had waited until the eleventh hour to receive his truth or anxiety or contrition.

⁝ ⁝ ⁝

Caba was a mediocre student but liked by his classmates, and his father was now part of the working class; no one had any reason to keep him out of the organization. On the contrary, he represented a rare acquisition, bearing in mind that most of the students came from peasant backgrounds: we would finally have a member from the working-class.

I expected a visit from him every day. I followed him. I watched over his every move. I answered him dryly and treated him rudely to disarm him, so he would have to ask for forgiveness, confess. I counted the days until the meeting. It was a frosty winter. Thursday afternoon the organization would receive new members from each class. The snow had frozen and crunched under foot. Night fell rapidly, a couple hours after we returned from school. I was alone with Donca. I remember everything that happened then, at the end of the first January that Caba lived among us. I had memory back then. I was powerful. People like Sebastian Caba should have feared me. So the new order demanded. I was expecting him to knock shyly on the window, ask for mercy, kneel in the snow to confess the truth, and withdraw to his destined place.

The window was iced over. Steps could be heard, but no one tapped on the glass. Convinced he would finally appear, I waited for almost two hours, looking at the frosty flowers and leaves covering the white field of the window. I couldn't stay in one place anymore; I had to do something to make the time to pass until I could welcome my classmate Caba, until I could listen to him with amazement and send him away—expel the disgusting, cunning Sebastian Caba!

I opened the book that the distinguished lady had lent me. *Time has an objective reality, even when objective sensation is weakened or eradicated because time "presses on," because it "flows." It remains a problem for professional logicians ... and again, one day, emboldened by youthful presumption, Hans Castorp tried to address the same problem ... to know if a hermetically sealed can sitting on a shelf is outside time or not. But we know too well that time accomplishes its work even on one who sleeps. A certain doctor mentions the case of a little girl, aged twelve, who fell asleep one day and continued to sleep for thirteen years. In this interval, though, she did not remain a little girl but rather awoke a young woman, for she had grown in the meantime.* I looked at the little seven year old girl. She was fat, a little balloon, with yellow hair and blue eyes. She had grown. She wasn't the same child. She had Mama's eyes and hair. Her first three children didn't resemble her. We were dark and tall. Dona's hair and eyes were black as night. She was slender, tall, almost transparent, but years had gone by and. Dona had become Donca, and she was small now, and fat, and she had blue eyes.

Still, I thought, Donca isn't Dona. It's not possible that Dona could have become fat and blond. And Eva had Father's eyes and hair. It's not possible that time fulfilled its work on those who slept. It's not possible that Eva could have acquired eyes clean as a summer's day and long hair, golden as summer wheat. It's not possible that time flowed through Dona's and Eva's sleep, while I should have been a hermetically sealed can sitting *there on the shelf outside of time.*

The little dumpling was ungluing stamps from envelopes and getting filthy again, as usual, with glue, water, and ink. We were home alone. It was winter; night came rapidly; the windows were frozen. Sometimes I could hear footsteps. I waited for them to stop in front of the window. *Even if you were more tolerant, it would not have been easy for you to distinguish between the present of a yesterday, of a day before yesterday, or of a day before the day before yesterday: all of them resembling today, as alike as two eggs....* Nope, it was easy. The days didn't resemble each other. I had memory then. I was powerful. I was not yet an office worker exhausted by sleepy days, who looked like everyone else, climbing the hill of the same lazy morning, bent double and apathetic, with bones strained by painful humidity: an office worker numbing his body among desks, drawing boards, and phones. I wasn't yet lost among confused, low, distant voices that rose like the extinguished cries of fugitives in a wood barely plucked from night. I didn't want to bear the exorcism of aloneness that would leave me with movements unspooled in the other air of an alternate planet where voices suffocate and tangled, useless gestures vainly fret in a mute choir of despair. I was powerful, upright, unbowed, like my sisters who turned to smoke, Eva and Dona; I went on expecting Sebastian Caba to prove to him that I knew how to refuse, which is to say *live*, like my sisters Dona and Eva, once vertical, vigilant, and viable.

I gave a start. Small timid footsteps were coming closer. Faint-hearted, guilty, the steps approached. I straightened my shoulders. They had passed by. It wasn't him. I understood: he wouldn't come. He knew he'd have to use any means he could in the upcoming struggle that would take place at the next session—and use them against those who'd decreed "the class struggle" the only solution. Like a powerful crocodile, he was entitled to fight, with teeth and jaws of steel, and he would have to bear expulsion, the response due to class enemies. There could be no trepidation in my movements. My thoughts mustn't betray me, even for an instant. Any respite would have been too much. *But what should we think of a son of the earth who on top of that is also at the age when a day, a week, a month, or a semester should play an important role and who, one fine day, should get in the ungodly habit of saying "yesterday" instead of "a year ago" and "tomorrow" instead of "in a year"!*

I wasn't entitled to a single concern: my sisters and I should have learned that yesterday is completely different than a year ago. In the camp, Dona, Eva, and I would never have let ourselves fall prey to the pleasure of saying "tomorrow" in place of "a year from now" because we knew that by the time a year had gone by we might no longer exist, which ruled out the perfidious pleasure of juggling with time tomorrow or a year from now. I was a son of the earth who knew: tomorrow will be Thursday, the day I'll publicly expose our popular classmate in front of everyone; I was of an age when every single day brings changes, and I would have to exhibit my progress in conquering my own cowardice and betrayals. I had no right other than to struggle, to be powerful. My position did not allow me to be lured, fooled, or lulled to sleep. I flung away Madam Minister's cunning book. Donca started to laugh. She was always throwing things around, making messes. She smiled at me, glad that I was becoming her brother.

The snow crunched underfoot. The freezing air burned my cheeks. When I entered the dorm room, my eyelashes melted. Droplets rolled down my cheeks. Sebastian Caba was playing backgammon with his roommates. Perched on the bed in a blue tracksuit, he'd wrapped his legs around the backgammon board, and his long, slim fingers shook the dice like magic beads.

My entrance gave rise to a certain amount of movement. From the bed near the door, one of the classmates signaled to me by waving his algebra book. He'd solved only half the problem assigned. I spent a quarter of an hour with him, and a few people had come to see what we were doing with the algebra. Only Caba and his adversary remained at the board. Eventually the dice rolling slowed down. I heard them hastily counting points. I stood. I spoke with our classmates a while. When the backgammon players joined our group, I told them all to let the dorm administration know that they would be late for supper the following day, that the staff should hold onto their meals. Then, since it was the eve of Caba's induction to the organization, his roommates started joking about him, the future hero, whom they cornered pretty well. Caba managed well, though, and even if he was on the defensive, he held his own. His replies were more powerful than the stings we honored him with, but such a lively reversal of circumstances didn't come as a surprise to his roommates or me. He always lived up to the faith they all had in his charm and lively wit, and he rose to their expectations this time, too. As for me, I'd put my faith in the future hero's cottoning on quickly when I pointed out that tomorrow's meeting would take longer than usual, so they'd be late for dinner. Our classmates sensed that even though we weren't friends, I had a closer connection with him, and he responded to my interest. Such amicability presupposed a certain complicity. While I wasn't making a public show of friendship, I never denied it either.

So, he conducted himself properly. The moment I moved to go, he thrust his feet into slippers to walk me out, and for a few moments we remained together by the dorm's wooden door, each waiting for the other to say the words the circumstances required. I wasn't sure I'd succeed in accomplishing my plan to flush him out of hiding. That would have cost a threat or a promise, but Caba raised his arm and leaned his thin white fingers against the brown door. He sighed and told me that the food in the dorms had become unbearable. He wanted to make an official complaint about this and was hoping his new friend would understand or maybe even intervene. The food in the dorm was unbearable, and as usual he had found the exact but moderate, inoffensive expression to lodge his protest in a decent way. It would have been excessive to affirm that he could no longer stand the food: he merely supplied impersonal information. He leaned his arm on the wooden doorframe, waiting for me to reply, or rather waiting for us to part in a friendly way. I looked into his eyes expecting him to say—once, twice, three times, like some deeply idiotic lament—that he couldn't stand the food anymore, not to mention his cold and filthy room, the stuffy air, the noise, the squalor and fatigue of a boarder's life. The food was unbearable, but he didn't say he couldn't stand it anymore. I kept waiting for him to repeat the impersonal expression that he'd chosen—proving through obsessive repetition that it was his responsibility, that the weight was on his shoulders, that he was among those who felt the consequences of the situation. Except he knew it was insulting and pointless to repeat the same thing over and over again, especially since the person he was talking to had avoided saying anything about it. He recoiled from repeating himself like a maniac. He didn't say he couldn't stand the food anymore, or that he couldn't stand the cold or the fog or the typewriters or the stupid moon up in the sky or the building's green roof anymore. That kind of tearing of a passion to tatters would only signal abandonment to the ridiculous, to childishness, to distorted ways of speaking—harbingers of maladaptation, isolation, perdition. I understood: he would repeat nothing. He spread out his fingers on the doorframe, having proven that he knew one's expectations had reasonable limits—and the point when silence becomes a bother.

So he asked me if tomorrow's math problems were really hard. Smiling, I told him to copy the answers from the notebook of our classmate near the door. I slammed the door. I shouldn't have answered at all. I particularly shouldn't have smiled at him before my final salute, full of promises as it was. Still, having learned to slam doors decisively, I slammed the door on time.

I'd granted the coward one last chance before cutting off his head, and tomorrow I'd crow and cackle over his corpse, like a coward.

⋮ ⋮ ⋮

The building with towers and narrow windows drew closer. There was no one on the street. Looked back again. No one. No one would be able to discover my fear of killing, cheating, running away, maintaining the truth, going to battle for it ... no one would be able to discover my fear of the pursuers' long arm and the pain of death.

I didn't want to bring anything to its conclusion or know that I was killing or lying out of fear. Dona and Eva were keeping watch. I knew it. They had guessed that I was fed up with being the favorite of fortune; so many times we had been loath to hold out against death any longer, to delay it further: it took so much power, oh, so much power, and so much lying to stay alive. Their shaved heads were suddenly near mine again. We were gathered together, three shorn heads, transparent as ghosts, three lifeless heads, frightened that we would have to be patient for another hour, another week. I had repeated this every day: all it takes is another day, another night, another week, an hour, an eternity, just that much, just that.

Later, in the long office choked with smoke, amid the clatter of voices like horse hooves and the patter of typewriters ... when sloth, tiredness, and renunciation dragged me down, and the days and weeks and tiredness had to be resumed again, it would be necessary to repeat the same exhausted refrain: *I cannot, anymore.* I have to break the lie, live innocently, simply, defend, adorn myself in the truth, to fire at the lie called Monica, the sublime Sebastian, Captain Zubcu's death, the parents and siblings eager to escape, to catch me in their stealthy game, in their guilty pleasures, in the complicities of survival, and the lies and the collective autism.

But back then, I would have to find Father and become his son again ... Maybe, I thought, maybe he won't repeat "*have to*" again today. Maybe he'll become my father again, so that I can admit all my mistakes, tiredness, sloth, and terror—the iniquities, the sins, the lies. Suddenly, he'll understand that having swallowed everything, duplicities had grown inside him, between thought and speech, as they have in me. He'll recognize himself in his son, and will have the courage to be satisfied with our mutual guilt, happy that we'll change, that we'll purify ourselves and live innocently.

Looked back again: no one there. The porter signaled me with two fingers and pointed to the second floor. The former Austrian town hall had wide, marble steps and thick balustrades. Arrived on the second floor. Two symmetrical corridors. Chose the one on the left. Uniform, polished doors. Opened the first door on the right.

Two desks, identical, both covered with red canvas. Atop one of the desks there was a book in a pocket edition. On one of the tables, a telephone. Opened the other door across the corridor. Two desks arranged at right angles. Opened the other door on the right, the next door on the right. Nothing. No one. Uniform décor. Opened my overcoat, loosened my muffler. Reached toward the book. Recognized it. Knew the sacred biography it contained by heart. Closed the door. My feet sank into the carpet—like stepping into a swamp. There were five more doors on the left, five on the right. Symmetry. Somehow found myself again at the head of the stairs. Was about to climb back down the stairs when the end of the corridor exploded. Boom-Boom! Boom-Boom! Voices went on chanting the sacred name from the sacred Kremlin. Now I knew which way to go. Father would be there, yelling with the rest, frozen in the barrage. A pattering of applause followed, like the rapid clapping of the rain, like the rush of typewriters. Entered noiselessly. They didn't see me. They were all looking at the orator, and even he didn't notice me. Stooped to the height of the chairs. Slipped along to the last place on the right, near the window. It was unnaturally warm, my forehead and body dripped with sweat.

There were three men at the table near the podium. Father wasn't one of them. Nor was Virgil Mehedinţi. Hadn't seen them in the auditorium either. Besides, it would have been hard to make him out: the auditorium was large. Sitting there, huddled inside my overcoat, the orator's words suddenly reached me, not because he commanded my attention, but because the words forced themselves on me; they came from inside me: I knew them so well it was as if I'd uttered them myself. I focused my attention, as they say, and followed the movements of the speaker's lips and arms. I wasn't crazy. I wasn't hallucinating. The speaker was repeating sentences, words that were in me, in my classmates, and in all the citizens of the Republic, uttered and repeated so many times by everyone—perfect formulations, transmitted and learned once and for all, so that the least deviation or supplementary accent would have amounted to profanation. Blasphemy! Young and old, large and small, feeble and grandiose, we all went on parroting the exact same phrases and words: proof of our fraternity. I knew the words that would follow, and indeed they came, and then the ones that would have to follow. I knew them all. I gave up anticipating and started looking at the high vaulted ceiling of the formerly Austrian town hall and at the stained-glass windows that narrowed into a sharp triangle—the lancet above me and the other windows at a distance. Though it was now full of chairs with writing arms, this part of the building had once been a festivities hall. This was the first time I'd seen its frescoed vault and narrow—rectangular, triangular, rhombic stained-glass windows. It was terribly hot, as if I'd fallen into the steam of a foaming cauldron, and I'd been sitting there for a long time shrouded in the heat of my overcoat when I suddenly leapt to my feet like the others, though my eyes were already closed. Then I fell back into my overcoat and heard nothing else—except later, the chairs being moved and slammed, like the rain's rapid-fire arrows on a rooftop or the overlapping clatter of many typewriters working together. My eyes were glued shut. I wasn't able to open them. Virgil Mehedinți's heavy hand was on my shoulder. I murmured, stuttered, muttered without being able to move a muscle.

—I'm looking for Father.

—Good. Come with me.

Groggy, listless, and ashamed, I followed him up one flight of stairs. I dragged myself behind his long strides. I counted the doors: the third on the left in the corridor to the right. Two desks, exactly the same, perpendicular to each other. Mehedinți passed behind the desk, lifted a chair over the desk, and put it in front of him—in front of me. Draped my overcoat over the back of the chair and sat down.

The two of us were face to face. Recognized his white hair, his thick black mustache and large hands: it was Virgil Mehedinți indeed, the one I'd followed for so long, and I had felt his large, powerful hands on my shoulders and his soft, calm voice. He was explaining Father's absence. Somewhere in the middle of his sentences I realized that Mehedinți was replacing my father. My folks would have to lose me and only retain the new offspring, Donca, to remind them of what they didn't want to forget: that they were reborn to life and had found the courage to forget everything from the past that needed to be burned and scattered, so the past could remain the past.

Comrade Mehedinți had already told me that Father would be away at a school for a while. Then he repeated himself, perhaps because I wasn't paying attention, though he didn't seem to want to draw my attention to the fact, and he added that maybe it was better this way. At the new workplace, Father would be able to highlight his honesty and discipline.

—Especially at the beginning, a former bank clerk doesn't get along very well in today's rather complicated context. After finishing school, which will be, rather, a way of getting up to date with the laws, he'll be our spokesperson in a place of utmost importance. He'll probably do that very well. He's conscientious and upright.

Virgil Mehedinți had a white shirt, powerful hands, and a warm baritone voice—not surprising for his large, heavy body. I went on listening to him and maybe I spoke as well. Maybe he said something else to me. I noticed a narrow black ribbon on the lapel of his jacket. He saw me looking at it, and he told me that his father-in-law, Ileana's father, had died several days ago. It was scandalous, this officially frowned on cult for the dead with its suggestion of protracted religious ritual, but he went on talking to me about his father-in-law, a big shot lawyer, who was, according to him, a delicate, cultivated person of exemplary probity. I didn't have time to be surprised. I was discovering that with gifts of money and shelter in hard times Ileana's father had helped him and his comrades and their subversive organization. Conciliatory and disturbing, my new parent, this Virgil Mehedinţi! What might I have achieved with this father who didn't hurry to make arrangements or thrust me onto the ledge of other *HAVE TO*s. Cold and fatigue caught up with me again: I was afraid of getting to know this man who was wasting time in such an unexpected conversation. I pulled on the sleeves of my overcoat to run home, to sleep in my warm bed. Mehedinţi took my hand. He shook it slightly, and clutched my shoulder.

I was rushing down the corridor when I heard his raised voice:

—Shut the door tight.

The door had been cautiously pulled into the edge of the door-frame. It had rotated slowly, noiselessly, so no one could hear, so the movement was imperceptible, so no one would realize—so no one would see my frightened face, my sneaky eyes, my hunched shoulders. Should have gone back to push the door, but didn't have the strength. Needed to hide, to slip away quickly, without being noticed, followed, and apprehended. Practically somersaulted down the stairs into the snow so his voice wouldn't reach me.

Donca had pushed off the covers, and she was breathing noisily. The light was extinguished in the next room. Shed my things in a rush to hide myself, sink under the soft, fluffy feather bed, and lose myself under the covers, which were thick, light, and kind. Stretched my legs on the narrow sofa, then my arms. Closed my eyes. My parents' whispers reached me through the door. They were discussing Father's departure and the prospect of his transfer as a demotion, a retreat toward the second line of battle. So now Mother's irritated voice was pronouncing the words "sickly correctness" and enumerating proofs that Father had refused the minimal "natural" advantages of the work with which he had been entrusted. Hearing it for the first time, it surprised me to learn how much wood was used to heat our damp, old, two-room dwelling, which might have been exchanged for something better a long time ago. Mama listed the debts they had accumulated before each fortnightly salary, and, being overly nervous, she named names—some of them in the public eye. She was talking about people who didn't have to go through the usual struggle to get supplies, "and, who knows, maybe something else on top ..." My guilty father wasn't answering. She kept on grumbling. He let her go on without interrupting. He whispered, "C'mon, let's sleep." Her voice broke off. Their words mixed in a low murmur, which couldn't be understood. The window was white. Donca was breathing with difficulty on her narrow sofa. A fine film of ice had settled on both sides of our bedroom window.

Like an athlete the night before a touch match, Sebastian Caba would go on sleeping dreamlessly under his rough blanket. Having prepared well, he'd be confident of victory. Father would go away to a place where he'd been long ago and from which I'd not succeeded in bringing him back. Mama would keep struggling with everything I'd ignored in my foolish overconfidence. Our friend Ileana's father had died; the once rich lawyer now had the luck to be mourned by his son-in-law; I had believed Mehedinți was harsh and unfeeling, but he had presented a new face, to my amazement. For just a few moments he had been this runaway's desired parent, until his voice became suddenly commanding. Comrade Virgil Mehedinți didn't need a son who wasn't able to close a door properly. No one rushed to adopt a self-imagined orphan who had wasted "earth and time" and who was ready to forget that today makes ten years and that tomorrow will be Thursday, the day when I must be alone with the enemy and break my sword in its sheath before the battle.

‡ ‡ ‡

March had come. Spring was late. The square was packed. We were all huddled closely together, gathered in our long, mournful loden coats. The air breathed powerful chords: mortuary cadences thundered overhead. The heavy, solemn sounds struck us from all sides as we waited, silent and gloomy. Clenched hands thrust in pockets, I kept moving my feet, dancing, to get rid of the numbness in my toes. Poking my head from my collar, I saw my classmate Sebastian Caba, who also wore a black armband. I should have bowed, overcome, like the thousands of men and women gathered in mourning around me, but I was no longer the same person as before. I kept seeing myself as disfigured, stunted, and punished, forced to lick everyone's boots, to crawl like a worm along the compact rows without missing a single foot. I would have to pass my frozen tongue over every cold and filthy boot, slinking along the cold and filthy roadway, so that everyone would find out I had committed an act of betrayal, that I was the only one in that grieving crowd who had defiled their suffering by permitting a sinner to remain among us. I was a Jesuit doomed to hypocrisy. I was ready to shrink, to contract suddenly to become powerless and lost among crowded legs and boots: that was the only way I could attend the funeral of the god.

We had lowered our eyes, however. I was contemplating Caba's grief-stricken face among the crowd of heads bowed under the weight of the megaphones, when I glimpsed her watching the crowd from a balcony, looking at me explicitly, so it seemed: our neighbor, the former minister's wife, tiny and thin Colette Triteanu with her fine, doubtful smile, looking at me—of course she was looking at me—which was, for her, a more interesting spectacle than the one offered by the crowd. She knew, of course, that I was a fugitive who hid himself when the enemy was received among us, for I was becoming a masked enemy myself, a deserter, a weakling. The lady had every reason to look at me in a maternal way: we were from the same placenta, we read the same books and smiled in the same tight-lipped, doubtful way. We were seeing, recognizing each other from a distance over the heads of all those orphans—allies in the secret funereal game. My classmate had known, too, for a long time, that he could count on me, that we would soon be side by side, bearing the same deceptive sign of struggle or armband. Like the other impotents, my parents allowed themselves to mourn loudly; they were no longer guarding themselves against me, they were no longer afraid of the son who would do anything the slogans of the day demanded. They could count on my discretion, the tolerance of a weakling—hunkered down inside himself out of fear, sloth, and sleep. They all knew me: Colette Triteanu, the lady who loaned me peculiar books, and Sebastian Caba, the insect who was stretching out his sly antennae toward other accomplices. And—abandoned by the Great Disappeared, the dead Father of the Struggle, the Illuminated One, the Intangible, the Red Star of the Kremlin, and Grandmaster of the Revolution—this crowd ignored me now, frozen as it was in an air-tight pain. I wasn't worthy of it. I shouldn't set foot there. There was *No Admittance* for me.

They knew in advance that they could leave me to play at the game of Memory or Virtue, for I would slip rapidly away, forgetting myself, them, time, and earth, somersaulting into a dark, dank tunnel where my outstretched hands would grope for any brother or sister, staggering on the bridge of a flimsy vessel, lulled to sleep by the suave voice of a lady traveler telling digressive stories about Tiberiu Covalschi, terrible kids in black limousines, an old woman driven mad by accursed memories, and the phantoms of children with shaved heads waving a wig of charred hair; and I would find myself again on the bridge of a ship, like a cell among lazy, liquid objects with a hand coiled around my throat, becoming hysterical in the orchestra of pursuing horns.

Brass instruments blared in the city square. Determined voices crackled through the loudspeakers, their foreign language sonorous and harsh. Shoulders heaved in memory of our parent, father of us all. Fists clenched in pockets, I saw the men and women beside me staring straight ahead as if frozen to the spot. Nails thrust deep into my flesh, I was a turned-to-stone hypocrite, like them. My chest rose. I could barely breathe. I was stuck with them, but they would never believe me again, ever.

⋮ ⋮ ⋮

Time lulled to a halt, lazed by the sun. Noisy, tanned, mad with the joy of vacation, the class galloped to the river. Donca rolled in the dust of neighboring courtyards. Bands of little troublemakers followed at her heels, clinging to her thick, blond braids. She kept secretly bringing other objects into the house. Patron of a scrapyard, she would bargain for boxes and mini-boxes: square, round, flat, tall, metallic, wooden, cardboard, colored, rusted, perforated boxes. Every three days the former minister's lady would raise her sallow hand to my lips and offer me a demitasse of sweet, Turkish coffee. She'd smile timidly and slyly, while I'd sip the candied poison. We had ratified a tacit pact: as I'd finish the coffee, she'd simper and offer me a square, flat book. I'd take it in my hand. She'd raise her warm, velvety paw once more for my goodbye, and the base of my nostrils would touch her fuzzy, aged hand. Like a perfidious page, I'd bow, almost down to the dirty parquet. Then, accustomed to the game, I'd turn my back on my Amphitryon. Like some kind of little unwashed soldier, I'd slam the door with a blow that worked for me every time, and the ramshackle building would quiver.

I used to gather the paperback, clothbound, and hardcover books. The stacks would grow taller than my head. Then I'd fling them back into the old woman's arms. She'd give me others. My lips would barely touch her fine skin, and I'd slam the door. I needed to conserve myself, hermetically sealed on my shelf. Lacking air, the books rotted inside me. With all its games and noises, summer wasn't getting close to the shelf where I'd perched. Everything stood stock still around me. There was no movement and therefore no time. From an infinitely distant beach where the waves crashed, a confused rumor would arrive now and then, the flutter of an immense bird, like a sailboat. I was cleaving the night, huddled in the compartment of a train where a toothless fortuneteller read my palm: I would return to the city to save my father from misfortune, but in vain. It would be too late. I didn't believe in this kind of reading without the alphabet, though. I was corrupted by vague hopes when, in fact, it was too late, much too late.

But all this happened some other time, many years after finishing the high school. Meanwhile, I had climbed down onto the bridge of a boat full of passengers and their luggage. Leaning against the rail, watching the greenish water slip back into the wake of our boat, I was alone, but near me, from behind, came the pitching notes of a piano. There was a cold wind blowing, and men and women dressed in heavy clothing. Those trifling, dreamy creatures had been abducted, like me, from their daily convoys by this giant metallic whale now dizzying in the waves, in the somnolent rocking of piano, pendulum, and old sounds.

—That's Handel's Chaconne in G Major.

Voice of water and wind. The fairy had stooped by my shoulder. Her murmur flowed into me. Was she the tall, pale-skinned girl I used to dream of on summer nights when the neighbor's books swallowed me? Her eyes big and black, her hair rough, long, and black. Impatient, she would hold out her arms to receive me after so much delay, to make amends for the delay and allow me to gaze upon the body expressly made to amaze me—a miracle, not to be disturbed by the slightest movement. I stood stiff as a board. The piano went on enunciating its fantasy. The waves played on. To one side, painfully alive, that voice of a pitiless suavity was real, alive, and undeniable.

—You know, I'm a music professor.

So there she was, disguised as a piano teacher on the damp bridge among those tired, noisy travelers. I could reach out and touch her. But no, I mustn't. She would soon put her lips to my ear and utter my name. I remained still for a while, with my back to her, as though I hadn't heard her call, and waited to feel the closeness of her breath and her velvety fingers. Paralyzed by emotion and something like stage fright, I waited too long, and when I finally became desperate, I turned quickly around, but it was too late. She'd already disappeared. Near me, there was a fat, ageless woman, a passenger in transit. She'd witnessed the entire scene and was looking at me. But these things happened at another time, long after finishing high school, when I hadn't yet become a hermetically sealed can sitting on its shelf.

One morning at the Polytechnic Institute, I met the unknown of my dreams again in one of the third floor corridors—on the arm of my former high school classmate. They were coming toward me. I didn't know how to vanish fast enough, to keep from running into them. Caba's cordiality would have come next. She, the unknown, would have recognized me. She would have understood that I'd been after her for a long time, driven mad to know her, to draw her closer—since the time we'd met on the boat, then in the train, then in the hall of the post office, which she'd just come out of when we bumped into each other on the lower steps. They were laughing, coming toward me without getting closer. Flattening myself against the wall, horrified, I went on listening as their steps sounded clearly on the floor—without getting any closer.

Years after finishing school, the memories are confused: the corridor at the Polytechnic Institute was different than the one at work where the thin, lunatic girl waited for me, following my movements with her big eyes from a hidden angle in the corridor with her hands still clinging to the wall. The mist penetrated to the bone. Body succumbing to wretched, rebellious, rheumatic chills, the job was now to keep staggering upstairs to a new morning, with jerky movements, pushed onward by distant voices like lost souls heard through the woods and barely plucked from the cold night, under the dew or mist, with small steps, stammering a few words, groaning like a monotonous spell. I stood up among desks, drawing boards, and telephones: the cadence of typewriters, drawers, the rustle of papers struck me. My fingers groped the corners of tables and rummaged through my pockets, found the pill—felt the earth under my feet again: on the peak of the hill, the light filtered into view, the narrow stripe of delayed morning. Suddenly: words, and telephones whistling. Went on running up and down, slamming doors, taking the stairs two at a time, three at a time, crossing the corridor on the ground floor, until caught by the dark gaze of the orphan girl, who was still waiting. She was waiting for me, following me … in the shadows, her hands on the walls, which somehow gleamed. My hands clutched my throat, to come back to myself, to return to the surface. For a moment, her large pupil trembled. Long, slender, pale, the girl sprang from her shadowy corner like a streak of yellowed light, bald, like Dona: shorn. And there was nothing to be seen but her brightly pale forehead, eyes, and fingers on the damp wall.

These mornings took place long ago, many years after high school, which trapped me and divided me from Sebastian Caba, and after the Polytechnic, where I met him again, and after years at the factory, when he had become my chief and I saw him daily, all the time. During the vacation when I let myself be crushed between the covers of delicate Madam Colette Triteanu's books, he was swimming in the river with my classmates—or maybe back home at Giurgiu, with his own friends, in the Danube. I met him again in his second autumn, and his second winter among us, and his second spring, when I saw him daily, and his last summer, when I met him again and we separated, in perfect understanding ... all these things have no connection to him. I must rediscover what that summer and fall had to do with myself in order to understand how we came to be in such a state of mutual understanding that we were able to meet again in apparently changed roles. I should recall how fall and spring went by and our last summer at high school as well, when I used to have memory—I wasn't yet hermetically enclosed on a shelf. Only, the memories aren't connected to him, nor do they have any purpose. They must and will be driven away. Then there will remain, perfectly clearly, the unknown of that autumn.

Our last juvenile fall, spring, and summer.

⋮ ⋮ ⋮

Back then, the windows streamed: liquefied glass—a fluid surface. No reason to wait any longer—there was no sign that it would clear up. Yet that was the first impulse, to stand on the threshold looking at the sky. The others had set out immediately, though. The dorms were nearby. I set out also, but too late: the school secretary was panting, headed in my direction, afraid of missing me. The director and my successor—the new leader of the high-school organization—were already in the staff room with a familiar, short, very dark political activist who taught at the school. I pulled up a chair. The activist smiled at me, so did the director. Still smiling, the director informed me that I had been called to help them in a difficult matter, and the activist added something about my experience and prestige. The director approved, nodding his head. They fidgeted on their chairs and turned toward the successor. The activist, yes ... I think he laid emphasis on the fact that my successor had not yet made his public debut, and it would be risky to do that under such complicated circumstances. Then in the ninth grade, my successor nodded in approval. The activist briefed me on what they'd discussed before my arrival. Then he told me that the assembly I'd have to run the following day was connected to events I would read about in the paper.

The activist raised a sheet of paper and read two names. One I knew, a scrawny freckled, nearsighted, excitable boy, who always got worked up over exams and was the son of a man who once leased large tracts of agricultural land. Then the activist read the two names again, adding that another name would have to be proposed. He looked at me calmly and smiled with his little teeth. I asked, "who's the second?" The director launched into an explanation about the second, who had just entered school that fall: he'd come up from the country where he had joined the organization, probably inadvertently. His father—a professor, a former colleague of the director's, and a former staff officer on the Eastern front—had withdrawn to the country to become a simple elementary school teacher after the war, in the hope that certain things would be forgotten this way, namely against whom he had fought and in what position: against our Soviet brothers as a member of the officer class. So the director affirmed, and they all turned toward me, waiting. I was still preoccupied by the name they were asking for. They waited patiently. Then, to give me time to think, they discussed the other details of the meeting: hour, auditorium, presidium, mobilization. I took advantage of the break. I told them that Saturday afternoon didn't seem suitable for such a gathering because many of the boarders went home for the weekend. The activist responded that all departures would be forbidden and after the meeting there would be a dance organized at the girls' school. I left the building in a hurry—it was still raining, and I got home wet to the skin from running in the rain.

The next day at three, the auditorium was full. The moment I stepped up to the podium, the hall murmured with slight surprise. Several months after the new school year began, I had become a simple infantryman again. Since students in the last year were exempted from leadership positions, I was a kind of president-in-retirement. I opened the session. The director read a page from the newspaper. The activist took up half an hour, more or less, talking about the significance of what had just been read. We passed to the second phase: the expulsions. I began with the son of the former leaseholder, the Zionist. The hall was mute. The guilty party spoke clearly, enunciating in a strong voice, and confirmed what had been said about him. He didn't stutter or turn pale. The commentators followed. The four designated speakers had been registered beforehand. When I looked up, I saw two more raised hands in the back. I added them to the list. The first spoke as I expected, with sincere fury. The second added several combative epithets. The third designated speaker carried on in the same vein as the first, but with a loud voice, red with fury. Although they were reciting prepared speeches, the words seemed different, enlivened with pathos. Then one of the people from the hall who'd signaled he'd like to speak jumped up. He agreed in principle with the others, but was proposing that there be more discussion because the former leaseholder was gravely ill and dying. The clamor died down. There was a long silence. The last designated speaker followed. He spoke calmly, perfectly punctuating the finale: "the leaseholder's illness has nothing to do with this meeting, nor does it matter that the sick man was a leaseholder long ago, in his own youth. The main thing is that we must rid ourselves once and for all of the shameful traces of the past!" The hubbub rose once more, particularly in the back of the room. I heard approving outcries, but other, confused ones too. I had been careless: I hadn't arranged the speakers well, which became even clearer when finally the second speaker from the hall took the floor and he hesitated ten minutes before declaring his verdict. He kept doubling back, just when he seemed to have decided. He'd go on finding a detail here or there that stalled him. He'd liked the guilty party's responses: the accused seemed honest and he had comported himself surprisingly, especially if we consider the difficulty his family was going through. When he sat, heads turned in his direction, seemingly in admiration. I let them wait several more seconds before intervening. I began by testifying that I appreciated the six speakers' interesting points of view, and particularly the dramatic conclusion, proof that they were serious about the decisions to be made. But we hadn't gathered simply to display our rhetorical skills, but rather, our resolution to decide, to neither pass over facts, nor commit injustice, nor to be superficial and hesitant. Precisely on such an occasion, we might show our force—our capacity to discern.

I stopped. I looked at them. They were listening closely. I asked them to think and to pronounce with a clean conscience.

—I will vote for expulsion! I said.

Out of all assembled, five arms abstained from voting. The freckled boy left the hall.

I presented the second case, and introduced the denounced, who spoke a great deal. This time, many more people had signed up to speak. I knew what some of them were going to say, and I interspersed the other unknowns among them. The balance oscillated. With his usual cordiality, the popular, long-fingered basketball player had attracted people's sympathy. He spoke convincingly, in a slightly passionate way. The last among those signed up spoke in favor of expulsion. I would have to master the crowd and influence it. I embarked feverishly. Everyone was breathless, shifting in their seats. I saw the impatience with which those in the first rows listened, following my twists and turns, my nosedives, breaks, and rolls, my lightning strikes. The accused was somewhere in the middle of the auditorium. I couldn't see him, and my madness in his favor seemed pointless if it wasn't rewarded with some sign from him. When I concluded and sat down, the hall was completely surprised. They expected something more. They were looking at me in bewilderment, as if I hadn't finished talking, and they smiled in confusion. I understood that I had sat down too quickly, like an idiot, giving the others a chance to refute me and knock me down. I sprang to my feet. I called for the vote. Convinced that it wouldn't be noticed, I forgot to raise my own hand as well. My vote wouldn't be marked by either side.

Having finished with the second case, I passed on to the third: the story of the staff officer. His son, the accused, barely had the strength to rise to his feet. He got tangled up in his answers, and didn't seem to understand what was happening to him. Everyone thought they should follow me promptly and categorically. Not understanding what had happened to him, the child from the eight grade staggered from the hall. The crowd scattered and I stayed behind to explain myself.

—There was no other way of proceeding … it would have been unconvincing. Everyone would have left with the feeling that something had been crammed down their throats: it would have been a formal acceptance, without effect.

They kept silent. The activist wasn't talking. The director beside him wasn't talking either. I detailed my motives. Everyone had hesitated over the first case. The second had been even more complicated. A person who accepts an unusual job for himself and goes to work in a salt mine without trying to find a way out is not straightforward, he is not a poor agonizing notary. Sensing that his lies would be used against him, the salt-mine worker's son admitted with thrilling emotion that he had made use of his classmates' ignorance of his antecedents in order to be regarded as one of them. But, he explained, he had lied not only because his father was now honestly paying for his sins, but also, more importantly, because he wanted to participate in the country's new reality and contribute to its luminous future. Repeating his words, I was beginning to believe in the passionately declaimed clichés: I was free to do exactly the opposite of what I believed and to pronounce words that contradicted my actions ... charming discrepancies, a realm where I was no longer obliged to torment myself and keep my weak and vacillating shoulders straight. I could sneak off anywhere, like a slippery reptile. The games for cowards were beginning. A realm was opening itself to me, a game for losers and weaklings displaced from the real world, for which they had proved themselves unworthy. The inhabitants of this realm were masters of an existence of contretemps and counter-spaces and counter-movements, free at any moment to stop the words on their lips before they were spoken, even from the moment of their birth, to change them for others, and to forget these too, fascinated by the countless transitory masks in the limitlessness of the game, strengthened by every new dodge. And this meant that I was more convincing than the accused had been, more convincing than I had been a few moments earlier, there, in front of everyone ... I went on inventing other arguments, some stemmed from others, multiplying in zigzags that would suddenly come to smash, plunging me into another curve, a crazy, captivating wager. I had saved Caba, and now I was trying to save myself.

The autumn leaves raced after me. I kicked at them; they danced, raising themselves from the earth in short spirals wrapping me in swishing ribbons. Autumn meant twilight, and they were celebrating me, like a son dragged through dusk, with long convoys of black wings, and running beside me like the dead feathers of yesterday's birds.

I had solemnly answered the activist. He was right to ask me why I had proposed Caba for the blacklist and then saved him. And I had replied that I had the right to bring the scoundrel before them, so they could choose if they wanted to forgive him or not. I had suspected that they would absolve him—and it was better for the public prosecutor to get his bearings quickly, as I had done, so that we—I and the organization—wouldn't be in disgrace with the masses. The instructor went on listening to me suspiciously. He had no idea how the ribbon-like words raced, how they whistled, how the rocking winds blew me forward, one word setting off from the other or from all of them. My thoughts weren't gushing from my eyes—they weren't betraying me. They were hiding, rushing: one spark, a second, rapidly replaced, playing with me, their plaintive plaything, asleep under damp leaves, sliding through the air like a bird dreaming.

The windows were lit. Music was playing at the girls' school. Wild hair, work boots heavy with mud, rough pullover—I shouldn't have gone in. I remained on the threshold. The voices traveled in pairs. Somewhere at the end of the dream, a dark lunatic girl waited, her large eyes, black and patient. Through the partially opened door came vapor, breaths, perspiration, noises, giggles. I skimmed along the walls near the gymnastic equipment, shaking hands, greeting, smiling. Sweaters and skirts, short, narrow sleeves, narrow, white peasant leggings, flower-embroidered shirts—national costumes—huge work boots, crumpled neckties, uniform dresses enclosed in the white of timid collars, all of them huddled into a swarm.

—Are you looking for someone?

I turned at the sound of my classmate's cordial voice. As we sat next to each other, his fingers kept time with the music as though somehow in time with events. He had greeted me easily, so I was only embarrassed at the start. There was no reason to reject his friendly smile. Everything was like before, as though nothing had happened. Those fine fingers went on juggling, and my classmate continued to dominate the conversation, a model of harmony between word and voice. It was remarkable how his eyes and lips served his thoughts. The same went for his body, hands, shoulders, throat. My classmate made himself the master of an agreeable closeness yet again. Our detour into small talk didn't need to be prolonged: the chitchat might have become boring. At the critical moment, the point (that little blow from askance) would have to be driven home, the sharp edge of truth, glittering suddenly among pleasant chatter—the gesture that would lend a necessary trace of authenticity. He knew the scenario.

—Have you been having a hard time?

My classmate was discreetly thanking his savior. Naturally, if I hadn't answered right away, he would have slipped away, and as far as possible.

A hard time? I'd been sustaining justice! I argued again, more convinced than an hour before, more convinced than an hour and a half before, and more convincing than he had been two hours before when he confronted the hostile crowd. I repeated his plea word for word. I hadn't defended anyone, as I told him—conclusively—I had only revealed the assembly's own hesitations, without tilting the balance, leaving them free to choose. Shaken by their trepidation, I had forgotten to vote myself. Then it was only a matter of his rising by my side and repeating the question to which no answer was expected.

—Are you looking for someone?

Following me from the dream where I couldn't reach her, the tall, thin girl wore her hair like a clod of black earth gathered on top of her head. She hid her impatient eyes. My classmate turned toward me again—it seemed we both knew how the other would gesture or reply, and yet we still made each gesture and reply. He became animated while talking about girls. Our female classmates were locked away in school uniforms, and they'd probably condemn us to chastity for a long time to come.

—We should marry quickly if we want to accomplish something. Otherwise, we'll fall right into the hands of the first coquette.

It was the moment to look him in the eye. I had to tell him what I thought, which is to say, I had to distort my words and phrases in such a way that it would seem I was lying or posing. Then the true thought would sink and disappear under a surplus of overly complicated concealments. I would wrap my thoughts in affected, precious phrases. I would look him straight in the eye, as I hadn't done a moment ago when I was replaying my speech for him with my eyes fixed on some distant angle that sight could never reach.

—I hope eventually to find myself in the same office with a girl. To get used to her way of walking, her face, so that she becomes necessary to me, so that she understands my silences, my preferences, and then a tacit engagement will arise between us—gradually and increasingly intense, and everything will be implied in our ordinary movements, so that there won't be any need for words. If it works out this way, one day I'll buy two movie tickets and before saying goodnight, on the threshold I'll ask her to stay with me forever. I hope she'll agree with a simple nod of the head.

He began to smile, as I had expected. I was accepting everything ass-backward, without caring, asleep on my shelf.

—You should study literature. In reality, things are simpler or more complicated—or in any case, more random. Seriously, you should get started on a literary career.

He was smiling, as I had expected. He had pronounced the expected words.

—Literature? It's only worth writing on walls anymore.

The sentence had to be finished with a slap on the back, and borrowing a gesture of his that he didn't have the courage to make, but which he'd foreshadowed in the complicated ballet of his courtly gestures, I gave him a friendly slap on the back—the ultimate sign of acceptance and trust, and particularly of encouragement to embark upon his long and victorious road, which I had played a small part in guiding him toward.

I had decided it would be our last conversation as high-school students, and it was.

I had made friends with myself in the end. Without hostility, I kept an eye on my movements. They were harmonious, to all appearances. A faithful, amazed attendant on my own steps, I counted them from a pace behind, overjoyed they were mine, with their decisive stamp on the damp roadway, successfully traversing conventions of traffic, proficiently executing whatever bounds, twists, or reversals the unforeseen required. I advanced along the serpentines of various ages, an obedient robot, subject to hours, cities, and people, the brother who indifferently regarded his blind twin walking a step or an instant ahead. Nothing was happening in the game of adjournment, acrimony, and anesthesia. Being neither one nor the other, I had acquired the freedom to be sometimes one, sometimes the other—the one who remained the same in all operations, the "invariant" who had been provided and who had lived long ago in some other time by someone else—or never, by anyone. And so I advanced monotonously along uniform spirals and uniform hours, alongside uniform people heading toward uniform cities, submissive, too, like the one beside me—the double, my indifferent twin. Opportune, prompt as the waters of Lethe, forgetfulness would quickly erase everything, and the whole business would start over again, like yesterday, like tomorrow—whenever, or at no time.

With my eye screwed into the back of his neck, I rode on the young corpse's back. The flesh was as flaccid as his arms. I accompanied all his staggering and his worn-out, falsified emotions. I fell in step with the suave, transparent twin who would agitate himself like a frenetic shadow on glass, ready to shatter. I tried to be a magnetic coating, able to intercept emotions, aspirate thoughts, able to infect his moods and ambitions, to concentrate and preserve myself in the depth, happy that nothing could be retained. All things happened in a watery, slippery way, or perhaps they had evaporated and were left-over bits of dust, unstable as the blade of a momentary wind.

I saw him—myself—pass through preliminary circles, as through Purgatory: I followed him into all the traps opened to him by her, *the third person*, the nameless, the only one that had a name—for the third person could have had any name, which is also to say no name at all—the bondswoman of his imagination, docile, foreign, and free of selfhood, cringing in grotesque little lying revolts, pointless attempts to increase the areas of irresponsibility in which *"he"* would trans-fer himself through her, the third person. I felt his body tested, con-vulsed, and electrically shocked by red spirals about to become heat and movement. He stopped on the spot, amazed by the intensity of his confrontation with the *second person* (*"you"*), who was flinging her hair over his eyes—his orbits—which was destiny coming to choose him, to test him. And with him I collapsed exhausted in the circle of such rings, in an ultimate vortex, reached only by the wind, the final boundary, the inferno of the interlocutor.

We were at the edge of a fortress with thick, high walls. Before the entrance, a massive gable, curved like a shield. We saw every detail of those walls and the colors of the morning that found us at the gates—the dimension, the form, and the color of the stones, the rattling of the cumbersome green metal gates, the road that carried us up its ser-pentine curves. I heard the words as if they were my own: *the oblong hole that remained in the wall closely resembled a crocodile.* And indeed, over time, the hole had shaped itself oddly, almost like a prank, into a long animal with short, barely visible paws and a wide, snarling snout. The decayed stones had grown jagged, like the greedy crea-ture's zigzagged teeth. "He" spoke haltingly, and "I" heard his words in myself, near every curve of the hole that seemed specially designed to embody the ferocious reptile's shape.

I and myself circled the fortress for several hours. Then we wandered the hills. We were setting out for the Big City in a few days. We listened to the undulations of our thoughts and saw the heavy green gate and the curious hole in the fortress wall once more. It was necessary to interrupt him, to interrupt myself, to contradict myself, to contradict him. The wall wasn't curved like a shield, but straight and sloped: the frustum of a square pyramid. It wasn't made of stone, but of brick worn by rain. The images had blurred. The memories: uncontrollable. I understood then that it had been a necessary occurrence: we could no longer unite in one being. We needed to remain separate though inseparable, halves. It would never be possible to be near him, and even less in him. Something definitive in me—forgetfulness—accomplished the wonder of our doubling.

The hole in the wall had not existed: it was a chimera, or so I thought. I had turned pale and listened to him describing the details: horrified, he gradually convinced himself that what I had seen was a spot of whitewash left by a brush. Bent over his back, suddenly hunched with age, I felt that he needed some verification. He wanted to return to that place. And, in truth, we really would return there later, but after many years, after uncertainty had already torn us apart. We gazed at the walls of the former fortress. Above the green gates rose the frustum of a truncated pyramid made of brick. He looked at the spot of whitewash on the wall. The hairs of the brush had created a crocodile. Our hands extended. Cold, clammy palms slapped our foreheads. If there hadn't been a hubbub of voices nearby, he might have collapsed. He didn't have the strength to turn in their direction. Panic had made him faint. He was devastated, pale as death. His unraveled mind let any kind of mental aberration through its serpentine coils. He was terrified by how easy it was to fall prey to imagined mishaps, and so was I.

A group of young tourists stood close by. They shed stray bits of information about the history of the fortress. Someone said that the restoration of the fortress had taken place several months ago. "He" turned, then, rushed toward the speaker, snagged him by the collar, and asked if the wall hadn't originally been made of stone and curved.

—Yes, it seems . . .

The young man wasn't sure: he hadn't had the leisure to recover. He was no longer sure what he had meant to say—the wall seemed to have been brick and straight, however, and "he" would go on believing this from now on: he was afraid to go back—everything escaped him so quickly. We kept forgetting in order to be free, in other places and at other times, without roots and duration: moving slowly, like a mobile point on a straight line rotated outward from a fixed pole, following spirals that tangled into a ball—the ash of closed serpentine spirals, rotations in a dark self, preliminary corridors. *The third person* and *the second person* gradually impeded access; the charred spirals deepened into a narrow remnant, contracted spaces, small, heavy steps on wires thin as humid trails of smoke, onetime slopes, stairs, spirals, and serpentine coils, scattered in a distant, black fog.

We would have to remain together, therefore, myself and I, as friends, opposite halves allied by necessity, unreconciled individuals, each struggling to inhabit me by himself. We were like a couple that might have seemed in agreement, but hadn't agreed on anything except indifference and the struggle for the life and death of the other, for whom existing at the same time and in the same place was impossible, unless this conflicted state was just a way for us to march in step and passively endure our own peaceful absence. The week of yesterday, the Friday of yesterday, and the year of yesterday would have to be forgotten. I would have to begin anew, as Father had taught us, for Eva's and Dona's smoke to rise, for us to be free, for Captain Zubcu to burn, for us to forget all those half-games in exchange for halves of each other. We should forget whom and what and why we forgive, and in this way it would be possible to organize the pantomime of the Saturday tomorrow and the day after that.

The walls of the Big City had therefore enclosed us. The alarm clocks shrieked at dawn ... damp, uniform mornings ... the shirt like a cold lash, hurried convoys climbing the same street, bowing tensely under the factory windows, heads lower than the porter's cap. Noises, drawers, voices, telephones, cigarettes, the pink ozalid paper, the industrial ovens in transverse and longitudinal sections, funnels, platforms, bunkers, circuits, cyclone collectors. I watched my other self, who knew my own laziness. I kept heeding the rheumatic pain that climbed slowly down the thin pipes to my knee, to my ankle.

The machines for beating time throb in the back of the neck, but tomorrow is a holiday, Saturday. It's worth gathering our strength for another "have to" and "a bit more," again, today, another hour, tomorrow is Sunday, the seventh day: we are born again, it will be a holiday, we're finishing school—like a grand finale, the youthful brow will be encircled by the ultimate wreath, the gates will spring aside before heads crowned with laurels. We will drag the triumphal car through the flattened crowd; tomorrow we are free to choose anything at all. Tomorrow is Saturday, the last year of the week, the great orchestra of typewriters will cadence the victory march, thousands of telephones will ring out like sirens saluting the backs bent over their work. We are a single philosopher: every year of the week we were an absent philosopher, every day we thought of the past and the future, and behold, it's Saturday afternoon: Father has come to congratulate his eminent offspring.

—You should take up philosophy. Your abilities would be of the greatest use to our comrades. That's their belief, too.

—The top of my class are going to the Polytechnic Institute or into medicine. It would mean finding myself among the bottom of the class, but you're right. I'll take into account the place where my abilities could best serve the comrades.

He should have been startled by the all too natural tone of my agreement. I could do anything with myself. My arrogance was boundless, ready to set out on the most capricious byways, just to see what would happen to me. Therefore, later, one Saturday afternoon when the graduates of the Polytechnic had gathered around the lists of relocation assignments, they asked me what factory I had chosen for myself. "Not one," I lied, but I wasn't lying when I confessed that my dream had always been to become a ticket seller at a cinema in Africa. The formulation had come spontaneously, and I had offered it several days ago to my former classmate, Caba, who was also graduating from one of the faculties at the Polytechnic.

And he revealed his future plans to me as well.

—I'm getting married. We have to do it now, chop-chop. Otherwise who knows what little coquettes we'll wind up wasting time with. My lady, Gaby, is finishing medical school, and I've got to make sure she'll be posted to the capital. I know I've come up with a real showstopper by choosing a job at the Zarea Champagne factory, but it looks like it could offer useful social relations all over the place.

After a summer and a day, it was Monday already and they were waiting for me as the jokes froze on the wage slaves' lips—they being Misha (the plain-clothes patrol), the chair like a coffin, and the industrial ovens where Captain Zubcu burned. I brought my hand to my throat, to defend myself; it was too late: the siren was going off . . . I lifted the receiver, it was the fat lady professor. *Quiet. There are other tenants.* I was in the street, orphan of the rain, holding out flowers to policemen and the black woman crooning *Summertime.*

I was a pale nomad, transparent, like a tall glass of water, defiant and suave. I found myself in a tram that would carry me toward sneering coworkers. Shadows kept climbing on and off. Their mirror images climbed off and on. The tram kept advancing toward the hill of another identical morning—casting me out onto the damp, unknown street before I planned to get off. I wandered into the fold of the streets to find the hours, the city, the people—to find the dream where the girl with hair as black as smoke, was waiting for me. And I was picking up the receiver, the cold receiver of the public phone, dialing numbers endlessly, certain that she would answer eventually, and then we would agree to find each other again. Evaluating my chances according to statistics, I was convinced that I could exhaust all of the possibilities and find her. I would go into coffee houses, movie theaters, tailors, beauty parlors, watchmakers and cobblers, taverns and groceries, jewelers and furriers; I would cross squares and stadiums, climb onto trains, into ships and flying fortresses, wait at the airport for that lucky surprise—the coincidence. I would have to blend into crowds, run around, make phone calls, put announcements in the personals. There would need to be a sufficient number of attempts, which is to say trials: the frequency of success tends to increase as the events unfold, which is to say the trial or also the attempt, the chance ... the greater the number of trials, which is to say attempts, the variables can wander further from the average, which is to say from certainty, they can be forced toward certainty, success: the monkeys that type away on a typewriter with 35 keys might produce *Hamlet* by chance with a probability of one divided by 35 to the power of 27,000.

Therefore, *the requirements include*: anything, anyhow, anytime, anywhere. I had no right to rest. I kept trying telephone calls—I would have to persevere, to heap up coincidences, deceptions, announcements, which is to say trials, to be everywhere at the same time, with those 27,000 powers of one alone. One autumn, I caught sight of her at a post-office window. I was standing in line. Several people separated us. I was looking at the delicate back of her neck. I became numb, looking at that sweet spot on her neck. I came back to myself as she went down the steps. I ran to see her face. It was she, indeed—she was walking briskly, people were looking at us, I was running, she climbed into a 103, and I lacked the courage to take the next 103. It was late, Friday evening. I had missed the opportunity.

The closeness of the festive day urged me on, leaving me flustered. Something would happen, again: tomorrow they might give me a promotion, a raise, increase my status, and I had no right to get lost, to be late, the week was ending. The failure could no longer be saved at the last moment anymore. I would have to calm myself and be punctual when—who knows?—they might give me other privileges, another residence, other wishes, and another obedience training. There would be upholstered doors, like in Sebastian Caba's office. Then, we'll slam the door and it won't be heard; we'll separate from the year Monday and the year Tuesday; we'll be free: nothing will be remembered—there'll be an easy, scientific, perfect flow.

I found myself in the street, flattened against the glass of the telephone booth. I'd left the office in a delirious state because I could no longer stand the 27,000 monkeys pounding their typewriters. I had to get to the street, immerse myself in rain, and get rid of the flowers that tethered my hands and impeded my memory; I had to arrive at the obese professor's lair, to kill the purgatory that Little Moni-pig represented—symbolically. I'd have to be brisk. My bullets would fire rapidly, my arms would quickly suffocate, the poison would kill quickly, without a trace. Then I'd run into the street again to encounter other hours, the city, and the police under the cold, uniform sky of the siege.

I wandered through the Big City's slums. The collegial bleating awaited me, ready to oppress me. And meanwhile I went on looking at the display windows of clothing and pastry shops, going into cinemas, schoolyards, following the pathways through parks, detouring around kiosks, cafes, and small shops, until I found myself in the square. Limousines kept sliding by, white, black, and green, and the chauffeurs—relaxed as a gang of grandpas—continued opening car doors, and the chubby, hysterical children lay siege to the school gates.

One morning, when I was still a somnolent Polytechnician, I

might have bumped into Monica Smântănescu; I might have seen her claws thrust into her white and bloated flesh, and the horrifying routine with the limousines, and the tyrannical students, and the cunning, guilty dwarfs. Back then, I might have been able to meet her and kill her, so that I would never have to see her again, never be obliged to recognize her as a potential double to be saved or killed, so that no one would discover we were passengers in the same fatherland, destined to meet again in a square surrounded by black and white and green crocodiles, revolving greedily like the ghosts of an infinite moment. Back then I might have met the giantess Monica Smântănescu and the sadistic dwarf, Tiberiu Covalschi, in an exceptional circus—with sleight of hand and hypnosis—but I was in too much of a hurry to pass through the colors of days without end, from one dawn to the next, through nights without end.

The end of the week and the end of the year would need to find me sufficiently tired. On the afternoon of the sixth day, the eve of the seventh, and the seventh day, I would not have been accepted at the festivities of pantomime and obedience training if I hadn't proved that I was suitably tired: hollow-cheeked, wrung-out, transparent—just as I was supposed to be. Time hastened rapidly with its streets and damp skies. The afternoon and the evening of the sixth day were coming. I needed to be at present at the climax of the weekly masquerades. Every week we'd celebrate another end: of school, of the war, of the family, the faculty, the end of the semester, the year, the five-year plan.... This Saturday I'll say farewell to the venerated schoolteachers Sofronie and Popovici, shake the hand of my parents' friends Mehedinți and his wife, Ileana the Fairy-tale Princess. I must bend my knees, kiss the hands of those who brought me into the world, while thanking them for the good raising and unraising ... I must embrace my sisters reduced to smoke in the old crematoriums, take Donca in my arms, then cry on the threshold of the house where I was raised, which I don't know if I'll have time to see again because next Saturday I will be far away, I'll have finished with my studies, I'll have chosen my next workplace, left my classmates, who I don't know if I'll ever see again, because another Saturday is coming: the weeks mount up with their Sabbath of pantomime and obedience training—only it's not time, one must take full advantage of every working day, from dawn to dark, using each of those 480,000 seconds to strike the 35 keys to the 27,000ththththth power and eventually we'll hit on the end, the masterpiece, which is to say the grand finale, crowned with black flowers.

I went on clambering into damp trams: I was setting out for the faculty, the factory, the cemetery; individuals and spies, patrols and pickets and pedestrians climbed on and off, like contortionists wrapped around me, crushing me, hurling me to the roadway before my destination; I would forget when and where I had started my journey through the damp streets of the Big City to meet the awaited chimera. The years flew by quickly: the Saturday would come when I would make the acquaintance of the illustrious artillery Captain, and with two movie tickets, he would begin teaching me how to watch a war movie, honoring me with his inquisitive attention, finding me worthy, with my mask of an aged child, admiring my great, livid, dark circles mirrored in the well's overturned bucket, giving me master classes in equitation, on tall horses, scattered along the curves of the shore, their damp muzzles searching the sea of apples by the seashore. The girl who appeared in our dreams would have to be found by Saturday, when I would become the confidant of the Captain who used to spend his nearly sleepless nights on the edges of forests and the banks of rivers, slunk away like some feral creature, and haunted by the nightmare of the skeletons he sacrificed among the convoys of deportees and detainees, so that I should learn to not slam doors, or shells or mines, to rotate doors slowly, without startling anyone, without making a noise, so that the smoke of the crematoria might ascend slowly and rest in peace.

I was looking at the long loden coats that hid the breasts and thighs of the girls in my class, searching for their white knees lost under immense skirts, their ankles squeezed into rough boots, their hair covered with rough kerchiefs. I wanted to be able to compare their bodies, foreheads, and gazes, to be able to recognize the pale girl, frail under the rain, with long black hair waiting to be pushed aside like a theater curtain. I would have to hurry from Monday to Tuesday, Wednesday to Thursday, until the two halves of Friday, as long as there was still time for the torment of chastity; for soon the curtain will be pulled and the sweet and filthy whores will pounce; I would have to writhe now, in hot, humid dreams, to take advantage of insomnia, to sink my hands and nostrils in the darkest folds of the damp sheets, to prolong the last endless days, to allow 27,000,000 trials, now, only now, when the nostrils of the young wolf were flared at every beast in the street, but without having the courage to approach. In the short dreams of the last, endless night before the festive day, I would have to draw a line, a fire, a finale, to begin another week and year and five-year life; the weeks will be five years long again and the years filled with an unaccountable number of weeks. Every five years, those years of mine, the five-year plans of delusion.

⋮ ⋮ ⋮

We rarely wrote. A message from them, however it might have seemed, was an appeal—an alarm. As it was, I hadn't been the eminent son crowned with laurels for a long time. I was now hanging onto my university exams by the tail. After graduation I would encounter my folks again in their established roles. I had left home one fall, then raced through vacations far away: at the factory, in the army, in student camps. But now the air was damp as it was back then. Maybe I'd find the strength to wear the old masks again.

The train had swallowed me quickly. The compartment rocked in the dark. The heavy body of the man on my right was rocking too, as were the long legs of the man in front of me. I had braced my shoulder against the door and was listening to their breaths mix together and the nighttime noises of their lips and snores. The volume of air had diminished; it was stuffy. Through the window, the landscape raced forward, and the bare, blackened trees, like abandoned old people, were now running backward toward the irrevocable nights of their youth. The train was chasing the night; it was easy to imagine that we would run into some other wild beast or be swallowed by the great holes of darkness that we couldn't quite reach. The travelers went on sleeping like babies in the train's metal belly. There would be no witness to the disaster. Two neighbors to the right whispered to each other. I drowsed, and it seemed I could hear them beside me. The darkness was total. I couldn't see them.

—He exited at the station in the morning. It was autumn, cold, like now. The carriage climbed the hill. You could hear the thud of horseshoes. They had entered the city: not a soul around. He had received a letter. It meant something had happened, so the wanderer thought.

—He had no way of knowing, but the quiet in the city seemed unusual to him. When he arrived at the main street, he raised his eyes to the windows of the houses, the two-story houses of the small town.

They were talking in whispers, huddled close together. It was dark in the compartment, and they continued telling the same story, taking turns.

—They were waiting for him behind the windows. He sensed it, even though he couldn't see their faces.

—The letter didn't say anything clearly, but suddenly he felt cornered by something evil. The residents had withdrawn from the windows, frightened of what would happen to him, or to themselves.

—He was trying to remember why he had come: in which of the letter's sentences had he found such a peculiar phrase that he had climbed into a train that very night?

—He had no way of knowing: it was a prudent letter. Thrusting his hand in his pocked to get it out and reread it, he felt the invisible eyes from the windows again and lost courage to look for the letter. He had a sudden premonition, a way of knowing to whom the misfortune had happened.

—He had no way of knowing ... because he, the passenger, was absent, apathetic.

Later, the heavy hands of a conductor shook me awake. The train was stopping. It was empty. I had arrived at the end of my trip. I belted my trench coat. The railway carriage steps were damp. I came out behind the station where buses or carriages usually waited. There weren't any vehicles, or any other travelers. Dawn was coming up damply. The church towers could be seen at the foot of the hill. A sea of white mist rose, the breath of the dawning day.

The sound of horses approached, galloping. In the cab, I lay back against the gnawed leather cushions: it was an old carriage, driven by a small coachman with red hair. Wheels grating, the horses strained up to the lip of the hill. The city seemed deserted. The carriage had taken a route through the back of a park. I climbed down in front of the Post Office. The house was several yards away. Mother ran toward me with her large coat hanging open. She was still panting when she wrapped her arms around me.

Confused, she looked through her pockets for the keys. When she sat down next to me, she was trembling. She took my hands and asked me how my trip went. She had heavy eyes with dark circles around them. As she came closer, she seemed to be guarding herself against me.

—How's Father?

—Well. Everyone's well. We have problems with Donca. Imagine—her ... she's such a lively girl. Her hair is falling out. Don't ask her about it. We've been to doctors. They prescribed all kinds of treatments. We had to shave her head. Pretend not to notice! You know how she was, always out in vacant lots with boys. Now she doesn't leave the house anymore. She needs to wear a wig for a few months. She locks herself up in the house, reads till dawn, keeps away from us. It will solve itself in the end, so don't trouble yourself. But tell me, how are you doing?

Her eyes were heavy: she was grabbing and letting go of my hands. So, Donca had a shaved head like our sisters used to have; the doctors would no longer be able to help her forget, to start over again from the beginning. Her blond hair, so new, so young ... Mama couldn't settle down near me: her eyes were heavy. We would need to hurry with our hugs, our despair.

—How's Father?

—Well, dear, well. Don't worry. Well. But you, how did it go, you, but you, which ... and she was suddenly in tears. I felt her shoulders against my own.

She got tangled in hiccups, her words ran together.

—It will be alright with Father, and with Donca, too. You'll see. Only, we mustn't lose ourselves—and she lost control again.... Don't despair. You'll see. It will work out. It was something scandalous, unjust: the whole world knows. He was always correct. The case will be retried. Have faith. Now, you're the one who *must*, who can't ... I'm so alone ... And she collapsed again, spluttering, dragging me into her terrible sobs.

Then, she went back to work. I remained alone—without knowing how to repeat the scene to myself—her pale, wrinkled face before my eyes. I was seeing her eyes, her sunken cheeks, her suffering. I looked at the window, the bed, the walls: I should have suffered. It seemed like just yesterday that she was pummeling him with reproaches: "This one did this, that one did that, this one got hold of such and such and got himself fixed-up really well."

Could it be ... do misfortunes fulfill certain predispositions or latent tendencies? My parents had found the strength to forget in order to start over, as Father said so many times. Then what had happened was neither surprising nor unjust. If he were reborn once, he could be reborn again. The cadaver might become a militant, forgetting again, starting everything all over again from the beginning; doing this or that and getting himself well-fixed, if that's what was necessary to start everything all over again from the beginning, tomorrow and the day after that.

Therefore, I had no right to pain, only to shame. In my new circumstances, there was no better way to atone for it than by visiting my former schoolmasters Sofronie and Popovici and the former neighbor, Colette Triteanu, not to mention the great Virgil Mehedinți.

Spent the afternoon alone with Donca. Spilling passionate phrases, she threw her arms around me and talked loudly. She had already accommodated herself to the role of wronged man's daughter, and she emoted compassionately with Mama. She told me that for a while now she hadn't been running around vacant lots, only reading ... Oh, yes, she was reading voraciously and feeling alone, gathered between the covers of books. She looked at me as though wanting to forgive me for all those nights of reading when my light kept waking her. Strongly confirming the signs of an emphatic kinship with me, she expressed herself negligently, used interjections, sighed often. Muttering French verses, she went over to the window. She swung her foreign braids. She was saying that she felt adrift like a drunken boat — past prison hulks' hateful eyes. That would have been the moment to tell her that the term should be ennobled, as the poet wanted: one says "drunken ship," not "drunken boat," but she came close to declare how much she loved me, her exemplary brother, and she embraced me with vast, youthful despair. Maybe if I'd had time for her mood that day, it might have been possible to do something. Mother came back in the evening. Signaling me to avoid any delicate conversation with Donca, she fluttered around the table with silverware and napkins, and in the end, she managed to reveal for my benefit the swindle for which Father had been so exaggeratedly punished. She kept assuring me that things would work themselves out: we would all be happy soon.

The next morning: saw myself stretched out in bed, alone, without the courage to offer Sofronie and Popovici the satisfaction of a visit, not to mention the delicate Colette. Went out into the city instead, and came back at noon. In the afternoon, my sister continued sighing over the noble victim of injustice. Now, she felt like a mad plank under sea-blue, spiral-flaming skies, as the poet, intoxicated by love, had said so well. She longed for the cold, black pond on which a sad child on his knees sets sail a boat as fragile as a May butterfly: she felt herself that child, adrift on the great ocean. She added suddenly that Father had been completely stunned by the event: he had never attended any trial and had therefore behaved badly. In the evening, Mother reappeared. She had prepared some warm packages of food for my trip; she assured me that her husband was well and his confidence hadn't been broken. Donca had heard this: her hair fluttered as splendidly as the stanzas she kept repeating. Returned on the same train. The little city had seen me for only several hours, but it was already inviting me for a reunion. My real healing would involve deadlines, meetings, and responsibilities. Time would pass quickly: five months ... five years. I had a target—I was becoming a passenger with a definite route again: I would travel to get somewhere, to participate in something.

My only duty was to not forget. Nor would that have been possible anyway. I was holding on for dear life to any obligation.

⋄ ⋄ ⋄

The reunion only lasted a few hours. Though the old city recognized its former star quickly, I didn't make my act of contrition. Not much remained of my former precocity, and I spared my old teachers the sight. I didn't visit Virgil and Ileana Mehedinți either. Now, all I could do was return to Sebastian Caba and kneel before him: I'd tap timidly on his window. I'd tell him what had happened. I'd become his disciple. I'd learn the secrets of serenity from the master himself. Of course, I'd go down on my knees in the snow. That's the only way he'd agree to direct my words and deeds in such a way that I'd regain the use of my fellow feelings and benefit from the misfortune that had thrust me so briskly from one camp to another.

Because there were so many detours involved, the descending star had to expend more energy on the way down than he'd used to climb the chilly heights. I was a dilettante, but the university clerks weren't too careful with the information they received, and I graduated. After that, we should have fallen into our proper places: I to the ticket window of a movie house, he to the champagne, furniture, or limousine factory. In the end we went where the wind blew; I to the worksite, he to the factory where we would meet again one bright, clear morning, like in the old days.

A large room with empty desks; it was spring. Caba's slender hands went on noisily rustling through new banknotes. My guide was a thin, silent girl, and I let her pass in front of me. I was becoming Sebastian's colleague again. We would see each other daily. And the years would pass quickly—I kept running on the staircase, up and down. There were circuits, industrial ovens, columns. And so I went on rapidly crossing the corridor of days until the cycles of rebirth suddenly came to a momentary halt in the long Buddhist corridor where my eerie sister's eyes waited to ambush me. I had no time. I went racing toward the orange afternoons: the cheerful whores of amnesia were waiting for me. Damp mornings, tram, crowd, desk, drawing boards, typewriters, slide rules, cigarettes, telephones, drawings, Monday, Wednesday, March, September, long mornings, short afternoons with the office sluts: Madam Whoozits, Comrade Whatzits, the former friend, the former widow, former wife, the former ice skater who sang in the evenings (opening the windows and letting down her red hair—as red as the Revolution), or the other one, the flautist with eyeglasses, or the other one.... My former colleague was serious, determined, preoccupied by family, meetings, and studies, up-to-the-minute with everything—what should be known and done; I was becoming increasingly dim, wiped-out, lazy, indifferent, opaque to anything that might have touched me.

Still, a slave to youth, skipping steps, opening and slamming doors: invaded by voices, laughs, telephones, and the persistent feeling of a cat's eyes lurking in the shadows. Hurrying, I pushed my luck: in a single moment of hesitation, everything would have fallen to pieces: the chief engineer would have discovered that I was braiding his wife's blond hair; the doctor would have caught me with the flautist, musically in flagrante delicto. I'd have collapsed on the spiral stairs. Sometimes suddenly the collar of my blue shirt would throb. I'd shudder. The days went on darkening.

It was probably a morning when the light radiated differently. My arms, throat, and collar felt cold. I turned suddenly to meet what seemed to be Dona's hands and hair, which I stubbornly persisted in not seeing. The light was faltering; metallic glints crossed each other from the corner of a corridor. My hands trembled. I found the cold knob of a door—a room.

Big eyes and a lusterless forehead: the darkness entwined her head as if it were Dona's black hair, as if she still had those long, powerful braids of yore gathered into a crown. Dona, my dead sister, was watching me from the end of the corridor to confirm I was living, running, skipping steps. She haunted my gestures to convince herself and me that I was alive and could see her—pale, beautiful, shaved bald. Mature now, I wasn't crying like a stupid little kid because they'd shaved her again and not a single strand of hair was left on her head or because we were dragging out our transparent days without the courage to release a door, a voice, a sound.

I was seeking voices, laughter, and doorbells so that people would find that I was hurling myself on the young body of the orange afternoons. Yes, yes, orange. I could wait for the phantom from the end of the corridor to come toward me, to rouse me, to take me by the hand, and for us to advance slowly, falteringly, in slow-motion, on the screen of a story in which I was turning into my formerly orphaned self with fierce, dark-circled eyes, slipping among patrols and horses on the edge of the dark water and the endless, black nights.

⋮ ⋮ ⋮

Had received the envelope Tuesday. Tuesday evening: was on the train. Wednesday I would encounter the old town's silent streets again. No one waited for me behind the windows. On Wednesday I met my mother's pain, my punished father's absence and shame, the illness of the one who was becoming my sister, the terrible illness that was corroding her skin, her hair, her romantically cadenced sadness. It was Wednesday that was hard for me—for them too, and for the roles waiting for us under the city's wide eyes. Eva and Dona had their sights trained on us; we had no more strength.

Thursday: picked up the courage to walk through the streets of the sloped town, where only yesterday I'd been a precarious little celebrity. I would need to meet Father so that I could talk to him. Every step through the autumn mud told me I should meet with him alone. Then I'd be able to say:

"When I was young, you avoided me and my overblown words.

187

You rejected my suspicions and reproaches. Great expectations sharpened the way I looked at things, and you must have sensed I'd catch you red-handed at the miserable games you played to readapt. You didn't have the strength for my kind of candor anymore—or reproaches or remorse either. And I was too young: I dreamed of cementing impossible moral absolutes, so I distanced myself from you. You were a man of duty, of course, so maybe our conflict was simply a generational affair, which would have made it remediable. Still, I saw you as an enemy. Sometimes I wanted to kill you—just like a real son. A lot of people feel that way during a teenage crisis. In the end, I saw your zeal as honest and stupid. I knew you were always completely upright. That was a reason for trust, maybe even pride, but in the battle against myself that I'd eventually lose, nothing but sarcasm would do."

Skidding, my rubber sole sank into the soft autumn clay. I gripped the auditorium's wall with my palms. Here, lifted in a whirlwind of applause, I had recited poems of assault and ardor to my fellow citizens' delight. I had been their hero, their resounding echo. Famished for spectacle and glory, my frenzy had taken this form, but I gave all that up the day I became capable of imagining what work would have been like in a salt mine. I suspected my Father of the discipline of submission and slavery. I thought he lacked fire and force. I was blind and young: it might have been fixed, oh, yes, our incompatibility might have been solved through minor adjustments—the confusions might have been cleared up.

"You didn't know that I was starting to stray into dangerous experiments, to see the unsuspected possibilities of the double game, to listen for anything off-key in the ambient arias—all those falsified false notes. I had discovered ways of using my weaknesses. Yes, I had discovered my weakness ... weaknesses ... I was no longer the hero: I had discovered the path of dissimulation; I was trying to make something of myself, proudly convinced that I could make *anything* of myself, and I was amazed and delighted, disgusted and subjugated by the farces I was preparing."

Narrowing, the street descended toward small houses with green, tapered roofs. Below, to the left, a shabby old abandoned building with elongated windows: the Jewish bathhouse. Before it, unharnessed horses chomped at the yellowing autumn grass, tethered beside carriage roofs, gray and damp. The street came to a halt in front of the former Jewish bath where another street curved up to the right. I was climbing up. At the crest, the two tiers of latticed windows: the high school.

It was quiet. Right now the little ants were listening to the schoolmaster ants and the police ants: they were waiting for recess, for the street—their brief dash toward freedom. Heard the grating of wheels behind me, the tossing of bells: a carriage.

—Greetings, young fellow, greetings! Let me know when you're leaving.

His cloth cap gleaming like leather, the little red-haired coachman grinned at me with his same old enormous teeth. He greeted me familiarly, and I wondered if he knew about my victories and entanglements.

Oh, Father, you weren't able to admit that I might be so impressionable that this man's greeting could rattle me. I hadn't the courage to show you this face of mine. From the very moment when I dared to tell you that any sister of mine needed to be named Eva or Dona, you let me understand— you wouldn't encourage my delayed reactions. Out of prudence for my life, you naturally wanted to shelter me from complications. You simply didn't have the courage to look at this gift of mine, even if it seemed negative from your point of view, so I tried to make myself the object of little prankish, premeditated games.

I was weak. I lacked tenacity. Maybe I lost my convictions too quickly, and imagined that this gave me the right to make anything of myself, anything at all. By the time the last "laurel"—legal adulthood—settled on my brow, I already knew: long ribbons of colored words unspooled from all the dirty streets, the moldy corners, and the filthy mouths. The words had blossomed, and they were proliferating, invading the wounded world. I couldn't be prey to the pairing of words anymore, as I had been, as you were; this was a good justification for my desire to serve only figures, hypotheses, numbers, methods, clear, rigorous, measurable results—at any cost. I despised you when you urged me toward a career of rhetorical speculations, of "ultimate learning"—that whole domain made of words. You had remained their slave. There was an instant when I could have loved you for such gratuitous staunchness. Only, if I'd been too young to defend myself from the glamour of words, my parent really couldn't have invoked any circumstance like that.

I was already separating myself from everything. You had no time to notice. You still owed me something, though, after a life that had tried you in so many ways because you were always ready to start over again: no matter where the thread had been broken, it would need to be retied. Father, you should have taught me that I had limitations, or that the cost of denying this is always too high. My alienation from myself ended by transforming me into a timorous beast, impoverished of beauty and innocence by too many old, innocent emotions. The shame I'm enduring now seems appropriate: it allies me with the lepers, who I can walk beside through trauma and silence, in defiance of the masquerade. The real education fondly reserved for my future only begins now.

The walls didn't answer. The small streets were slippery in the damp autumn morning. I was eager to speak to him. A lump in my throat seemed to keep me from breathing. *I was afraid of the enslavement that befalls overly correct people—starting from the night when I understood that you were listening to Mother without protesting, while she fed you examples of people who found time to arrange housing for*

190

themselves, and goods and benefits. I listened, afraid of everything that might happen, waiting for the aftermath of silence—the beginning of hesitation. My terror was no longer forceful; I wasn't invulnerable anymore. If we'd been able to get close to each other back then, maybe we could have helped each other, and I wouldn't have gone astray trying to return and reverse what seemed to be my destiny.

Hung onto the metal grillwork by my nails. A sense of suffocation … a longing to have my revenge on the father who'd forgotten to love me at the right time and on the Party idol I'd been ready to choose as a surrogate father, but who, like Father, had been overly occupied with all the principles, words, and conversions of the day. Like Father, he'd shut himself up till late at night in the peculiar municipal building. The gate of the Austrian town hall was just a few steps away. Wrote a furious, insulting note. Hurried to a newsstand. Bought an envelope and glued it shut. Then it was a matter of writing the name of the one from whom I was separating with a blunt pencil: His Excellency, Comrade Mehedinţi, from whom I was separating, and there was nothing to do then but hand it to the porter as if handing over an ultimatum. Didn't give him time to ask me questions. It was windy. Stomped through puddles, chilled me to the bone. Detoured around the stadium through the park full of bare, black trees. Sat down. Leaned against a wet, green backrest. A soft hand caught me around the waist.

—When did you come? Why didn't you stop by our place?

Ileana Mehedinţi was pale. She was wrinkled now, with tired eyes. My astonishment was impossible to articulate. There was nothing to do but offer silent reassurance: I hadn't forgotten her beautiful hands, or her voice that taught us to laugh again, or the way her Madonna's face pursued us through the lairs of the war. There was no way to manage the fleeting images of the past that overwhelmed words and thoughts. There was nothing to do but let myself be led by her warm, aging hand. Hadn't answered her. She remained silent. Neither of us speaking a word, I walked her to the front of the balconied house where she lived.

—Tell me, Ileana, would you still be able to do it today?—and out of pure friendship, out of the goodness of your heart? And you were so young, so ...

—I've thought of that myself, many times. I don't know. Maybe I wouldn't be able to anymore, maybe I wouldn't have the same strength or as much trust in others. I have no right to answer. Only the events could tell—if they repeated themselves. It's unknowable, and there's no longer any need for me to know.

Of course, she might have imagined that the question touched on the present as well, that it had been put intentionally, that I wanted to force her hand to help us now, too. But her eyes were wet, and she didn't suspect me of leading questions.

—I looked for your husband. I wanted to talk to him, and left him a note.

—Didn't you know, he's not there anymore? He was sent back to his old work from before the war—low-level work, as they say nowadays, at a carpentry workshop. It's better, in a way. He's been very sick for a long time. It's his heart. He wasn't getting any rest, day or night. If he wouldn't distress himself so much ... it makes him sick.

I found the strength to cover her mouth, to stroke her white hair. I was an imbecile who writes idiotic notes to people with heart disease and leaves them at the wrong address. I would have returned to the official building to pick up the note, but gave it up. It had gotten late. Mother was certainly waiting with lunch. There was no point in my adding tension there.

Presented myself to the porter toward evening. He recognized me, even though we'd only seen each other for an instant. He had the experience that goes with being an official watchman.

—This morning I left you an envelope for Comrade Virgil Mehedinți.

—Yes, you gave it to me.

—I'd like it back. I've learned he doesn't work here anymore.

—Well, I was telling you that earlier, but you ran off, so I put the envelope on view here, at the information window.

—Yeah, I was in a rush.

—Well, that's clear. Rushing around like that do you any good? He smiled roguishly. Anyhow, here's the envelope. Take it.

He bustled off to the window, came back and held out the envelope, which I was about to tear in half.

—What's up with that? First you write, then you rip? That's not very thoughtful. Better if you don't tear it up.

Written in crooked sprawl with a badly sharpened pencil, the name Virgil Mehedinți had been crossed out with a diagonal line in ink.

—Anyhow, the comrade just passed by here. He comes from time to time. He read the note. Left you an answer ... He thought you might come back to get it.

If, therefore, I should find myself at the best hotel in city B, it would be possible to allow myself the joke of asking if any letters had arrived for me. The receptionist would hand me a letter with my own name, addressed to Room 307, the room I'd just been assigned to. Then it wouldn't be possible that the preceding resident coincidentally had the same name as me, but it would seem that the previous tenant and I had common acquaintances, since the note left for him would have been signed by a good friend of my father's ...

I didn't have any other choice, so I opened the envelope: "You've gone rather overboard. Stop by my place in six months. V.M."

Without wanting to, I'd rolled six twice, in two different throws of the dice. Should we find these coincidences *interesting*? Perhaps yes, if the appearance of the event truly concerns or *interests* us. The fact that Father's arrest coincided with Mehedinți's dismissal was a matter of interest to me, and I was glad to have my deadlines, occupations, and responsibilities.

Now I knew that someone would be waiting for me in six months time. I could let myself leave, again, at the mercy of any night train.

⋮ ⋮ ⋮

It was probably April when the train took me again. Left at night, arrived at dawn in a dirty, deserted station. There were three hours before being able to proceed. It was cold. Went into the waiting room. Huddled near their luggage, a few passengers slept on wooden benches. Numb from traveling, propped my feet on a bench like the others. The dull light stung my eyes. Saw the remains of a book down at the other end of the bench, by my shoes. Pulled it toward me. Pages were missing. Someone had probably forgotten it. The fragment began on page 58 and ended at 91. The hero, it seems, wanted to get to a secluded place where he would meet an important character. Proper nouns were not mentioned: perhaps they had been mentioned at the beginning, but were no longer being used. It was necessary to cross a body of water. The hero had found a boat. The night before the crossing, he came down with a curious illness the locals called "fog sickness." The young man was shivering and trembling; he had fever and talked about himself in the third person, as if narrating someone else's story. The meeting could only take place at specific times, over great intervals. Anyone who missed one meeting couldn't count on living long enough to see another. It seems that the hero had a meeting with his own self, and that a kind of retribution or resolution would take place at this distant spot. The fragment ended on page 91, just when it was starting to get interesting.

The waiting room had filled with other passengers. Many people were standing—propped between suitcases—the noise had increased. Looked at the clock: there was another hour to go. Stretched out my hand for the book again and bumped into someone's shoulder. The bench was occupied. Had dozed off. Went out onto the platform, then behind the station. The bus came shortly afterward. We crowded aboard. The driver was ripping tickets from a book. Managed to find a seat. Our route crossed several villages and small towns. We traveled for two hours. Arrived at a small fishing village. From here we could cross to the other bank by boat in the afternoon. The bus had emptied in front of a place called The Village Buffet. Looked at those disembarking passengers. Judging by the way they moved and by their parcels of food and necessities, it looked like we would make the next portion of the journey to the prison together, too. The boat was leaving at noon.

The muddy water ran backward, ground by the boat's paddles. A powerful smell of gas came from the motor. Had eaten nothing. The movement of the boat, the smell of gasoline, and people's flapping clothes were making me dizzy. Sat down on one of the benches. The travelers were sharing disaster stories: the biographies of the prisoners they had come to visit. A damp wind struck one's cheeks.

Had prepared a speech. Would assure him that misfortune had brought us closer together, and that the errors and injustices couldn't last much longer. At the end of his suffering, he would find an honorable place in society, once again, and another son, too. My voice would be kind and reassuring: it would all be nothing but love. The boat bobbed and danced. Leaned against the rail, closed my eyes. Somewhere close, a piano lilted through a speaker.

—That's Handel's Chaconne in G Major.

The wind whispered near my ear: it had the voice of my sister, resurrected from the smoke in which she'd vanished. In a moment, I'd feel the silk of her hands to assure myself she was alive, her voice would be real, to assure myself of being alive.

—You know, I'm a music professor.

Disguised, on this damp boat? But there was nothing to be afraid of; it was just a lady passenger, a music professor.

Didn't budge. Didn't open my eyes. Had heard nothing, seen nothing ... there was nothing but to be the essence of patience ... expectation. Might she disappear suddenly, the same way she came—out of smoke—as if she had never existed? It was too late. After managing to turn toward the left, to open my eyes again, there was no longer anyone there—a delusion, then, and only the piano coming from the speaker and the murky water waving.

Viewed from the side, the woman looked tired: hair hidden under an ugly, blackened scarf, tied under the chin, like an old lady. Her gray overcoat hung long, straight, and wide as a cloak. She probably wore slacks: there was a scrap of material that stretched between the hem of her overcoat and the top of her work boots. Didn't look at her anymore. Then she addressed me: a familiar voice, a very well-known voice ... ah, yes, from the children's broadcast. Red, soft, puffy cheeks, wrinkled, double chin, thick neck, and yet still, yes, she still had something childish about her, something tender, naughty, and appalling. Glanced at her lively, mobile, green eyes. She was talking, explaining herself.

We got off on the other bank. She came close to me and sat down.

—And what exactly did the friend you're visiting commit?

—How can I put it ... it would take some explaining. Actually, he stole a pair of shoes from a store.

My eyes opened wide. To me, interest in such curiosities seemed possible. She was waiting for this, to tell her story. Director of a school until several months ago, Professor Tiberiu Covalschi had many shortcomings, and he turned out to be a kleptomaniac. The shoe adventure had been attributed to this condition. There couldn't be any other explanation. They'd been colleagues at a special school: the pupils were dignitaries' children, and Covalschi had used his position to terrorize his subordinates.

—It's not like that anymore. There are other children at our school now, too. But since then I've been left with a kind of . . .

Unable to find the word, she gestured with her hand to chase away the confusion.

—You're probably indebted to him if you've come this far.

—No, no, not at all. On the contrary—he always behaved badly with me. He did me a lot of harm, as he did to others.

They had gotten close, however, at one point: she had a perpetual need for advice, for someone else's understanding, since her mother had disappeared into an asylum for the mentally ill . . . yeah, the old lady had suffered a lot: she had seen her husband killed before her eyes after he had been forced to dig his own grave. Maybe Covalschi wasn't all that bad, only deranged: after everything that had happened since that miserable night when he'd terrorized her, she believed he was sick . . . he had made her fear those privileged kids, those cars that had brought them to school . . . even now, when some limousine happened to stop in front of the school, even though it was rare— and, actually, many people have cars now—she'd begin to tremble the way she used to, yes, she continued having trouble managing the children, the classroom, the classes full of kids who sensed her weaknesses, who blackmailed her and put her in compromising positions. They were terrorizing her—what more could you say?—that was the word. The bags under her eyes were twitching by now. Her eyes had turned gray. Day was passing into dusk. A great, postponed terror dilated itself; she was trembling. Her voice had lost its clarity. It wheezed, deepened.

—Then why did you come here? Still, it seems that . . .

—You know, we were kind of friends. I'm attached to the memories.

Little, white balls of foam had blossomed in the corners of her thin, cracked lips.

—Actually, he's alone. Yes, that's it. He has nobody. I'm alone too. I wanted to see someone, anyone, to leave home . . . I couldn't stand it anymore, and I think it will please him. I'm also on the way to see Mama, far away in the mountains, at the asylum.

She couldn't add much more. People were lining up. We rose. The woman had been focused on her confessions, which was fine with me, since she hadn't asked about the reason for my visit.

The hour approached. We had to climb a hill. There was a long, brick barracks on the peak. We couldn't see the canal embankments that the prisoners were being forced to build; they were probably far away, and the dormitories where the prisoners would have to be brought were far away too. At noon, right after our arrival, a list had been drawn up with the names of the detainees we were trying to see, and someone had brought it up to the barracks. It was almost evening now. The women were crowding to get to the front; the convoy's impatience had grown.

We remained in the barracks for another hour, in a state of expectation. Naturally, it would have been best to avoid being in the same series with Madam (or Miss) Professor. Her name fell at the end of the alphabet, mine at the start. The patrol called my name among the first. Hadn't expected the names of the visited being called, and not the opposite, but Tiberiu Covalschi was in the first series of eight as well, so the professor was near me at the wire grill that separated us from the detainees. The door opened. Gray caps in hand, heads and beards shaved, they entered as they were called.

We were separated by no more than a spider's web: it was clear that the man across from me didn't have rich, curly hair anymore. His lenses had gotten bigger. The glass: thick, spiraled, focalized. Maybe this frightened me. He smiled. A wave of scorching heat came over me, but everything that had to be said was clear in my mind. Had all my words already prepared at the moment the signal was given to begin talking.

Opened my mouth, but to my right, someone else spoke before me—whistling through his teeth.

—You cretin. You idiotic woman.

Felt compelled to look at Covalschi, a pale, boney dwarf with twisted lips, large eyes pressed into a heavy, rickety head, hunched forward. There was a weak, livid light and no way to unglue myself from the image. That went on for a few moments till a faint came over me ...

Woke in the morning, the next day or the day after that, in a peasant's house on a hard, clean bed. My bolster had been watched over by the lady professor with the "big heart," the master of the house told me and "all thanks was due" to her and not himself.

Returned to the University, without accomplishing the meeting that was the reason for my trip. Therefore, my other plans went astray as well. The faint had made it impossible to leave for home, for my planned meeting with Virgil Mehedinți.

Five months or five years later, Father visited me—reestablished, or rehabilitated as they say. He was ready to work again with all his strength. He explained to me that he had been implicated in "the Mehedinți deviation"—by no means a matter of personal guilt ... association with an old friend who was forced out of leadership ... too highly valued, though, to be found guilty of non-existent illegalities. Vulnerable from several directions, acolytes of flimsier positions had been targeted. But it wasn't like other calamities of the moment, he added. Some had been condemned to do hard time or had even been executed ... it's a difficult period. It'll pass ... we've been through so much, we'll get through this too ... we've got to be ready to begin again, to stay alive. He hadn't given up the grade-school rhetoric.

Had graduated, then, and was dreaming of selling tickets at a movie theater in Africa. Left for the worksite. Had little news from home. Only returned to the old town when they celebrated Donca's coming of age. Was already working at the large new factory in the capital. My afternoons were hurried, full—they vanished, rapidly.

Declined the music professor's invitations to chat, except once every couple of months. It was a matter of perpetually listening to her confessions: she considered me a friend, poor thing, and she went on complaining of loneliness, though she was very active and always falling into complications with new and old acquaintances—which turned into dilemmas, and she wouldn't abandon them at any cost— and she always complained about the school, the little terrors.

For me, it was hard to find the smallest scrap of suitable advice.

⁂

Really, the light vibrated differently then. Mornings from another time. The starched shirt collar fluttered like the stiff wing of a bird. My wish was to be flying in a fairground ride in the middle of summer, up, up, high as can be, almost to the sky. The steel rods would scream and screech, hit the peak, then whir whizzing down, striking the wooden floor. Setting out on the stairs: every time the void in my stomach rose and fell.

We saw each other again in the afternoon. Then the evening wind chilled her shoulders. She trembled. The windows blew open with a sound of wooden applause. Together, in the deserted corridor, crushed under a heavy, white ceiling and the little room's lingering sky: the same gentle nightmare for daydreaming girls. The smoke of night chased hesitations away. We were caught in a bewildered embrace of orphans, and it couldn't last.

Everything was the same as before for a while: nothing had happened—this was proven in everyone's cordial interactions, with neighbors from the office and apartment, with former classmates, former relatives, former professors, former wives of some former pals, with the punctual Armenian woman who would bring me her sly little smile, and with the chief engineer's blonde woman. No one reproached my hypocrisy. The spy, Mişa, followed me without gusto; the flautist visited me between concerts. Eyes following me perpetually, the girl with rough hair and big eyes continued to smile at me.

We would meet in the corridor as if nothing had happened, sometimes having time to joke, without really acknowledging each other and without forcing recognition. Several months after her peculiar departure from the factory, I noticed her absence, however. She had a kind of codified smile, a timid gait, pale hands, and—yes, it was only natural to miss her. She had left with excessive discretion, and hadn't seemed disturbed: a colleague visited the factory where she had been transferred and confirmed that she looked well, charming as always, on the quiet side, and still young. This addition, "and still young" sounded strange: a consolation that seemed like a reproach.

For a while now, the afternoons had been boring. Got rid of the flautist, gave up the blonde too, and no longer smiled at the woman who worked in the same office as me. Closed myself up in solitude for several months ... several months or more, it's not clear to me. Meanwhile, Donca had become a university student, and she seemed to need more money. Quite cheerfully, she asked me for small sums each week. Surprised by my sedentary and lethargic moods, she became worried and suggested spending New Year's Eve with a group of her classmates from the Spanish Department. There were a lot of nice-looking but very young girls chirping around her. Didn't think it would be possible to win their confidence. In the end, agreed to attend a "preview" with my sister, a kind of pre-party meant to help those who didn't already know each other.

Donca stopped by to pick me up. She was wearing a big black beret that looked like a wig. The way it contrasted with her blond complexion and blue-green eyes suited her perfectly. She caught me staring at her, and ripped off her hat and started flouncing her long black hair, which stopped me, dumbfounded, as if seeing her for the first time. Then she rushed to calm me down.

—Don't be scared. It's my real hair. You can pull it. See! I dyed it, and everyone says it looks great. Finally, a veritable Dolores Ibárruri, to go with our department.

Silencing faint echoes, the name struck me. Donca had a carefree way of referring to the illness that had secluded her—or so our parents maintained. Still, I saw no sign of those past crises, either because of her ability to hide them or my lack of subtlety.

Naturally, I had to ask, "Where's Fred?" Donca shrugged her shoulders in a way that suggested, "He'll be there too." She already seemed disinterested in her fiancé, for whom she'd confronted our confused parents. To me, her fiancé had seemed attractive enough and a decent guy. On the awkward side, it's true, but really taken with the charms of the girl who found him "extraordinarily profound," "extraordinarily cultured," and "extraordinarily sensitive"—which said more about her than him.

In any event, found myself in an elegant house, with many rooms that were connected by sliding doors. The carpets were rolled up, the lights turned low, and people broke off into groups or couples. Animated by the atmosphere, Donca kept inciting everyone to dance. Her own body vacillated unexpectedly, as if she felt herself in danger. Eventually she withdrew into a corner—near an unknown man, while her fiancé was occupied with the tape recorder. Naturally, the middle-aged guy who was courting her kept pouring her fresh drinks—and she emptied them while he told crude jokes in a very loud voice. He was trying to cancel their difference in age, and he was succeeding marvelously with the girls around, who found his tough libertine type *très jeun*, just what they liked. The other girls envied Donca, the favorite of the moment. The two of them got up again to dance. They entered each other's arms impatiently; he took advantage of their closeness and the dark with both hands. He was a slimly built man, a bit over forty, with a lightly pockmarked face, thick hair over a strongly lined brow, narrow shoulders, big hands, and a youthful laugh. He moved lightly, bending his partner's body.

—Are you really her brother?

Two sticky hands grabbed me by the shoulders, turned me around, and pulled me into a slow dance. My partner was trying to steer me toward the other room. Let myself be directed by her and wound up near the tape recorder. Raising her arms and bust, my partner danced on tiptoe. She had slipped off her shoes, like Donca and the other girls. Even Donca's gentleman was sliding around in socks. We stopped near the door. The melody had ended. The girl leaned against me. She had twined her arms around my neck, pulled me down near her ear: "That man's a forestry engineer. He has a lot of success with the ladies. Married, of course. Has a very chic stupidity. Women love it. As a matter of fact, you older guys have an advantage over these boys who are just too young and inexperienced."

And indeed, as the engineer dexterously palpated his prey, it was impossible not to notice several rings on his long, bony fingers. On the other hand, his charm had it's uses as it seemed to have rubbed off on me and attracted this young girl, though you couldn't call me young anymore. Only laziness kept me from taking advantage of this disadvantage. My dance partner exhibited a dry, direct humor; she was easily approachable and playfully, provocatively elastic. She kept brushing her breasts against me, and I was ready to make a pass when Donca's fiancé showed up beside us, hair on end, bottle in hand, and eyes red with fury.

Unbraiding her black hair, Donca had stretched herself out on the floor and her low voice made itelf heard: "I can no longer, bathed in your languors, O waves ... *De vos langueurs, ô lames ... en vuestro languidez* ... Nor cross the pride of pennants and of flags, Nor swim past prison hulks' hateful eyes ... *Je ne puis plus* ... Drunk with love's acrid torpors ... I can no longer ... *Ya no puedo* ... sail ..." She was spouting her favorite verses and rocking unsteadily like a boat about to face the storm. She'd let herself go too far. Scandal would soon erupt.

The girl's arms pulled me again. Then, she took off her stockings and showed them to me, holding one in each hand like trophies. Her bare, white feet twitched to the music, which blasted so loudly the room seemed to shake—a feeling like screws being twisted into the back of my neck. My head was heavy. Clenched my hands, my nails, so as not to fall. Slipped near the wall. No one saw me. They were all overcome by fervid, nervous expectation. Made it to the hall. Tugged at the sleeves of my overcoat. At that moment, the girl grabbed me by the buttons.

—You're unfair to yourself. You're not getting any younger. Why don't you want? Why don't …?

She had nestled, full of warmth, under my coat. She was uncovering herself like an enchanting, helpless child with sad hot eyes. Stroked her cheeks, then her lashes, and promised to come back in an hour.

—If you run away, you'll get old. It's stupid to grow old.

She scratched the wall with her nails. With warm eyes fatigued by longing, she remained behind the door. She had offered me an invitation to a night of healing: the girl would have shattered the courage it took to confront a new bout of insomnia. Climbed down the steps, wanting all the while to return. Came back to myself in the freezing air outside. Sank into the snow. Thought about Donca and wondered why we'd never managed to talk together for more than ten minutes at a stretch: she was always confused, distracted, exalted. Hadn't done my duty to her, either. Recalled the evening when she had celebrated her graduation from high school, and remembered myself too—myself back at that age—preoccupied exclusively with my own flounderings.

⁝ ⁝ ⁝

My parents were living in a new apartment, and through the open windows, evening could be heard far away, beyond the hills. The young people were dancing. Their embraces seemed daring for the time. They were kidding around in a familiar way. Hands joined. Their lips sometimes seemed to meet by chance. Didn't notice any trace of Donca's previous illness; on the contrary, she seemed perfectly integrated with people her age. She talked loudly and a lot; she moved lightly. She had a provocative way of twining her arms around each new partner. Mama took care to quiet the perplexities I didn't have:

—You have to understand her. She exaggerates. She has complexes from the things that happened. Anyhow, for a girl ...

This new vocabulary startled me. One could only nod stupidly, not having suspected her of such modern investigations and understandings, which were evidently dangerous because they stretched too far in the direction of error and indulgence. But there was no time to sweat the small stuff. I was waiting for a certain guest, and when I heard, from the next room, that his wife was taking her leave of a nurse, who was our guest, I understood: there was no chance he'd appear. Back then, in the year when Donca was finishing school, if I'd had time to watch her closely and had found a way to get closer to her, it might still have been possible to do something for her, just as it might have been possible to do something for me if the guest that I'd been waiting for had come. Simple, gratuitous suppositions, both.

Came back home for Donca's first engagement, having been urgently summoned—and again, when things had taken a turn for the worse. Winter had raised snow banks in the streets. Allowed myself then to look for the guest who hadn't come to the summer party. The truth is, my visits weren't for the sake of "winning back a sister for myself," as my parents used to say. They had wanted this daughter and never tired of starting over with her again; but my goal was to find the guest who had been absent on that summer night when Donca was finishing high school. Meanwhile, people had singled me out as a "defective model," a shell of myself, what was left over after an "imbalance" freed me, and my peculiar search took advantage of the prevailing impression.

It wasn't easy to find him, but in the end he received me. He was in charge again, although the five years hadn't passed. He had a suitable office and the same responsibilities on top of new ones. Any normal person would have been terrified to approach a high official freely, and only a madman would have been able to aggressively approach a man whose wife was dying.

—You probably know the reason for my visit.

—To see me.

—And to apologize for the delay. Five years aren't five minutes or even five months. You once arranged a meeting when I wasn't able to appear. That probably doesn't put me in good standing. You're not a person to summon someone without having a serious reason.

He raised his eyebrows, but to my surprise he quickly entered into the tone tacitly proposed by me. The apparent rebellion hadn't put him off.

—Indeed. Back then, I called you for something important. As proven by the fact that I had granted myself six months, in order to be able to present myself with all of my bases covered. Given my circumstances back then, it was an act of defiance, out of pride. Things have resolved themselves in the meantime. The conversation no longer has an objective. Your father's suffering went on for more than six months, I acknowledge, but ...

—Since I came ...

—I wanted to tell you that your father is not guilty.

—Which is to say, less guilty than it appeared.

—It could be said that way, too. But I wanted to tell you that he's really not guilty.

—Six months or five years of deliberation were necessary for this?

—I felt you were rather susceptible. I didn't have the right to affirm his innocence till he'd been freed. If I'd done anything else, you might have easily slipped into the role of the victim—and with a certain pleasure.

—To one like him, it would have been possible to forgive any weakness. And that was evident.

—But it wasn't clearly a matter of some guilt or weakness—but something else. If friendship is a sign of weakness, then the word itself has an entirely different meaning than the one we're used to.

The moment had come to let myself lean back in that imperial armchair. It was proper, however, to keep quiet for a while. He understood, and when he believed that the ritual allowed him to continue the performance, he spoke again.

—Your father didn't tell you anything?

—I didn't ask him. He said a word or two. He isn't giving up the role of victor, so I can't offend him with the questions I have. At one time, I was ready to lay a heap of affection at his feet, but he would have seen that as suspicious.

—Don't you consider yourself a victor? he asked me, heaving irritably on his throne.

—Then he really should have spoken to you, he went on. I don't like you. You must know, I-DO-NOT-LIKE-YOU. Your father suffered a fall back then as a result of an inability.

—Of course. He was barely initiated in the strategies and tactics of "abilities." It wasn't easy. A former bank clerk can't change into something else easily.

He looked at me, like an ogre, and stood up with clenched fists. I thought he would hit me, but he paced around the room and the soft rugs seemed to absorb his fury.

—I'm using "inability" in a completely different sense that you want to understand. After finishing the school we sent him to, your father received, as you know, the mission of working in the justice system.

There he received anonymously signed tips about abuses committed by people with important positions. He contacted me, asking if informing higher authorities was the right thing to do. The only person who could resolve this matter was a dangerous individual, a comrade who had abused his own power. Nevertheless, I advised your father to go to him, and I felt responsible for what happened. I didn't know that there were things about me, too, in that denunciation. In his exaggerated correctness, your father didn't tell me. He wanted to be principled. That cost him his freedom. He wanted to dissociate himself from what he understood was going on, and he took the initiative, in the negative sense.

—What would have been the positive sense?

—In point of fact, your father delayed a certain minor payment. We don't live in heaven. We wouldn't have anything to do there. The person to whom your father presented himself assured him that measures would be taken. He gave him freedom of action. False freedom, naturally. Your father hurried to react, and, as I told you, ineptly, provocatively. They stopped him, isolating him in a jail cell. That's about it.

Yes, that's about it. I was ready to ask about the more serious cases that Comrade Father had mentioned: condemnations to do hard time, great show trials, executions. There was no sense in that. In these imperial armchairs, in this upholstered room, and before the new chief who was the old boss, the discussion stopped exactly when it should have. We had to be quiet, take our time thinking, look at each other cautiously. And that's what we did.

—I'd like to ask you something too: is there any truth to what was said about the crisis you went through?

—Everything. Nothing of what's said was exaggerated enough. Not enough was imagined, and I'd say that it wasn't a big deal. It would take too long to confirm every detail. Anyhow, this meeting remains an honor for me. I have no right to abuse . . .

—Indeed, I'm hurrying to stop by the hospital. If you like, we can talk in the car.

—No, the car goes too quickly.

He looked at me and smiled.

—Good, we'll walk.

On the wide stairs and then on the street, everybody who saluted the leader saluted me. At the exit from the former Austrian town hall—now the activists' office building—the porter looked at me as if I were the crown prince. I didn't have anything else to discuss with the authority who accompanied me, nor did I want to elaborate: the only solution was to imagine that I was talking with Ileana and not her comrade husband.

—You had an exact intuition, Comrade Mehedinți, imagining me as someone predisposed to sliding into the role of the defeated. I feel like a newborn. Do I have any more chances to lie, which is to say, to defend myself? May I ask how the unexpected identification took place?

—Don't worry. Only tell me what you want. My so-called intuition about your character was something I had figured out. It seemed unnatural that a young person who was finishing high school wouldn't be able to close a door properly.

—Ah, yes, I tired quickly, too quickly. Gestures didn't follow me. I remained behind them. I believe that if I'd been left alone or maybe if I'd let myself simply vegetate in some room, I would have forgotten how to write, how to count: I would have forgotten my name and desires. To avoid total vegetation, I imposed obligations on myself in a perpetual panic; to go to the office, to work, to bed alternately with other women—a kind of habit—to shave, to check my address book daily and call someone, to remember my own voice and remember the faces of friends, colleagues, an aunt, a flautist who I was expecting to see after a concert so I could go to bed with her but whose features I forgot as soon as she left. Only, this isn't really what I'd like to tell your husband. I'd like to ask if he'd allow me to speak in a public square, to confess in front of a crowd.

The words were for Ileana, in fact. Ileana kept quiet. Her husband kept quiet. I kept quiet.

—I'd let you speak.

—You're relying on their indifference. It would be dangerous to count too much on the indifference of the masses. Their indifference is limited. All their possibilities are limited. Don't count too much ...

Got frightened, almost screamed, though there wasn't anything to be heard as he walked by me side—tall and calm.

—I'm not counting on indifference. I know it's a matter of environment, not absolute ... something transitory, peripheral.

—A matter of environment? Peripheral you say? The mass of comrades gather great mountains of objects, clench heaps under their poor plastic jackets while forgetting that they produce these objects as well, and similarly, they're blind to how they themselves dwindle in prefabricated dwellings, rarely self-reflecting, and when they do it's reduced to a "functional" vocabulary, as they say, which means woodenly, in fact. I'm no better than they are. The perpetual chill, disgust with myself and with them, the standardized, uniform, sweaty faces, the roars of the partisans: all these things have gnawed at the weak fabric of *my* being too. I can't be blamed for having inherited the characteristics of a parent who's capable of making perpetual efforts to seem the victor—over and over again. The defeated victor, I mean. The real father has nothing in common with the hypothetical one: the one who couldn't alter and modify himself or his senses after returning from the crematoriums and the great bazaar of blood; I mean, the one forever afflicted by what they had done to him and his daughters, and by the kind of person he'd made of himself—the one who's only free now to scatter himself in the flames of a new pyre.

Would you allow me to talk to them—those who might want to listen—about this hypothetical parent of mine?

Ileana wasn't answering. I was captured by my own defiant words. It was better not to look around. The sick man listened silently and made no reply.

—Maybe you'd allow me to say anything whatsoever, in order to prove that anyone can say anything, but then you'd install some articulate militant, a dime a dozen in these heroic times, on a platform nearby: a militant with the same qualities that I once possessed. He'd point toward this city in a sweeping gesture, which was formerly so miserable, but modernized now: with hot water, cold water, theaters, institutes, industrial complexes, the population doubled, and the water of the river suffocated by lye and sulfur. I mean, in school I acquired a solid understanding of the theory of the typical, of the representative, and I once wanted to kill a poor, typical, not at all heroic victim of our paltry confusion and panting subordination. You know, my defeat is personal, a failure that regards only me. When that militant denounces me, the victory will be everyone's—a synthesis of the great collective triumphs. Statistically I don't count: I am an anomaly, and the appearances of anomalies are not always interesting—it depends on who selects the results.

Mehedinți's big hands rested oppressively on my shoulders. He looked at me severely.

—We're going to Ileana. Don't tell her about our discussion. Look, I have the strength to sustain losses.

Yes, we were going to see Ileana. We were in the park. Monica's case would have interested Ileana: the unfortunate day when I wanted to kill an innocent piano teacher. I rested my hand on a snow-covered bench where, not long ago, I had met Ileana Mehedinți. Meanwhile, Comrade Mehedinți had carried on ahead, bored by my silence and slowness. It was imperative for me to go see her—although I didn't have the strength for something like that. That woman who had rocked me as a baby was now helpless as a child, weighted with the presentiment of death.

I should have told Comrade Virgil Mehedinţi that, like him, I loved her too. Her voice from long ago still lingers in my ears.

⋮ ⋮ ⋮

In the end I managed to chase away the phantom from the head of the stairs. The gaze that had returned from the other world to save me had disappeared. It obsessed me no more. In the early hours of the day, I follow the same routine: I manage to drag myself into the convoys that press onward from all sides; I arrive on the hill of the same eternal morning—the cigarette smoke, voices, steps, telephones, typewriters, and the rustle of skirts and tracing paper seem like the hushed whispers of forest rising from the mists of dawn. I take the round white tablet, drink coffee, and begin to feel. The rheumatic pain drips slowly through my bones, starting at the heel, moving through my knees and spine, and then back down again to my heel. I'm blessed with the misfortune of seeing Mişa, who follows my every move, which is what he was trained to do.

For a long time I've had a letter in my briefcase that I've put off opening—from before Donca turned into a slut: the letter of a whore, who finally found courage to become one. Even though she's my sister, it doesn't horrify me. On the contrary, it might bring us closer together because, after all, I was as bad as a whore—I mean, who isn't? What the hell. I'm still attracted to young people, I want to understand them, even if it's hard for me to adopt their frankness, their hunger for the present, the effectiveness of their affective operations . . . no, affective isn't the right word. I was therefore afraid to open her letter, because she wrote it when she didn't yet realize what she was becoming: she was in a stupid phase when shamelessness

212

kept feeding on illusions. She's going through another phase now, the equally disgusting phase of reconsideration. She's picked up her university studies again, grinds away day and night, and doesn't leave the house. Tomorrow, I'll see her among the leading students in her class and a model of morality—which will be nothing less than jaw dropping, no?

One day I got a call from the music professor I sometimes met—to listen to new stories and complaints. Her desire to cry was inexhaustible, and I realized that she only wanted to seem sentimental and stupid to make fun of those who wanted to torment her, and this game contained hidden, masochistic pleasures: to be blunt, the joys of humiliation. This idea interested me, actually, and, using her wonderful voice, she read out some sugary letters to a newly besieged beau. I began to suspect that the letters had been treated with special effects, pushed with verisimilitude to a point where pathos swelled to revenge. She was also writing children's stories. They were a kind of transposition of her failure to mate, played out in the realm of bunny and squirrel, sparrow and bird fancier.

Anyhow, she begged me to stop by her place. She needed to participate in a school assembly, and wanted to make a tape recording—on a certain borrowed machine—of a story of hers that would be broadcast that evening on the "Goodnight, Kids" show through the intervention of one of her former colleagues, a certain Tiberiu Covalschi, who was also a former teacher (with the rank of professor), former principal, and former jailbird. I'd given up trying to tell her that her messes were a complete embarrassment—especially at her age: in the past, she'd begin to cry, declare that she was sick and alone and that her old mother was mad and far away. In the end, I just shrugged my shoulders.

Once, when she had infuriated me, I shouted at her that if she'd chosen the way of "amour," it should have been her duty to learn something about men and couples, from her countless humiliations, as well as the related strategies for coupling and manipulation. She had a fit of hysteria right away. It horrified and disarmed me. Out of fury, I yelled that she was fat and ugly—but then I saw her as if for the first time: an ordinary woman, neither ugly nor beautiful, completely average. It might have been a good bet to say that she would have done better as a regular housewife with several sniveling kids tugging at her skirts. She had lively eyes, a pleasant face, and a relatively well-made, navy-blue dress with a little white collar. At that moment, I understood that everything I knew about her had kept me from actually seeing her.

My surprise was even greater when, after she had calmed down, she said: "don't you realize, my vitality can only be tempered by the multiplication of defeats? Tiredness, misery, tears! Happiness would amount to nothing for a person like me. You need much more strength for the role of the unhappy woman." The surprises didn't stop there. I spotted her on a busy street several days later. She was creeping past the passersby in a state of total negligence, hair in disarray, great crocodile tears flowing down her fat, childish cheeks—dirty streams of continuous tears.

In any event, I didn't promise that I'd make the recording, but our discussion . . . her entreaty had made revulsion rise in my throat, and just like that, suddenly, I opened Donca's letter. She had run away to the mountains three months ago, following a certain forestry engineer, Dan Vasilescu. I'd had the misfortune of seeing the conqueror at the dance party my sister had dragged me to.

The letter was full of exclamation marks and ellipses. Amid so much blank space I recognized a few words that might have been the professor's: "The cigarette butts remain in the ashtray on the table. The other ashtray is still on the bed. Both remind us that we exist: the madness of our merging is not just a dream." She thought I was the only one who would understand her. She told me how the engineer called her Dona and carried her around the room in his arms, beseeching her: Dona, Dona, Dona. She even signed the letter with this borrowed name.

Workroom noises broke over me in waves. Staggered upstairs to the boss's office. This former classmate was an amiable guy. Though very young, he'd worked seriously and advanced rapidly. He'd claimed an enviable position for himself. As on other occasions, he seemed to understand what was happening to me. Left the building, wandered the streets, and stopped off at the professor's.

The key was under the mat, as she'd said. Hadn't ever seen her place in such a state of filth and disorder. A little pigsty, suffocated by too many things, all mixed together. Found all kinds of books and letters. I even received a visit from a pretender to the resident's hand whom she'd fished out of the personals. After several hours, I had become part of the chaos of rags and words, destined, it seemed, to remain there forever, to communicate with the dust—the stinking leftovers of the cell. I understood then that I'd kill her. The thought wasn't completely new. I knew (and in moments of discouragement had often repeated to myself) that I had no right to judge her, that I was, in fact, a kind of "brother"—panting in the sludge of subterranean caves, humbled, silenced, accomplices. We had no right to judge people like ourselves. Our common apathy and sleep wore so many faces, and her falsifying, false agitation was just one side of our complex figure—and who knows how much more wretched it was? So now I felt a need to kill her at any cost—as if I could destroy our collective culpabilities, our compromises and degradation: the dysfunction or dementia of soiled, abased, betrayed good intentions. I would poison, strangle, or shoot her with the sounds trickling from the tape recorder, and I would commit suicide myself, accompanied by *Summertime* from a black woman's thick throat.

The doctors took this shock most seriously. I hadn't killed her.

Instead, I'd gone quietly out of her room before she returned.... I climbed down the twisted, narrow stairs and wandered the streets till late. It's true that I was missing from the office and from home for a while, but that can happen to anyone. It didn't seem important to me that I would sometimes bring my hand hurriedly to my throat. It was an inoffensive tic, in fact, and they helped me get rid of it quickly. The investigators (the doctors and others) asked me how the movie theater was and if there were really so many apples down by the seashore. *Of course Death isn't waiting. Give Death a kiss from me*, I told the Sisters of Charity, *she rocked me so many times ... Look, she leans heavily on my shoulder. She shook my hand till my fingers cracked, and then smiled at me.* It was for the best, I knew, that I now remained alone. In the course of things, they asked me why I'm always cold. How do I explain the cold, this perpetual chill? Why should it seem that when my workmate laughs he'll freeze in place, showing his teeth? Why do I feel fear and cold in crowds, when the agitation produces heat? Of course, friction should produce heat—where in hell does all this cold come from? Continuous damp cold—where the devil ... Poor inquisitors and guards, they asked me many things, but kept returning to this: Why does everything look frozen to me—hands, hair, lips, all ready to snap off with cold and all around, cold, sleep, and inescapable frost. In the end, they took a letter out of a drawer. No, it wasn't from Donca. They showed me the envelope. I recognized it. I knew that letter by heart. They had found it in the coat I'd surrendered when I entered the hospital. It was from the professor, Liliana Zubcu, the Captain's wife. "Mr. Engineer, I am the mother of the girl you ruined ..." That's how indiscreetly—no, no, indignantly—the letter began. "Her pure soul cannot endure this violation. After the death of her father, she placed her trust in you, a guardian angel, she believed." I listened to the doctors' indig ... no, indiscreet reading, and hadn't the strength to protest against this invasion of my coat's lining. "How could you do such a thing? Do you know what it means to rip out a girl's unborn fetus? Do you know what happened to her body and soul? And the danger? The abortion is now followed by prison, but she told you nothing, nothing. She took the risk completely alone. You didn't love my daughter enough, and you will never be free of this guilt!" Mrs. Liliana Zubcu was right: I didn't love that sublime sister enough. I cannot love enough, it's true. The guilt she's talking about is real: I carry the burden in myself. I didn't want to answer any of the doctors' questions about the letter. It's not their business to get into my coat's lining. Eventually they accepted my silence and told me to get some rest.

The hospital authorities maintained that there was a way out. I should change environments, get out of the house, go out for walks, chose another place to work—outside, in the fresh air. I should be patient, very patient. In any case, I should not stay in one place for too long, nor is there any reason ...

This miserable wooden bench is full of snow. Only a few green stripes are visible, as if it were a dead crocodile caged in fallen snow. So there isn't any point: I mustn't stay long in the same place.

⋮ ⋮ ⋮

They proved to be understanding, and they really worked miracles with their science. The effects appeared quickly. In less than three months I was another person—or rather the person I had been before. I am grateful to my father for saving me from the common room, where I might have seen all sorts of macerated faces, which is how they looked sometimes in the corridor or the courtyard, making speeches and waving their hands, blinking horribly, bringing their hands to their hair, their throats with a full range of coughs, tics, twitches, and salivated gibberish. As a caregiver, Father proved careful and particularly efficient, as he knew how to be: orderly, restrained in suffering, which he mastered like a shameful secret that might have been able to unite us. The cheerful, young, distant nurse would pop into my clean white cell from time to time, or her boss would come with his thick lips and his characteristic way of contracting his cheek and shifting his thick, rectangular glasses in a single movement. He held out his hand to shake every day and spoke in a baritone voice that vibrated with reserved force. Sometimes the higher-ups visited me as well: the diagnostic professor, the emergency radiotelegraphist, the expert in analyses and recuperations, and the reeducation and requalification instructors. They listened to me with great attention. They asked me questions to find out where the malfunction was and what I was thinking. I was a bastard. I lied. I cheated. I coveted … no, appropriated my neighbors' work and wives. I didn't help my near and dear. I wasn't capable of love. I didn't respond to love. That girl with the big eyes wasn't like the others. It was no laughing matter. What would I have done with such a woman? We would have been afraid of each other. She thought I'd remain perpetually worthy of her protection, to fondle and diddle this weak body: a scrawny boy, transparent with deeply ringed eyes, passing through the rivers of the night in the shadow of the patrols, with big bad cinematographic eyes. They nodded. They understood, the conversation tired me. I hadn't the strength, the patience, the appetite. The people around me stared—hideous, ravenous, haunted. They understood right away. They had come across cases of this kind.

They succeeded, of course. So I slept: I slept a lot. It was important for me to sleep, and they succeeded: I kept sleeping. Then they explained to me that I wasn't guilty. Such monstrous atrocities happen daily—no, they didn't say monstrous atrocities, they said it differently, movements, not movements, not mistruths, not motives, yes, marvels: marvels of this sort happen all the time. Mysteries, mutations, *meshugaas* ... yes, yes, minor problems. Which is to say, the girl will eventually find someone else, and I another girl. We'll mature, so they were saying. We will mature. Such things solve themselves with time. Maybe it was all for the best. She was an overly sentimental girl, no, not sentimental, sensitive. That's all I needed. I was better off out of it. Yes, but I ... not by much, I explained to them—in fact, I was always indifferent, forgetful, not that I feel ... no, not that I care, the proof was the way I behaved: like a brute, like a blessing, because she was alone, in fact. They nodded their heads and gestured with their hands. They understood what I was saying. They were right: I had no connection to the Captain, nor to Monica's mother, the old lady, Rebeca Smântănescu locked away in her madhouse, and it's no good to go see war movies, either, or those horror movies—that's way too much. The reason was that I had worked a lot; probably I'd worked too much. I explained to them that it wasn't true: I was working sometimes, but playing hooky often, and that wasn't important—probably I didn't like what I was doing. I shrugged my shoulders, but they were right.

One afternoon I had an interesting discussion with the doctor. He came, adjusted his glasses, and talked to me about the formidable power consumed in playing the role of the defeated—the weak, powerless, frightened one—which is altogether greater than playing the role of the solid, steadfast, stoic, severe, character—the victor. The doctor who came to keep an eye on me was right, and that lady professor was consequently right too—ha! She wasn't stupid, the daughter of the crazy old woman who spent the rest of her life bent over the grave of her executed husband, Monica's father. Look, Little Moni wasn't dumb. But change was advantageous from all points of view. I listened to the doctor attentively, and I understood him. He had a gentle voice and was the subtlest of my caregivers.

They considered my intention to kill the professor grievous but interesting, and they didn't interrupt me as I told them about it. I continued telling the story coherently, logically, and they didn't contradict me, no, not at all: they'd been reviewing this matter for a while, and that was normal. They told me that the shock (the moment when I lost control of the reins) ... that was the problem, but, still, it was only an effect. They were searching for causes, or in other words the etiology, so that they could prescribe the right treatment.

And the treatments were very good. I managed to sleep. That made them happy and calmed them down. After several months I understood that it doesn't help to rush in and out of treatment if certain details are still eating you alive. And it's not good to pay too much attention to details either. You have to work in an orderly way, get some rest, have some fun (within reason), keep yourself busy, and work without fail, otherwise, you're screwed. But first understand what you like, what suits you best, and busy yourself with that, though not abusively. The principle is to cure yourself of *tristesse*, no, of triumph, no ... of temerity, that's it, to cure yourself of temerity ... to stop believing that you can make any old thing of yourself or that the others have to do who-knows-what, and in general for you to keep to your place, and embrace that order, which is to say, you shouldn't be looking left and right all the time. You should see to your business, work for specific results. This can be achieved and enjoyed.

Of course I couldn't change my trade. It was a wonderful trade, like all trades, except that I should work in the open air, which could be easily arranged, of course.

They always smiled in a friendly way. They told me I should work in a place where I wouldn't have too much time for idleness or trifles— it was better like that— because you shouldn't have too much time, and you shouldn't get too concerned, either. You see to your business. Don't let yourself wander. We can't solve everything. And those people who were watching over me, most of them young, like me, that's what they were doing: they had a great deal of patience, really a tremendous amount, even with a person like me. I would need to become more sober, no, more sociable—I was still messing up letters, words, ideas; I'd stammer occasionally, but I was getting better: when the treatment was over, I was thinking and expressing myself clearly.

That's the main thing—I mustn't isolate myself, I should seek people out, observe, as one should, their lapses, no, not lapses, their lives, and life in general. And the inverse of that: I shouldn't spend too much time looking left and right, but that was only an apparent contradiction. They told me not to observe too much, but that I should still look. I shouldn't get into details. In short, I should be engaged with others, but in a certain way. Ultimately everything revers ... no, revenges itself, rots and decays—look at the evidence. I agreed with them that everything depended on my attitude. An effort of will was needed; after all, I wasn't a child. I'd work patiently and precisely, and to find pleasure in this would be even better ... even the smallest things. For example: shaving. That's been disgusting for a while, of course. Hair keeps on growing, perpetually, and every which way— black, blond, red hairs, white hairs, some longer, others shorter, dirty, sweaty ... again the foam, the blade, the alcohol—you can lose your mind. On top of that, you keep seeing yourself in the mirror, too— that bloated, aging, sleepy, yellow face. This is exactly the place for willpower. Once. Twice. Then things begin to feel normal again— you stop thinking about everything. Shaving is a hygienic operation, a daily ritual. Just don't stop and think about every motion or analyze every single strand of hair. The razor, the foam, and the alcohol are organized in the mirror: don't study your face, but avoid nicking yourself, too. It's the same with everything. Matters have to be solved efficiently and quickly, without dedicating yourself wholeheartedly to them. Only I wasn't stupid, and there was no solution except the exercise of will.

From my small cell, every day I saw a small rectangle of blue, and there was no other solution. Therefore I helped them with my recovery. In the end, I would need to gather my strength, the will to work in a useful, therapeutic way. I had the will, indeed. It wasn't too easy for me to follow all their advice, then or afterward.

But there was no other solution. I got healthy.

⁞ ⁞ ⁞

The crane driver and the workers from the concrete station are the first to arrive. They check the state of the aggregates, which should be in optimal proportion, without any impurities. They test the cables, the lifting hooks for the bucket, the control levers. And the drivers have to arrive at least half an hour before the others. When work begins the buckets must start, the concrete has to be prepared already, and the trucks need to be ready to start.

When the concrete pouring begins, we carefully prepare the surface, or in other words, treat the old concrete over which the fresh batch will be poured. It is washed. With several hoses at once, pressurized water removes any foreign substances. Then, the surface is scrubbed with wire brushes till it's perfectly clean. A thin film of mortar is poured, a kind of "cement milk," over which the concrete is poured. The preparation of the surface, which needs to be as rough as possible for maximum adherence, takes a while, so the other workers end up arriving an hour or two later, but they stay later, too.

The best days are those when we pour. The high-capacity buckets sway above us. Full of concrete, two come from one direction on one cable, and then two empties leave in the other direction on the second cable. Noisily, the concrete flows near us. A powerful mass descends suddenly, and you can tell right away if it's well prepared: not too runny, not to thick. We drop in the concrete vibrators: the granules knock into each other, scattering and blending, and liquefaction occurs gradually, a continuously better mixture, until—perfect! We hurry to pour as much as possible. Some people don't pay close enough attention to the concrete vibrators: they don't adjust the RPMs. I've warned them about this many times. The pouring days are the most stressful, the fullest. The bustle peaks: everyone's nervous; they run around and become negligent. They don't always check that the screens—the soldered carcasses of the armature— have been mounted in the correct position and if they were brushed for rust and dirt. They're glad when a lot of concrete is poured without interruption in an accelerated rhythm. They work without talking, and their gestures take on a kind of obstinacy. Only when there's some problem at the station or the electricity cuts off—who knows why—and the buckets hang suspended in the air, do they finally start getting mad. But they also get mad if you ask them to straighten something, or to double-check something—in other words, if you hold them up in some way. When the concrete comes out too runny, it has to be communicated to the station right away: the ratio needs to be checked, the proportion of water to cement or gravel or sand has to be altered. It takes a while to make these changes. It happens too that the bucket doesn't close perfectly. Cement milk pours out of it. The concrete becomes weak. The bucket needs to be repaired.

It's hard to calm the workers down in such cases—even while they're pouring cement. I've tried to explain to them that the vibrations only affect granules up to a certain dimension. But as the frequency rises, the smaller particles start to oscillate, too. At 3,000 vibrations per minute the granules up to 15 millimeters start oscillating. At 6,000, up to 4 millimeters, at 12,000 up to 1 millimeter. Bored, they give me annoyed looks. They say they've understood, and it even seems they do. It's not too difficult: the frequency has to be adjusted according to the composition of the concrete. In the end they forget, they hurry, they're heedless.

In summer, the pouring days are the most beautiful. *Summertime*

... *summertime*. The sun burns, the bucket rocks on its cable like a small flying ship. Two buckets come; two buckets go. We protect the concrete, for the elevated temperature increases contraction and causes cracking, particularly as the material starts to harden. I have explained this to them so many times. They hurry, though. I saw one of them glaring at me furiously as I repeated for the third or fourth time that the closing of the capillaries stops the evaporation and limits the contraction—meaning, let's follow the rules. This is what we have to do. Otherwise ... otherwise, how ... this is the rule, the relation, which is to say that this specifically sustains us, stimulates us—it's very important.

At one point the site management proposed that I should move over to the technical department, in an office. I'd be better suited to the work there, or so they claimed. I'm meticulous and methodical, as they mentioned, particularly when a bucket suddenly dropped, raining down cement from the clear blue sky.

They have a terrific way of rocking in the sun, these buckets—a bunch of dizzy boats. They shine. Two buckets come, two go. If you don't pay attention, they unload—once, the concrete fell right on top me, and it seemed like the bucket opened on its own, without a command.

They asked me if I wasn't looking elsewhere, somehow. They insist I was daydreaming, that I was preoccupied. I'm convinced that the bucket opened unexpectedly. The hitch must have sprung on its own. Luckily, I had a helmet on my head. We all wear protective helmets. During summer some workers leave them off. It's too hot. If the cement happens to splash you, your hair gets grimy and immediately dries with a film of cement dust. I look at one guy: it's as if he no longer has hair, you see a safety helmet, no, not a safety helmet, a gray cap, a mass of dust, a strange wig. Perukes of powder, powdered perukes, petulant and petrified. Of course I didn't agree to move into an office. I like to feel the cold, the sun, the snowfall, the rain; I like to wait for the concrete, to see how it flows, how it hardens, how it becomes petrified and powerful. It's something real and alive. The pouring days are the ones we enjoy the most, after all. Our movements bring us together, they communicate: we're whole. You feel the sun and wind and rain on your cheeks: the body responds to commands.

The cranes, the compressors, the vehicles, concrete mixers, and cement vibrators rumble on all the time. Sometimes I can hardly wait for lunch. Tired but joking, we go to eat, together.

In the mess hall there's a great deal of noise—lots of noise. You can hear the machines and the vehicles: you have a hard time talking with anyone. We wait for the food. We're famished. We don't put on airs. From time to time the food is too greasy, or it has too much sauce. Once, I went looking for the boss to tell him. I didn't find him. He'd gone to get food somewhere else. I spoke with the woman who did the cooking, since the food ultimately depends on her. She had her back turned—bent over a steaming kettle. I approached and asked if I could speak to her. She was tasting the food, and she paused with the big, metal spoon in her hand. She wiped her hand on the corner of her apron, which was dirtied with all kinds of spots and stains, and offered me her hand to shake. She had an unexpectedly small hand, a chubby pincushion of a hand with short, thick, sausage-like fingers ending in long, blackened nails, which curved like animals'—a hand that disturbed me.

I didn't touch it. I got flustered. The cook smiled at me. She had small teeth—white, very white—a round, greasy cheek. She asked me what I wanted. She had a surprising voice—it was slender and slight. She herself was fat. I didn't know what else to say. I stammered that I was looking for whoever was in charge. She answered something, but I had already retreated back to the kitchen door.

I'd probably behaved strangely because she remembered me. After that, she made a habit of coming out of the kitchen. She'd come into the dining hall and observe for a while, and if she caught sight of me, she'd give me a smile. She had white teeth, very white. Sometimes, if there weren't many people, that is, if I were late, she'd come to my table. Huge as she was, in her spectacular, thin, soothing voice she'd ask if I wouldn't like to eat something special: she'd fix it for me. She would bring it to the table, and I would keep watching those fat little hands with short fingers like sausages and long, twisted, black nails. I missed lunch several times for this reason. It was unpleasant for me. The others had noticed too: it nauseated me. Once I stood up and left while she was talking to me. She realized I was annoyed and backed off, but she still follows me with her eyes. She follows me secretly, from the kitchen door, without coming closer anymore — except rarely. Sometimes she still asks me how I'm doing, smiles with her little white teeth, and heads away.

We finish work late. The afternoons are short, particularly toward the end of autumn or in winter. In winter the working conditions are more difficult. We are very careful with the pouring. The "catching" and hardening of the cement happens slowly. The water in the concrete dilates and disorganizes its structure. The concrete needs to be checked carefully to make sure that it's properly prepared. I go to the workstation to check if they have reduced the ratio of water, if they have selected the aggregates, if they are heating them correctly. Sometimes they heat the concrete. The temperature has to be measured every two hours. I've reminded them so many times. It's not my business, but I know they rush. They overlook important details. They're heedless, hurried, keen on immediate results. They force me to keep an eye on them.

Even in summer. Maybe particularly in summer, when they want to pour as quickly as possible and then go into town for a few hours before nightfall. They don't care that on dry summer days the concrete's surface needs to be sprinkled with water after it has been covered with matting or a layer of sand or sawdust. It isn't a huge deal, but it needs to be done. If they rush to arrive in town before nightfall, they do a sloppy job.

The town isn't far away, ten, maybe fifteen kilometers. It doesn't tempt me. Still, they took me with them one day, almost by force. It was pleasant outside. The weather was beginning to warm up. It's a small city, and having the worksite barrack nearby has made it more lively. A few streets, a small downtown. By the time we arrived, it had cooled off again. The wind blew. We walked in front of the stores, the movie theater. We were an odd group, the way we walked in worn-out, grayish uniforms—like dusty, tired prisoners—but the locals had gotten used to us.

I don't know how, but I got separated from the others. I had remained behind. Maybe I had been distracted, looking at the houses and shop windows. They'd probably gone in somewhere to eat, to party. I headed up a street that seemed busy and headed toward the center.

The houses were solid. The people were returning from shopping with bags of bread and beer. I stopped on a street corner and leaned against the wall of a small building, a dairy store. I watched the passersby with their curiosity; perhaps they were asking themselves who I was and why they didn't know me. What was I doing in their city, on their street, leaning against the door of that particular building?

I headed up a narrow, perpendicular street. The sun touched me suddenly, the sun was touching the houses, too. It was a faintly glowing street, under the arms of tall trees waving large, cool leaves ... short houses, each hidden under a red, orange, or green roof—severe, calm houses under a peaceful and unwavering sky.

The small street descended toward a park. There were several empty benches. I sat down. I stayed on the bench and looked at the children who were shoving each other. They were skipping rope, falling, tripping each other. The mothers were running around making peace. I went out of the park and took several steps, just a few. Near the park was a tall, massive building, a school. Probably the city's high school. Just a few steps ... I hugged the concrete wall. A car sped past me, a car ready to run me down. It braked in front of the school. Another green car shot past. Two well-dressed young men got out—black suits, white shirts, neckties. They were laughing. Bouncing, they set off toward the school. The car sprang forward. Another stopped. Tall, supple girls—wearing either long heavy dresses or very short dresses—got out, too. You could see their young white knees, and their authentically curly, golden, or chestnut hair fluttered. I withdrew. It was a graduation celebration, I imagined. Kept moving, and went into a courtyard. The metallic gate slammed behind me.

I climbed a step. I had walked into a building with an upper floor. I started climbing up the steps. I stopped on the staircase. It was dark. I stayed like that. I didn't know which way to go. My hand clutched the cold bannister. I heard voices. Someone would come downstairs. A door slammed somewhere above. A step could be heard descending. One step, yet another. I was waiting for a light to be switched on. Someone panted. The person was coming down with difficulty. It must have been someone sick, asthmatic, some unbearable ... some unacceptable wretch, some ugly, gaunt, and sweating swine who was moving step by step, waiting. Maybe that person felt my presence. Now that person was bleating, breathing disgustingly, some bad stench. I jumped aside, down two steps. I was in the courtyard, in the street. The gate's iron latch closed behind me.

The street was clear, quiet. The weather had grown cooler: it was cold. In front of the school there wasn't a ... there was no one. I wiped my brow with my hand. I walked up the street again. It was drizzling now. The raindrops fell along my footpath and enveloped my sleeves and shoulders. I arrived at the intersection, at the corner where the dairy stood. I stayed there. The rain had energized me. Couples walked past arm-in-arm. They had a festive air: the women had ridiculous hairdos, and the men strutted stiffly. They looked at me reproachfully. My outfit wasn't exactly suitable ... not quite correct. The raindrops slid down my cheeks and my hands. Who knows? We must be prepared. When it rains the pouring of concrete becomes more difficult. The material has to be protected, covered. The rain shouldn't liquefy the cement. Autumn and winter are coming quickly. We don't have enough time. We'll cover the concrete with mats, with sheets of tarp, as is proper. We must work in any weather. No one has any reason to shriek ... no, to shirk, to get shook up.

Hugged against the corner of the dairy, I watched the couples moving along the street, which headed down toward the park, toward the school, yes, toward the school. They were going, perhaps, to some celebration, yes, they were going to a banquet, to the graduation banquet. That must have been why all the taxis were rushing: the young graduates were celebrating their separation from the rigors of school. That's how they do it nowadays: each one comes in a taxi. Motionless under the rain, in their way: they would have thought I was a lost tramp or something like that, with a dusty beard, disheveled hair, and a filthy uniform dabbed with cement. The couples kept passing, less frequently now, walking at the same brisk, uniform pace. They were late. They were in a hurry. I should have had armfuls of flowers to offer them, large bouquets of blue flowers to give to the girls and boys. They should've understood that my bizarre appearance had nothing defiant about it. I'm a person from here, from close by, one of them. My lazy gestures lacked any violence. Only the uniform had drawn in too much water, like a sponge, a cold bandage.

From somewhere nearby, a saxophone reared suddenly—a warm melody, perhaps coming from the school, a low, raspy woman's voice:

a harsh, hot song from a warm, metallic mouth. I remembered my comrades. They had finished their little pleasure long ago. I shouldn't have wandered away from them. I shouldn't withdraw, stray from them—I must return to them. Now in the fog and rain, our dormitories are like barges, somnolent, rocked by this hot, desperate melody. In this weather, sleep is deep—very deep. I must return as quickly as possible, I must find some vehicle, some van, some dump truck to get there fast. All things are reconciled there. I have a roof and bed and comrades, which is to say, my duties.

⁝ ⁝ ⁝

The roof and walls are damp with the breath of night. And roof and walls have woken up with me now that the cement mixers' rumbling has just ceased. So often, the walls' sleep and my own seem protected by the mixers' noise. Night passes fast and peacefully among the sounds behind the walls. Once it's quiet, the walls open their pores, suck in the damp, black air that slides along the windowpanes. It rarely happens that the cylinders' rotation gets blocked. Then silence invades and forces me to feel the midnight.

My sleep is usually long and total.

The day's rush from the one section to another, back and forth across improvised stairs, the running for concrete, welders, drivers, and materials is backbreaking, leg-breaking work. I don't hear anything except precise orders, the gnashing of the crane, the horns, the crackle of welding, the splashing of concrete, and the delightful drunkenness of water. I drop, exhausted and happy: a section has been filled, tomorrow another. My fatigue has a clear and ascending name. It's good this way. They were right to send me here to work outdoors. We communicate simply and precisely. We hurry. We have no time. Tomorrow we will raise the flat block of another morning. I love my team. Our solid movements, uniting us like brothers in the concrete colossus that rises under the inexplicable light without season. For an instant, the friction of our stiff bodies and hoarse voices seems warm and powerful. I float now for a short period of rest, in the dark of the wooden barrack, as though in a hot air balloon among the clouds. Soon the noise will begin again, and I'll sleep. Until then I can imagine this happy flight over the earth that carries no obligation with it. In the dream of tomorrow, I, with my duties and my rights, will rotate again, uniformly, from a fixed, rigid pole. Moderately, as is proper, I'll climb with uniform footsteps on the frigid, rotating, damp ray. Again there'll be an agitation of ants under a somber, streaky sky: clouds, convoys of clouds, strange contours, cusps like clippers, chimes, or castles, camels, craters, crania, crocodiles, and—who knows?—maybe we'll rendezvous, recover, hear from each other, finally, we'll ignite, immolate, be born, insatiable, unchecked, maybe even tomorrow, with my brothers (semblables or siblings) still safe and satisfied. Look, the drumming of the building-material mixers have begun to boom again ... with the bongos of the tamerial bixers ... with the bongos and gonbos, and ... oh, let's grab another hour of sleep till tomorrow, till morning.

Translator's afterword

THE LANGUAGE OF Norman Manea's *Captives* can't be discussed without an excursion into history. History animates *Captives'* unhinged voices. Time after time, we hear the untrustworthy speech of people cut lose from their moorings, who try to make "anything" of themselves, anything at all demanded by the moment, just to stay afloat. Having come through the Second World War and living through its communist aftermath, many speak in hypocritical or self-serving terms.

Captives is tacitly Stalinist Romania (1947–1965), and *accommodate or flounder* is the unspoken motto. Party membership is the key to success, and many are ready to hide or lie about "class enemy" antecedents.

Those unable to join the Party seek to be on good terms with it: in the novel, two high school teachers—a fascist ex-legionnaire and a former priest (e.g. a representative of the old order)—grovelingly hide their true natures in order to blend into the new order. Those in relative favor with the Party rationalize their attempts to take advantage of their position. And those who fail to adapt end up drifting: the narrator's sister, born as a replacement for the children lost during the Holocaust, emblematically changes her appearance and goals at the drop of a hat and feverishly quotes Rimbaud's "Drunken Boat." Her identification with the poem tags her as an unmoored vessel, a person born in denial of her family's natural identity or trajectory.

Like *Captives'* narrator, she is unsettling, not out of malice but as a result of her own instability.

The characters' chameleon-like self-invention and apparent lack of inner solidity comes of their having lived through the novel's implicit backstory. Like *Captives'* first readers, the people in this novel live in the knowledge that having been scorned by the Allies, Romania joined the Axis Powers and fought on the fascist side until August 23, 1944, when Romania's young King Michael staged a coup that over-threw Marshal Antonescu, the fascist-allied leader. Disaster (and, for some, opportunity) came on the heels of heroism. The communists quickly ousted King Michael.

Long before the endgame politics of the mid-forties, though, in alliance with Hitler, the Antonescu regime deported Jews and Romani from the northeast of the country to concentration camps in Transnistria, which stretches from the Dniester River in Moldavia to Moldavia's border with present day Ukraine. Hundreds of thousands of people died there, most of them Jews. While the (better known) captives in the Nazi camps ultimately fell victim to the Final Solution, those in Transnistria were left to perish of hunger, disease, and the random brutality of the guards. The survivors were liberated by the Red Army, *Captives'* author and his parents among them.

The unmoored mentality of Manea's literary captives is partly self-willed. One sees it in the language they use to think about the past. A quick trip through the text turns up many statements like these, each from a different character:

"It was necessary to gather memories, to rummage through them, to understand them so they could be forgotten, and then the amnesia would have to be checked again and again, for it would have to cover everything so there'd be no need to cheat or engage in the farce of little, passing deceptions."

"We have to forget in order to start anew."

"Forget it, banish it, erase it all ..."

Thinking about the past leads to self-induced amnesia, which is comparable to coma, as we are repeatedly reminded. Here's a key passage from a philosophy book to which the narrator frequently recurs:

> *Time has an objective reality, even when objective sensation is weakened or eradicated because time "presses on," because it "flows." It remains a problem for professional logicians to know if a hermetically sealed can sitting on a shelf is outside time or not. But we know too well that time accomplishes its work even on one who sleeps. A certain doctor mentions the case of a little girl, aged twelve, who fell asleep one day and continued to sleep for thirteen years. In this interval, though, she did not remain a little girl but rather woke up a young woman, for she had grown in the meantime.*

The narrator/protagonist considers that he himself has spent a large portion of his late adolescent and adult life in a hermetically sealed coma. He describes the effect of hermetically sealed reading:

> I used to gather the paperback, clothbound, and hardcover books. The stacks would grow taller than my head.... I needed to conserve myself, hermetically sealed on my shelf. Lacking air, the books rotted inside me. With all its games and noises, summer wasn't getting close to the shelf where I'd perched. Everything stood stock still around me. There was no movement and therefore no time.

The narrator's preoccupation with hermetic sealing derives explicitly from a passage in *The Magic Mountain*, and expresses a deep concern with the relationship between trauma and forgetting, which have severed these characters from what would have been their normal course of development. What results both in their direct and in their reported inner speech is a trajectory toward stasis: the denial or refusal of personal growth. Communist Romania, *Captives* implies, isn't just a hermetically sealed can inhabited by the comatose because of its citizens' inability to leave the country. It is a self-made psychological vacuum.

Operating in this psychological vacuum, *Captives* itself exhibits a mentality that is unstabilized, unmoored. The book is ostensibly the semi-therapeutic writing of a madman who suffers from attempts to disconnect himself from his past. The result is language that continuously tries to make "anything"—to use the narrator's word—of the world around the narrator/protagonist in his doomed effort to keep psychologically afloat. Consider the following passage, which spans two subsections of *Captives'* final chapter:

> A day has gone by, a week. Am still a somnolent high-school student. No, only a day, a week, a Saturday has gone by, and talk of confusion would be justified. Machines for typing and checking and intercepting and photographing and following and reproducing: their monotonous patter is here, and myself … fugitive, lost, stalked from every corner, unable to sleep.
>
> *"You walk, you walk forever, you have lost time and it has lost you … a terrain, sprinkled with seaweed and tiny shells; hearing thrilled by that unbridled wind that freely roves … we watch the tongues of sea foam stretch to lick our feet."*
>
> Under the waves, under the stroking foam, the sea roars in the great castle of water.
>
> ⋮ ⋮ ⋮
>
> The sea boomed. The thick castle walls kept out the noise of waves, but other sounds collided and crossed paths in the great hall: the release of bolts, metallic clanks, keys turning in locks,

latches, heavy springs. Between them, odd, erratic breaks. One, pause. Two-three, pause. Four-five-six, pause. One, pause, two-three, then four-five-six, pause. Over and again, perpetual clanking, a continuous murmur from the right. To the left, short breaks; to the right, the crowded taps of many fingers, hammering.

Raised my eyes. Found myself on a chair placed to the right of a medium-sized table.

Here, the narrator allows himself to flow through several states that include almost simultaneously recalling events from high school and from his working life, while also entering a hallucinatory state or a timeless dream of walking forever by the sea, only to find himself back in his office, seated on a chair. Talk of confusion would indeed be justified.

In this way, as if it were science fiction (which it certainly is not), *Captives* exists as a world in which versions of reality melt into each other in a continuous series of visions and revisions. Entering *Captives'* first section, "She," for the first time, the reader will be surprised to find the narrator/protagonist going upstairs to the apartment of Monica Smântănescu, Professor of French and Music. He makes two approaches, and each time the apartment is different. On the first try, his visit goes like this:

> ... The building's staircase: step, riser, step, riser—chunks of ice. The final threshold, the wooden door covered in arabesques, angels sculpted from edge to edge on its wide margins. The door opens toward books heaped on heavy iron shelves, vases with slender flowers, a narrow table, a tall chair, a piano raising its oblique tail, the ceiling painted with pastel squares, the slippery parquet: everything accumulated with the serenity of a fairy tale, until chaos imposes itself, until the path from the street corner must be taken again, killing reveries, reestablishing the brutality of things,

On the second attempt, better anchored in reality, the apartment turns out to be a pigsty. Similarly, there are to two versions of the narrator's initial meeting with Ms. Smântănescu: they meet on a train— or is it a boat? By the third section, "I," the reader will have to decide if a woman known only as Captain Zubcu's daughter is either (a) a mystical avatar of the narrator's sister Dona, long dead in Transnistria, or (b) an office girl he seduces and abandons, though given the novel's deeper themes there's no reason why she can't be both.

Captives is remarkable for saying everything and nothing: there is no historical backstory. We never hear that the action takes place in Romania—the country is not named. We are not told that the protagonist's family is Jewish. Joseph Stalin's name is not mentioned once, although he is referenced in the subtle details: the narrator's show trial is Stalinist; the narrator stumbles into a political meeting where we are given to understand that the attendees chant *Sta-lin, Sta-lin*; and the narrator attends a mass outdoor commemoration in honor of the Beloved Leader at the time of his death.

This language of omission obviously owes something to the climate of censorship in which *Captives* first appeared. It's also a safe bet that *Captives'* omissions wouldn't have pulled the wool over anyone's eyes, which more than suggests that the language of omission is a strategic, literary act.

Even though *Captives* was written to appear in communist Romania, even though its characters are Romanian, and even though it passed through Romanian censorship, still, *Captives* is not only (or primarily) a novel about Romania, or the Holocaust, or communist dictatorships. It is these things, of course, but freed of the explicit by omission, *Captives* creates its own world and can be read on its own terms. It demands that we experience life in a world of things unsaid, which makes silence one of the "loudest" voices in the book. Deafened by silence, we experience captivity, and silence becomes the gadfly of protest.

If silence is maddening, so are the implied and the tacit. They play games of "I dare you" and "now you see it, now you don't." At the level of conversation, *Captives'* language is quicksand.

The office spy, Misha (who is presumably in the pay of the Securitate), plagues our protagonist with seemingly inoffensive remarks. At one point they engage in the following non-dialogue:

> —I've been thinking, everything they're saying about Kennedy is a bunch of shit. Robert, the brother, is hiding the photographs of the autopsy, and saying they'll only be revealed in '71 because they're *horrible*?
>
> Unobtrusive voice, fixed gaze, astonished.
>
> —What exactly can be so horrible? If it was Oswald who shot him or the other guy, who cares? What's so horrible?
>
> He asks and answers, poses and resolves dilemmas meant to provoke his interlocutor.
>
> —It's clear that Johnson shot him. Otherwise, there'd be nothing horrible at all.

What does the informer want his interlocutor to say? Something about the Kremlin's responsibility for the Kennedy assassination? Whatever Misha says is untrustworthy, not least because it's incomprehensible. It's impossible to find the core of his remarks. Silence is the only safe response.

At another point, the weakened, self-doubting narrator attempts to resign from his office job. His boss, Caba, meets this crisis with apparent cordiality, but Caba's cordiality seems entirely suspect: "The old games of cordiality would have to be maintained at any price, along with the well-known lines of attack, defense, and encirclement. He knew how to engage the old laws of cordiality. " The most the protagonist can expect of Caba is the entrapping, famously "wooden" language of communist rhetoric: "This formerly eminent colleague should have been the light of his generation. Through what evil, unsupervised game have all those hopes and promising signs come to naught?" To answer these questions with their tacit threat of political risk (and possible prison) would amount to walking deliberately through a minefield. The only answer: silence or flight. Our narrator chooses flight. There's more than that, though. The unwieldy, wooden question, which the narrator attributes to Caba in the first section of this novel, circumnavigates its true answer, which only becomes clear to the reader in *Captives'* third section. The narrator has betrayed his potential to rise inside the system by damaging himself in the course of an initial game of rhetorical circumlocution at the show trial. His rhetorical swoops and dives rescue Caba and result in the destruction of his own mental stability, but the core of the two characters' relationship remains painfully locked away from discussion. It hovers between them as a closed center around which they revolve.

Ordinary communications aren't what they seem either. A bedtime story submitted to a (then real) radio program for children holds fanciful and deliberately idiotic disguised messages about disappointed love. A love letter written in connection with an ad placed in the personal columns is a tissue of lies. Our protagonist's parents' communication with their son about a name for his new sister are implicit denials of the Transnistrian past—they insist that the boy cannot remember his murdered sister, whom he remembers perfectly well. The real center of each discussion and interaction is seen and unseen, shut away, so that all talk and action revolve around these "closed centers." I use this term advisedly. It comes from the novel, and it belongs to a key figure: the trope of the spiral staircase. Romanian cities abound in winding staircases, and *Captives'* natives ascend and descend them constantly. Here is the narrator going up stairs:

> The high iron gate strikes its latch; the narrow, serpentine, spiral staircase devours itself. Hand on the cold metal balustrade, the climber coils within himself. One flight up. Again, the steps rotate uniformly again in the shape of a fan: a point flowing at an even rate along the radius of a circle. Rotating evenly, slowly around the circumference, dizzied by the curved trajectories, the climber's body turns in on itself toward a painfully closed center.

Just as their feet make their way up and down so many twisting staircases, the denizens of this novel are forced to spiral around truths closed to (or enclosed inside) themselves by trauma, obfuscation, or denial.

In this sense, *Captives* is a spiraling dance of sealed-off subjectivities. Although a dark bildungsroman can be dug out of *Captives*, the novel is actually organized as a chaconne, and indeed Handel's Chaconne is *Captives'* signature piece of music. When the narrator and Monica Smântănescu meet for the first time (on a boat or in a train), music pours from a portable radio, and Monica announces her presence by saying, "Handel's Chaconne in G Major." A dance in moderate triple meter form, the chaconne is based on the continuous variation of a series of chords. The musical definition describes the novel very well. Organized as a set of multifarious and evolving variations on a theme, *Captives* is composed of three chapters — "She," "You," and "I" — and follows a series of thematic modifications that includes (but isn't limited to) its narrator's resignation, differing versions of the narrator's encounter with Monica Smântănescu, ruminations on the narrator's obsessive relationship with Captain Zubcu's daughter, as well as his preoccupation with both his own childhood loss of his sisters and his decision to save Sebastian Caba, the defendant at the show trial who becomes his boss. The *She* of these variations is, of course, Monica Smântănescu. *You* is the Captain's daughter as a revenant of the narrator's lost sister, Dona. *I* is the narrator. As for *sealed-off subjectivities*: to qualify as a main character in *Captives*, you must have your "I"/ego hermetically locked away, and this is not just a matter of a sensation felt on climbing stairs or comparing oneself to a jar in a novel by Thomas Mann. For the translator, the most striking feature of Manea's three characters is signaled by their frequent lack of subject pronouns.

While sparing subject pronouns in general, *Captives* is especially chary of the words *she*, *you*, and *I*. It should be said here that a lack of subject pronouns is both easier to accomplish and much less jarring to read in Romanian than it is in English because Romanian is a highly inflected language. Whereas English present tense verbs, for example, tend to inflect only in the third person singular (I go, you go, he/she/it *goes*, we go, you go, they go), Romanian verbs feature personal endings. The Romanian for the present tense of the verb "to go" (*Eu merg, tu mergi, el/ea merge, noi mergem, voi mergeti, ei/ele merg*) has five forms for six "persons." This means, in practice, that, thanks to the signal value of the verb endings, standard Romanian can be spoken without too many pronouns, and it can be written without them as well.

The absence of pronouns ordinarily presents no special challenge for the translator. When translating standard Romanian into standard English, the translator simply supplies pronouns when necessary. *Captives*, however, presents a particular challenge. Manea's narrator tends to reserve the subject pronouns *she, you*, and *I* for climactic moments when identity is an issue. At other times he takes advantage of Romanian's ability to do without subject pronouns or finds objective correlatives like "the professor of French and piano" or "the wandering son of earth" to substitute for the mysterious subjectivity condensed into an asserted *she* or *I*. In a similar way, the narrator tends to slip into the third person and to use objective correlatives — "the visitor," "the orphan girl," "that girl" — to avoid words like *I* and *you*.

In this translation I have tried to cope with the author's use and avoidance of pronouns on a case-by-case basis. In a few instances phrases have been rearranged to avoid awkwardness. A Romanian sentence that reads "In vain had [she] arranged her class schedule in order to avoid this insufferable courtyard motorcade," has become "It was a matter of vainly having arranged her class schedule in order to avoid this insufferable courtyard motorcade." In one case I followed the pronounless Romanian telegraphese to emphasize the narrator's frenzied madness:

> Let him rattle for a moment or two. The visitor evidently feared a trap. What fun to watch him deal with Madam Professor's husband! Farces leapt to mind: all equally good. It was hard to choose.
>
> — My sister told me about you, the madman finally remarked. Personally, I don't live here.
>
> — Mhm. She didn't write anything about having a brother.
>
> Should have seen that one coming. The end of the letter had been clear.
>
> — Make yourself comfortable. Perhaps you'd like to wait. Have a seat.
>
> Proceeded to pick a pile of the chair. Miscellaneous trash. Couldn't find a place for it. Threw it on the bed.

There is no way to write the English second person without using the word *you*, however, and I have simply used it when the narrator's prose apostrophizes Captain Zubcu's daughter.

Readers not preoccupied with the blood and guts of translation and the differences between languages may see these final notes as technical details, and that's as it should be. For any translator, what really matters is bringing the spirit of the writing into the new language. In this case, the language is swirling and mysterious, for *Captives* does not aspire to be a traditional novel. It expresses the dementia induced by the captive state. Part novel (verging on roman-fleuve), part musically inspired composition, *Captives* leads the translator to grapple with the text as fluid, polyphonic writing, for it includes many kinds of speech, nearly all of them unstable.

JEAN HARRIS
AUGUST 2014